# Re:ZeRo

~Starting Life in Another World~

"Welcome—
Tell me, what
did you gain
from the time
you spent
facing your
own past?"

"—I must say, you came far sooner than I expected."

# Characters

Re:ZERO -Starting Life in Another World-

The only ability Subaru Natsuki gets when he's summoned to another world is time travel via his own death. But to save her, he'll die as many times as it takes.

## *Frederica*

Senior maid of Roswaal Manor.
Perfect domestic skills as a maid.
A capable servant.

## *Garfiel*

Guardian of the Sanctuary.
His manner of speaking is gruff and he
is quick-tempered, prone to hasty action.

## Echidna

The Witch of Greed.
Her pure-white, seemingly bleached hair
is her defining characteristic.

## Ryuzu

The representative of the Sanctuary.
She dotes on Garfiel, whom she calls
"Young Gar."

# Re:ZERO -Starting Life in Another World-

The only ability Subaru Natsuki gets when he's summoned to another world is time travel via his own death. But to save her, he'll die as many times as it takes.

# CONTENTS

# -Starting Life in Another World-

# VOLUME 10

# TAPPEI NAGATSUKI
### ILLUSTRATION: SHINICHIROU OTSUKA

NEW YORK

Re:ZERO Vol. 10
TAPPEI NAGATSUKI

Translation by Jeremiah Bourque
Cover art by Shinichirou Otsuka

Re:ZERO KARA HAJIMERU ISEKAI SEIKATSU Vol. 10
© Tappei Nagatsuki 2016
First published in Japan in 2016 by KADOKAWA CORPORATION, Tokyo.
English translation rights reserved by YEN PRESS, LLC under the license from KADOKAWA CORPORATION, Tokyo, through Tuttle-Mori Agency, Inc., Tokyo.

English translation © 2019 by Yen Press, LLC

Yen On
1290 Avenue of the Americas
New York, NY 10104

Visit us at yenpress.com
facebook.com/yenpress
twitter.com/yenpress
yenpress.tumblr.com
instagram.com/yenpress

First Yen On Edition: June 2019

Yen On is an imprint of Yen Press, LLC.
The Yen On name and logo are trademarks of Yen Press, LLC.

Library of Congress Cataloging-in-Publication Data
Names: Nagatsuki, Tappei, 1987– author. | Otsuka, Shinichirou, illustrator. | ZephyrRz, translator. | Bourque, Jeremiah, translator.
Title: Re:ZERO starting life in another world / Tappei Nagatsuki ; illustration by Shinichirou Otsuka ; translation by ZephyrRz ; translation by Bourque, Jeremiah
Other titles: Re:ZERO kara hajimeru isekai seikatsu. English
Description: First Yen On edition. | New York, NY : Yen On, 2016– |
Audience: Ages 13 & up.
Identifiers: LCCN 2016031562 | ISBN 9780316315302 (v. 1 : pbk.) | ISBN 9780316398374 (v. 2 : pbk.) | ISBN 9780316398404 (v. 3 : pbk.) | ISBN 9780316398428 (v. 4 : pbk.) | ISBN 9780316398459 (v. 5 : pbk.) | ISBN 9780316398473 (v. 6 : pbk.) | ISBN 9780316398497 (v. 7 : pbk.) | ISBN 9781975301934 (v. 8 : pbk.) | ISBN 9781975356293 (v. 9 : pbk.) | ISBN 9781975383169 (v. 10 : pbk.)
Subjects: CYAC: Science fiction. | Time travel—Fiction.
Classification: LCC PZ7.1.N34 Re 2016 | DDC [Fic]—dc23
LC record available at https://lccn.loc.gov/2016031562

ISBNs: 978-1-9753-8316-9 (paperback)
978-1-9753-8317-6 (ebook)

3 5 7 9 10 8 6 4 2

LSC-C

Printed in the United States of America

# PRoLoGUE
## TOMB

The cool, placid air in the ruins greeted Subaru with a strange tranquility.

The *clack* of his shoes rang out with each and every step. The rather jarring echoes of his footsteps were causing Subaru's unease, but they also helped him stay grounded.

When he couldn't even see anything right in front of him, those sounds were the only things that reminded him he truly existed.

"…"

The place was completely shrouded in darkness. Quite some time had passed since he'd lost track of the wall he'd found by touch earlier. He walked and walked along a path without end; for Subaru, it was almost as if he were actually standing still, as though his movements were mere hallucinations.

Hearing his footfalls abated that concern. More importantly, Subaru's reason for being here urged him onward.

He continued to walk, relying on the echoes of his shoes. He couldn't stop—he wouldn't allow himself. No matter how deeply resignation had rooted itself in his heart, no matter how heavy his burden weighed on his shoulders, he had to grit his teeth and keep walking.

If he didn't, how could he ever face her—?

\*    \*    \*

"—I see. This is the desire that drives you. How curious, I must say."

Suddenly, a voice rang out.

The moment he heard it, Subaru froze. The unending eternity he had felt suddenly fell away.

In the blink of an eye, the darkness he'd thought would continue forever quickly faded while the world that had been drained of color now seemed painted in a dazzling array. There were tufts of green beneath his feet and a cloudless, blue sky stretching out far overhead. Subaru realized he was standing on a grassy plain that should not have been there.

He felt a gentle breeze stroke his hair, and then his throat constricted in shock.

"—Ngh."

"Would you please stop playing around and come here?"

As Subaru stood there frozen, a voice called out to him from behind.

When he turned around, his noticed a slightly raised knoll. At the top, a parasol had been set up to provide shade for a white table and chair underneath—and in that seat, he saw a girl.

"..."

Her figure filled his mind with thoughts of white—pure white, as if all color had been bleached from her existence.

The long hair reaching all the way down her back and her barely exposed skin were like porcelain, more than enough to seize attention; a pitch-black dress veiled her slender limbs, like an outfit someone might wear to a funeral; her black eyes shone with an extraordinary intellect—these were the only things that seemed to prove the ephemeral girl was actually there.

White and black: her extraordinarily stark beauty was expressed by those two hues alone.

It would only take a glance for her captivating appearance to put anyone under her spell—but the sight of this girl injected overwhelming fear into Subaru's soul, the likes of which he had never felt before.

Even his first encounter with the White Whale had not struck him this way.

"Oh my, have I surprised you?"

"..."

Subaru didn't say a word to the girl who had come so close to him. When she saw his reaction, her eyes filled with amusement. The girl paused before nodding, seemingly taking stock of the situation.

"Ahh, I see. I have yet to introduce myself. How embarrassing. It has been so long since I've spoken to anyone, my emotions seem to have gotten the better of me."

Unlike the tone of her voice, the girl's expression barely changed at all as her tiny shoulders dipped slightly.

She turned to Subaru, who was still silenced and frozen in utter terror, then touched a hand to her breast as she calmly introduced herself.

"My name is Echidna..."

The girl's lips softened into a thin smile as she added:

"Or perhaps it would be better to call myself the Witch of Greed?"

# CHAPTER 1

## AT THE PLACE OF RETURN

1

To Subaru, the cloudy sky above seemed to be an accurate reflection of his mind.

"This place shall feel emptier without you."

As Subaru stood in front of the mansion's gate, a woman in a dress spoke those lonely-sounding words.

The woman was distinctive, with long, flowing green hair and amber, almond-shaped eyes.

Subaru still couldn't set aside his unease at the delicate way Crusch Karsten faintly lowered her eyes like a stereotypically proper young lady.

All in spite of knowing full well why this was happening.

"Crusch, I'm grateful to hear you say that, but…"

Subaru scratched his head as he averted his gaze, looking straight ahead instead.

Multiple dragon carriages lined the grounds of the Karsten estate; aboard were the villagers who had evacuated to the royal capital to escape from the cultists under Petelgeuse's command. The Archbishop of Sloth had since then been defeated, meaning it was safe to return to the mansion and Earlham Village now. For that reason, they were scheduled to traverse the highway back to the village—with Subaru accompanying them back to Roswaal Manor.

Put bluntly, a mountain of problems lay before them, even setting aside the Witch Cult. Crusch's sudden change was one of them, but—

"I hate leaving at a time like this, but nothing's gonna get solved if I stay here. I don't want to abuse your hospitality, either."

"If it is Master Subaru Natsuki and Lady Emilia, I hardly mind if you stay at my residence as long as you desire… But it seems that is not an option."

"I'll accept your kind words and leave it at that. We both have a lot of issues to face right now, yeah? Especially you, since there's that greedy merchant's crew to deal with. If you don't handle it well, they'll steal all the credit for the White Whale and Sloth right out from under you."

Shaking his head at Crusch's request, Subaru urged her to be wary of Anastasia's followers.

It would be most accurate to call the victory over the White Whale and the Archbishop of Sloth a joint operation by the forces of three royal candidates. However, at the moment, Anastasia was the only one to have emerged as a clear victor.

The Crusch faction had established supremacy over enemies who had gone undefeated for over four centuries—but the price their leader Crusch had paid was not low. Subaru and the rest of Emilia's supporters who had led the way to Sloth's defeat had taken casualties as well. Subaru wouldn't say that his loss was as critical as what Crusch and her people were enduring, but at the very least, Subaru had suffered a grievous wound that agonized him at that very moment.

Meanwhile, Anastasia's faction had both candidate and knight intact even after playing a large role in dispatching both foes, taking minimal damage while reaping great rewards.

Accordingly, everyone would need to keep an eye on Anastasia's movements from then on. That was simply one more reason to maintain the secrecy around the alliance between Emilia's faction and Crusch's faction.

"We need to head back and get our ducks in a row before we discuss anything. We gotta have a little talk with Roswaal, Emilia's sponsor, and I wanna bring the worried villagers back home, too."

"It must be a trying time for the families that have been separated. It would be best if you could help them."

Crusch showed him a slight, fleeting smile as she turned her gaze toward the villagers aboard the dragon carriages.

Half of the village had been evacuated to the royal capital; the other half had been evacuated to another safe area by a separate route. Just as Crusch had mentioned, families had been separated in the commotion. Subaru wanted to reunite them as soon as possible.

"I'll come back to the capital once we have that settled. I guess this is goodbye for a little while, then."

"Yes, I shall be waiting. When that time comes, I will be pleased to finally repay the great favor I owe to you."

"Aw, you're making a big fuss over nothin'. We're helping each other out, that's all. Plus, I already have my reward."

Subaru put on an awkward smile for Crusch as he pointed to the dragon carriage at the head of the column. This carriage seemed of a higher class than the rest, and a beautiful, jet-black land dragon was hitched to the front.

The black land dragon was what Subaru had received as his reward for his part in the hunt.

"You ask for too little. To think you would ask for a single land dragon as a reward for defeating one of the three great demon beasts."

"Hey, I owe this dragon my life. I haven't been with her for long, but I've been on the brink between life and death with her more than anyone...and maybe the reason for that is 'cause I'm one hell of a nuisance to Patlash, but..."

"An unnecessary concern, I believe."

As they spoke, Subaru and Crusch watched over the land dragon, Patlash. That was the moment the aged swordsman, Wilhelm, walked over and gently voiced his disagreement.

Having finished checking on the state of the carriages, the Sword Devil bowed as he joined the conversation.

"The Diana breed is said to be the most temperamental of all land dragons, and few grow this fond of someone in such a short time. It would seem Sir Subaru and this land dragon are most compatible."

"I suppose you're right about that. When I was picking a mount before the fight with the White Whale, I only picked her on gut instinct, but…"

The compatibility part was likely a fact. Subaru felt like it was a match made in heaven. He didn't think he could have made it past both the White Whale and Sloth with any land dragon besides Patlash. Subaru had been saved by that wise dragon so many times he was convinced.

"In other words, I won't be satisfied with any land dragon other than you…!"

When Patlash nestled close, Subaru stroked her neck with renewed gratitude. As he did so, she rubbed the side of her proud face against him, which unfortunately made her hard scales feel like a file sliding against Subaru's hand.

"Guaaah! Those scales hurt more than I figured! Now I know what radishes must feel when run against a grater!"

"Hmm, land dragons find such playing to be quite pleasant. This is simply another way to deepen mutual trust."

"Are you serious?! Won't that make the power in this relationship like when a cat keeps toying with a mouse?!"

Perhaps, even with the land dragon shaving away his hand, this was mere child's play to Wilhelm. The Sword Devil's pleasant composure made Subaru scratch his head with a guilty expression.

"Well, setting aside the issue of how Patlash and I should get along for now… Wilhelm, it's sad, but I have to say goodbye to you for a while, too. Take good care of that wound, okay?"

"Thank you for your concern—judging from how the bleeding has now largely ceased, it would seem that I am farther away now. It is difficult for me to speak about that as a fortunate thing, but…"

They were discussing Wilhelm's left shoulder—the spot where his wife, the previous Sword Saint, had wounded him.

The fact that his old wound had opened up filled the Sword Devil's eyes with a maelstrom of complex emotions. As to what it meant, there was no way to find out except through questioning the Archbishop of the Seven Deadly Sins who had attacked Crusch.

The Archbishop of Gluttony—if something other than the White Whale had been responsible for the death of the Sword Devil's wife, that archbishop was the prime suspect. And considering the doctrine of the Witch Cult, Subaru and his friends were sure to clash with them again someday. The cultists were the true enemy of their alliance.

They had to defeat the Witch Cult and take back what had been lost: Crusch's memories, and more—

"Subawuuu, I've secured Rem to the bed. Come see for yourself."

His thoughts interrupted by the calling of his name, Subaru turned toward the speaker. It was Crusch's knight, Ferris, his iconic flaxen-colored kitty ears visible as he leaned out of a dragon carriage.

Obeying his beckoning hand, Subaru walked over and peered into the interior. Upon examination, he realized that seats had been removed from within the wide carriage and replaced by a simple bed.

A lone girl slept in it. Seeing her made Subaru's heart ache.

Instead of her usual maid attire, the blue-haired girl's body was wrapped in a thin, water-colored blanket. She had been left unconscious by a slumber from which she would never awaken, her very existence forgotten by the people around her—

"Rem isn't going to fall out the back or anything while we're moving on the road, right?"

"I'm telling you that I made preventing that a priority already. Believe it or not, Ferri is a genuine healer, so I'm kind to all my patients... Though I'm not sure if calling Rem a patient is...accurate."

He gazed at the girl's face as she seemingly slept in peace, and Ferris's shoulders sank.

Though his tone of voice was lighthearted, Ferris's face bore deep, unconcealable grief and disappointment with himself. Subaru wasn't the only one who resented being powerless. Here was another who felt great pain at not being able to do anything to help.

Ferris still regretted his inability to protect his master when it mattered most.

"You're really returning to the mansion?"

"Yeah. It's not like Rem's going to be cured by staying in a place like this... Uh, I didn't mean that to sound rude."

"It's okay, Subawu. I get it. You're just that terrible of a person, *meow.*"

Ferris forced a smile when Subaru tried to explain his poor choice of words. After that, his eyes immediately grew more serious as he thrust a finger at Subaru.

"More importantly, it's not just Rem who needs rest. You do, too, Subawu."

"I do?"

"Yes. Did you forget why you came to the royal capital in the first place? This time, all the commotion with Sloth that made you abuse your gate... Does your body feel...sluggish at all?"

"No, not especially, but..."

When Ferris posed the question, Subaru stretched his neck and shoulders as he replied that there were no apparent problems. His external wounds had already been treated, meaning his body felt fine. As for Ferris's concern about his gate...

"In the first place, I didn't rely on magic for day-to-day life, so I'm not really gonna miss it."

"Something only a non-magic user would say. Speaking for myself, I think using magic is a good thing, including for emergencies... Well, if you're not concerned about it, that's fine."

Ferris sighed with a look of resignation at Subaru's indifference and his lack of a sense of danger.

"But I will say that nothing has changed. You must not abuse your gate by using magic. Mark my words, the poison inside the gate has been cleanly drawn out, but that doesn't mean it's healed. Let's see. You should rest your gate for…two months."

"Two months, huh? Pretty low hurdle for a human being who's lived for seventeen years of his life without any magic."

That was when Subaru remembered that technically not even two months had passed since he'd been summoned to this new world. Though he'd personally experienced something like four months' worth of time, chronologically speaking, it was right around two—

When he reflected on all that had happened during those months, he wasn't sure whether two months of rest was a low hurdle or a high one.

"Well, there's no way incidents like that will just keep on happeni— Wait, was that an event flag just now?!"

"Unfortunately, healing the inside of your head is outside of Ferri's specialization, *meow*."

While Ferris was verbally laying into him, Subaru shuddered. His physical reaction made Subaru realize that they needed to bring the chitchat to an end. He reached out a hand toward Ferris.

*"Meow?"*

"You've been a big help. I don't think I've ever addressed that properly. You healed my wounds and my gate, but more than that, I never would've made it past the White Whale and Sloth without you… Thanks for Rem, too."

"…You probably didn't mean that in a mean or sarcastic way, but that's what it sounds like, *meow*."

"The moment I said it, I thought it totally came off that way, too."

But he genuinely felt grateful. Certainly, Subaru had his differences with Ferris, and each had posed an existential threat to the other at some points. But when Subaru added it all up, his gratitude to Ferris far outweighed any hard feelings.

For a while, Ferris remained silent, looking down at the hand Subaru had offered. Then—

"…Your fingers are thin! Your hand's super-small! Guess I can't say, 'Oh, your fingers are the only manly thing about you!'"

"Ferri is adorable, so why would you be hung up on something like that?!"

After a moment's hesitation, they shared a handshake that left Subaru surprised by the feel of Ferris's hand while Ferris wore a suspiciously charming smile. It was adorable. When you added in his slender limbs and light skin, Ferris seemed like the ideal beautiful maiden—

"But, you're still a guy. Damn it, what the hell..."

"Hey, it's Lady Crusch who wanted Ferri to wear this. She said the outfit suits me and makes me shine the brightest... Besides, it reflects my entire body and spirit."

"But that's..."

Subaru had been about to say, *not something this Crusch knows*, but he stopped himself midway.

Ferris knew that without Subaru's having to say it. It wasn't something for which mere words sufficed. Subaru flapping his lips and acting as if he understood would only upset Ferris.

"Regardless of what happens with the royal selection, I will protect Lady Crusch no matter what."

"...Huh?"

The unexpected cold words that rang in Subaru's ears drove him into silence.

It was a quiet whisper, echoing emotions that had frozen over. Even though he had been talking with Ferris right up until that very moment, it took a moment for Subaru to fully realize who had spoken those words.

Ferris's head was lowered; Subaru couldn't see his eyes past his hair. But the palm in Subaru's grasp was very hot.

"Ferris...?"

"And thaaat's why you have to keep your promise, right, Subawu?"

However, that ominous presence lasted but a single moment. Subaru was still at a loss for words when Ferris's head seemed to bounce back up, his demeanor the same as usual. His eyes had a mischievous glint to them as he continued.

"You'd better, or I'll make you suffer before killing you by making the mana inside your body go craaaazy."

"Could you stop saying stuff scary enough to kill people with such a cute voice and that pretty face of yours?!"

Ferris pulled back his hand, laughed as he disembarked from the dragon carriage, then bowed. Subaru felt weary just watching him, though that brief instant where he'd seen an unknown side of Ferris still weighed heavily in his chest.

Those intense words had to be how Ferris truly felt, an expression of both his tenacity and his resolve.

And Subaru was no bystander in the matter—that was what both believed.

"Ah, Subaru. Is Rem's bed all ready?"

It was just after Ferris hopped out of the dragon carriage that Emilia appeared at the front gate.

When the dragon carriages were ready to depart, Emilia came over. Her silver hair was bundled into a triple braid.

"Does everything seem fine? Will it hold up until we make it back to the mansion?"

"No problemo. Patlash and I are pumped up and ready for some stunt driving. I'll pop a wheelie."

"I don't really understand why, but I have a reeeally bad feeling about this 'wheel-ee,' so I forbid it."

"Aww, that's too bad. And I was planning to use some risky driving to set Emilia-tan's heart aflutter with the suspension bridge effect."

Replying with typical jokes like he usually would, Subaru gave the dragon carriage a tap to knock on wood. His reply made Emilia's violet eyes slightly worried, but she didn't say anything.

"Yep. Anyway, though with some lingering regrets, it's time to get this show on the road, *meow*?"

With a clap of his hands, it was Ferris who brought an official end to the awkward pause. When all eyes gathered upon him, attention immediately shifted to Crusch, standing right beside him.

"Now, Lady Crusch. If you have any final things to say to Lady Emilia…"

"Yes, I suppose I do."

With Ferris ceding the stage to her, Crusch took a step forward. With the men who served her—Ferris and Wilhelm—at her back, she stood at attention as she turned toward Subaru and Emilia.

"First, though I have said this many times, I am deeply grateful to both of you. I may have lost my memories, but I believe it is thanks to your cooperation that our lives have been connected, intertwined with my desires from before I lost my memories. Thank you very much."

"N-not at all… There is nothing you need to thank me for with such words, Lady Crusch. I spent most of the last several days out of the loop rather than doing anything."

"It's a fact that you were out of the loop for the main events. But, relax, 'kay? I got a lot of stuff done right. Any credit I earn belongs to you, Emilia-tan."

"All Subawu's sins belong to Lady Emilia, too, *meow.*"

"Don't pick at my scars!!"

When Subaru moved to reassure the apologetic Emilia, Ferris swiftly inserted himself into the conversation, poking fun at him for what had transpired at the royal palace. Laughter erupted in front of the gate the instant Subaru raised his voice.

A few days prior, Subaru wouldn't have even dreamed of laughing those events off.

Of course, that didn't mean he could just forget about how and why he had acquired those scars, but—

"It's all right. From here on, I have many things I need to properly talk about with Subaru."

"…"

Emilia, the only one not to laugh, spoke those words with a sincerity in her eyes.

They seemed to say that whatever the results of Subaru's actions, she would face them head-on. This was proof she had truly accepted Subaru. In name and fact, Subaru truly stood by her side.

"Let us be sure to meet again in the near future. Lady Emilia,

Master Subaru Natsuki, I believe we shall maintain friendly relations for a long time to come."

Crusch smiled pleasantly as she offered those words, turning a gaze toward the pair that left no room for deceit.

Even after she'd lost her memories, her nobility remained undiminished. Crusch, whose existence radiated honesty, did not deal in lies or conceits.

Perhaps that had been conveyed painfully clearly. Emilia lowered her eyes, her lips trembling.

"I...am a candidate in competition with you, Lady Crusch. Even with an alliance, we will someday become enemies again."

"Yes. I must strive to do my best so that I do not lose to you, Lady Emilia."

"Besides that, I am a half-elf, with silver hair at that... You're not...afraid of me?"

"Emilia, that's..."

Subaru tried to stop whatever she was trying to say, but when he saw Emilia's expression, he said no more.

Emilia had posed that question with a desperate, serious look in her eyes. At that point, no one who understood even a tiny fraction of her feelings could thoughtlessly intervene.

Besides, Subaru knew Crusch—and knew that even now, her soul remained unclouded.

"—The worth of the soul is determined by the worth of a person's actions. Whether for themselves, or for others, we should all live in whatever fashion makes us shine brightest, to live in a way that brings no shame on our souls."

"..."

"Or rather, I apparently used to say that often. Hearing it now...from the perspective of the listener, the words sound rather pretentious, do they not?"

Unable to help herself, Crusch let a smile slip as she talked about her own past statement. While listening to the words, Emilia had pursed her lips in silence, likely considering them emblematic of a deeper truth.

"Lady Emilia, do you believe the way you live now is shameful?"

"…I…do not. I have lived this far believing that whatever others may think of me, at the very least, I must not hate myself."

"Then there is nothing for you to fear or regret. Hone yourself, strive harder, and walk straight and true on your own path—you possess a…wonderful soul."

Once she had finished speaking, Crusch unflinchingly offered Emilia her hand.

"I am pleased to have had a chance to come to know you. I feel no fear."

"—!"

As if she felt pain in her chest, Emilia's cheeks stiffened as she stared down at Crusch's hand. Crusch quietly awaited Emilia's response without any attempts to hurry her.

Finally, Emilia very, very gently touched Crusch's hand, exchanging a handshake with her.

"I hope you remain in good health. I look forward to meeting you again soon."

"I… No, I do as well. Most likely, I will be able to stand firm before you when that time comes, Lady Crusch. Until then, please be well."

The two royal candidates swore to do their best, exchanging promises to meet again.

As he watched them share those oaths off to the side, Subaru's chest was filled with a sense of accomplishment. Subaru had suffered, struggled, and endured much agony. This was the moment they had finally gained something tangible for it.

He hadn't been able to manage a perfect finish, but—

"I don't wanna regret anything I've done, or forget what I've accomplished and make you feel like it's somehow your fault."

Subaru glanced back at the dragon carriage before he closed his eyes, imagining the sleeping Rem.

This was a place for celebration. He couldn't use Rem as an excuse to feel sorry for himself. She wouldn't want something like that, either—or perhaps he was selfish to think that.

"Master Subaru Natsuki, I hope you remain in good health as

well. I pray from the bottom of my heart that...your future exploits help this girl recover as soon as possible."

"It's not really a good thing if it requires my exploits in the first place... I'm a useless man except for extreme situations, when I'll borrow anyone's help to get things done... What happened to Rem, and what happened to you, Crusch, aren't someone else's problem. I'll make sure to find a way."

Crusch smiled pleasantly, seeking a handshake from Subaru as well. Too embarrassed to place his hand over the one she offered, Subaru did not shake her hand; instead, he briefly met her palm with his.

A small, dry sound rang out, and with that, the touch between Subaru and Crusch was over.

"Let us certainly meet again."

These words spoken, Lady Crusch and retainers bowed, seeing Subaru & Co. off on their way.

2

A delicate, stifling atmosphere filled the dragon carriage on its way back to the mansion.

"..."

Crusch had added the large dragon carriage to Patlash as part of his reward from her. Wide enough to seat ten passengers, it was total overkill, with plenty of room to spare.

At present, the only occupants were Subaru, Emilia, and Rem, who slept on the simple bed. With Subaru sitting beside the Sleeping Princess, and Emilia sitting a short distance removed in silent consideration for the unconscious Rem, a rather awkward air had spread throughout the carriage.

"...Feels like it was a mistake to put the brats on a different carriage, huh?"

The village children who had ridden in the dragon carriage with them on their way to the capital were in a different one for the return trip. He'd arranged it out of consideration for the villagers, thinking they wouldn't want to hear talk related to the royal selection, but this had backfired on him.

There certainly was a lot they needed to talk about. But a trigger was nary to be—

"—Um, by any chance, is the absence of a topic putting you in a bind? This oppressive silence, this heavy atmosphere, I simply cannot bear it."

"Why are you butting in all of a sudden? Wait, you were here?"

"I was indeed! Of course, I have been here the whole while! In the first place, how do you think I ended up cooperating with you and getting abused by the Witch Cult, Mr. Natsuki?!"

"Personal hobby of yours?"

"Not even a cat has enough lives for that kind of hobby!!"

Peering in through the intervening window from the driver's seat and letting a grandiose amount of spittle fly was a young man—the merchant Otto Suwen, who had cooperated in the final battle against the Witch Cult.

Subaru smiled mischievously at Otto, who'd volunteered to accompany them as their coachman for the return trip.

"I'm kidding. Your objective is to talk with Roswaal and have him buy up all your cargo. I didn't forget."

"I am truly counting on you. Truly, my very life depends on it!"

Otto was all worked up for a big showdown, but Subaru could see no future for him save Roswaal leading him around by the nose. Having been aided by him, Subaru wanted to lend a hand, but…

"I can't speak for the man himself, but your odds are pretty slim…"

"I can hear you, you know?! You meant to hide it, didn't you?!"

When Otto, eyes bulging, overheard Subaru speaking to himself, Subaru's shoulders sank. When she witnessed this exchange between the pair, Emilia's big eyes went wide as she spoke.

"I'm so surprised. Somehow, you two reeeally get along with each other."

"I don't get along with him at all. He's just someone who saved my life, that's all."

"You can't deny it, so don't explain it away!!"

When Otto had been captured by the Witch Cult and was on the verge of becoming a human sacrifice, Subaru was the main person behind his rescue. Strictly speaking, it was the Iron Fangs who had saved Otto's life, but that was something of a tangent.

Either way, thanks to Otto, the awkward atmosphere inside the carriage had greatly abated.

"And while I thank you for the current mood, it is time to bid you farewell for a while."

"Hey, wait a—! You keep treating me like a pest at the drop of a h—"

Subaru closed the shutter, cutting off Otto midshout. With *Well, that job's done* on his face, Subaru looked back. Emilia wore a surprised look as their eyes met. And then—

"Pfft." "Ha-ha-ha."

Unable to take any more, the two abruptly broke up in laughter. For a while thereafter, the pair's laughing voices echoed inside the dragon carriage. When their laughter finally died down, Subaru said, "Reading the awkward atmosphere and keeping quiet, that's really not like me, huh?"

"No, it really isn't like you, Subaru. The Subaru I know is more… a boy always full of energy and doing reckless things, stirring up trouble with almost no regard for my feelings at all."

"I feel like that translates to a braggart who can't read the mood to save his life!"

In point of fact, this was without doubt an assessment he could not refute. Laughing awkwardly as he scratched his face, Subaru slowly sat down beside Emilia. She narrowed her eyes toward him.

"…Subaru, you sit next to me like it's a natural thing."

"—? Huh? Something strange about that?"

"No… At first, it made me nervous, but for some reason, it doesn't now, so it's all right."

Emilia shook her head as her thoughts on Subaru's sitting beside her trickled out.

For meals at the mansion and the conversations with minor spirits that were a daily ritual for Emilia, and in many other everyday settings, Subaru had stood and sat by Emilia's side as was his wont, but…

"All that hard, painstaking work finally paid off. I'm so moved…!"

"There you go making light of things again… Even though I don't want you to do that weird bluffing."

When Subaru clenched a fist and murmured, Emilia's cheeks puffed up in dissatisfaction. Then, after ever so slightly moving her hips away, she turned her eyes to the simple bed at the back.

"You've been thinking about Rem the whole time. You don't need to hide it."

"Ta-ha-ha…"

With Emilia's sullen gaze sealing all avenues of retreat, Subaru conceded with a listless laugh.

"Yeah, I have been. I've been thinking about her a huge ton. I think she's been on my mind this whole time because I felt *I've gotta do something*. I want to think of Emilia-tan first and foremost, but…this time I just couldn't keep things in the right order. Sorry."

"I'm not upset about that at all. I said it back at Lady Crusch's mansion, too, didn't I?"

She'd said she wanted to understand all the concerns and worries Subaru harbored.

Yes, he remembered Emilia had spoken those words to him. He had been so happy, he'd cried.

Even so—

"She's very precious to you, isn't she?"

"Precious, super-precious. As precious as you are to me, Emilia-tan."

"…Do you realize that's a reeeally selfish thing to say?"

"I do. To be honest, I feel so bad about it I wanna roll over and die. But I'm super-serious, so…"

He conveyed his honest, undisguised feelings to Emilia loud and clear.

Scoundrel though it made Subaru, Rem's presence inside him was simply that large. Without exaggeration, it was every bit as large as his feelings toward Emilia.

Hence, he continued praying for Rem's recovery, glad that he had not upset Emilia in the process.

To find a way to make that recovery happen, Subaru Natsuki would take on any trial.

"—I'm sure you'll find it. A way to bring her back."

"Emilia-tan?"

With Subaru engaging in that extremely selfish reasoning, Emilia gave a thin, charming smile and nodded. She ran a finger through her silver hair as she stared straight at Subaru's raised face.

"I think, in the sense of being motivated by selfish reasons, you and I are probably very alike, Subaru... I'm well aware I joined the royal selection for a selfish reason of my own."

"A selfish reason... You mean, a world of equality without any discrimination—that reason?"

Subaru reminisced about the desire Emilia had spoken of when she declared her beliefs at the royal selection conference.

As a half-elf, Emilia had been exposed to discrimination like few others. Was it not natural for her to want an egalitarian world?

However, Emilia sadly shook her head in the face of Subaru's understanding of the matter.

"Not that. I started this with something that was reeeally personal..."

"..."

"...I'm sorry. I can't really explain it with words. I don't want to hide it from you, Subaru. But I'm not sure what I should say."

Emilia was at a loss for words, vexed that she could not speak well about what was in her head. If there was no tangible answer to be had, Subaru didn't want to try to force her to give him one.

If the details about the emotions welling in her breast were secretly related to why she had entered the royal selection to begin with—

"—We'll talk about everything after we catch up with Roswaal."

"You'll forgive me, then?"

"You haven't done anything wrong, so I don't need to forgive you. If anything, the stuff I talked about is more of a problem... Besides, Roswaal might know something about the Rem issue, too."

So far as Subaru knew, there was no one in that world better connected to both the top and the underside worlds than Roswaal L. Mathers himself. Considering the detail that the clown-looking eccentric had nominated Emilia for the royal selection, it was about time they got him to spill his guts.

There was also the matter of what the hell he had been thinking, not even lifting a single finger during the Witch Cult attack.

"But if we're putting that off until after we get back to the mansion…"

"Yeah?"

"If you don't mind, Subaru…I'd like you to tell me about Rem."

—For one moment, the suggestion sent pain running through Subaru's chest.

But this was not because he rejected Emilia's suggestion. It was from pure worry and hesitation.

Could Subaru speak words that could truly suffice about Rem, the girl who had saved him?

"Ahh, yeah, that's gonna get a bit long, but I'll tell you all about it. To me, memories of Rem are as precious as my memories of you since meeting you two months ago, Emilia-tan."

Hiding his sentiments behind his words, Subaru began to speak of day-to-day life during those two months.

When, after meeting Emilia in the royal capital, he'd awoken in the mansion, greeted by Rem and Ram—

"_____"

Once he started telling the tale, he couldn't stop. Emilia continued quietly listening to Subaru's story.

And in the end, he continued without pause until they arrived back in the Mathers domain.

3

"Hey, you two, we've finally arrived at our destination."

When Otto shared that news from the driver's seat, it was evening, half a day since they'd departed from the royal capital.

The report through the shutter made Subaru break off his story and turn his eyes to look through the side window.

"Oh, really? Faster than I thought."

"It seems you were caught up in your story. We made excellent time down the highway as well. Perhaps, thanks to departing in the early morning and arriving before nightfall, everyone from the village will be that much more relieved."

"I'm so glad. Otto, thank you very much. It's a relief we made it to the village safe and sound."

As Subaru leaned forward, Emilia was right beside him, gazing through the same window as she thanked Otto.

"I am honored that you would say so, Lady Emilia... I wish Mr. Natsuki would praise my endeavors in a more straightforward manner."

"Hey, don't be that way. My personality means I say a lot of things that don't match what I'm actually thinking. Catch on already."

"How can those words come from your mouth after all the things you've said to date?!"

Otto's voice rose at Subaru's poor treatment. "Now, now," said Emilia, scolding Subaru for his attitude toward Otto. "I'm sorry, Otto. It's Subaru's bad habit to tease the people he is fond of..."

"Wait, wait, you've got it all wrong! I don't do that to you, Emilia-tan!"

"But you do it to Beatrice, don't you?"

"Considering how much of a loli that girl is, that statement's all kinds of wrong!"

In terms of experiencing Subaru's teasing, Beatrice and Otto certainly had something in common. But how he felt about either of them wasn't related in any way to his being nice. It was simply an issue of the company he kept.

"Mr. Natsuki, Lady Emilia."

"What? Right now, I'm busy clearing up Emilia-tan's grievous misunderstanding..."

"We've arrived at the village... But there seems to be something amiss."

"_____"

The abrupt call in a low voice made Subaru and Emilia make eye contact. When they hurried to follow Otto's gaze, they were drawing near Earlham Village, their destination right down the road.

The village was a familiar sight. The lack of human presence made this eerily similar to the last time Subaru had seen it: an uninhabited village, right after the villagers had been evacuated to flee from the Witch Cult. In other words—

"—Ram and the villagers in the Sanctuary haven't come back?"

That was the conclusion they reached after Subaru and the others split up to check out Earlham Village. Concern stood out clearly on the faces of the returning villagers after they failed to find any sign of the others—the ones who had split off and fled to the Sanctuary midevacuation, and who should have long returned by now.

"According to Ram, the Sanctuary is a seven-to-eight-hour trip from here. To not have returned ahead of us after we spent three days in the capital..."

"We mustn't be hasty. It might be simple prudence until they're certain the village is safe."

"Would Roswaal act that passive once he heard the circumstances? During the demon beast incident a while back, he immediately ended it with brute force. It's just weird that he hasn't done anything this time."

Roswaal possessed magic that gave him the ability to fly through the sky. That was a simple and effective way to reconnoiter his own territory, even if he was being cautious. Even discounting that, Ram, with her Clairvoyance, would be right by his side.

It was obvious he had already learned about their victory over the Witch Cult. The fact that he had not returned to the mansion despite that meant—

"There's a reason he didn't come back... Did something happen in the Sanctuary?"

Subaru and Emilia turned their faces toward each other, both having arrived at the same point of view.

The pair's concerns were shared by the remaining people of

Earlham Village. They had hoped to be reunited with the family members who had returned to the village ahead of them. Considering the villagers' mental state, they all had to find out what had happened as quickly as possible. They had to, but—

"So, Emilia-tan…do you know where the Sanctuary is?"

"Eh?! S-Subaru, don't you know where it is?"

Emilia's surprise at Subaru's question raised a fundamental issue. It was simple, and large: they didn't actually know where this Sanctuary was actually located.

"It's kind of late to be asking this, but this Sanctuary, what sort of place is it?"

"I don't know… Roswaal said it was kind of like a secret hideout. Besides…"

"Besides?"

"…No, it's nothing. Sorry, I wish I'd asked him more properly at the time."

When Emilia made that rather awkward-sounding apology, Subaru shook his head and reflected on his own sins. However much in a hurry they'd been to evacuate the villagers, it was Subaru's fault a thousand times over for being careless. Worst case, they'd probably find some sort of clue about the location of the Sanctuary inside the mansion, but…

"For that, too, we'd better go to the mansion for now. I want to put Rem where she can have proper rest… Otto, you don't have a place to stay, do you? Come with us."

"Ueeeh?! T-to the marquis's mansion?! I-I would be more at ease sleeping in the dragon carriage!"

"Oh, shut up and play along. —Sorry, everyone! Just wait a little longer!"

Squishing Otto's tearful words flat, Subaru called out to the people of the village. His appeal to them could not wipe away all their anxiety, but they sent spirited voices back Subaru's way nonetheless.

With the villagers watching them go, they had the dragon carriage gallop once more—and ten minutes later, they saw Roswaal Manor in all its familiar splendor.

"It is even larger than it appears to be when seen from afar... I feel even more out of place..."

"Don't chicken out after coming this far. Even if you do, you'll never make it all the way back home."

With Otto struck by the majesty of the mansion, Subaru offered those words of persuasion as they headed through the front gate onto the manor grounds. They proceeded to stop the dragon carriage outside the front door, inside which, in a sense, the mansion of old times awaited.

"It's supposed to be three days for me, same as Emilia-tan, but..."

When Subaru looked up at the mansion, deeply moved, he murmured as he felt complex emotions in his chest.

As a matter of fact, Subaru had returned last to the mansion four days prior, engaging in an elaborate act to get Emilia to flee. However, emotionally speaking, he didn't want to think of that as *coming home*.

It was at this very instant that he felt he had finally returned.

"Well, that's what I think from the bottom of my heart..."

"Mr. Natsuki, setting aside whatever you may have thought, shall I put the dragon carriage in the stables? As for Miss Rem sleeping in the bed in back..."

"—I'll carry Rem. You don't need to do anything."

Subaru closed his mouth, realizing he'd unconsciously let out a hard, barbed voice. Otto, who had no doubt his own suggestion had been a good one, appeared stern at the sharpness of Subaru's reply.

Subaru couldn't help having an exaggerated reaction where Rem was concerned, even though he knew that Otto and Emilia had shown plenty of consideration for her to that point on their journey.

"...Sorry. Please put Patlash and the dragon carriage in back of the mansion. I'll get things ready on the inside."

"Understood. Think nothing of it, Mr. Natsuki."

Otto accepted the apology, heading for the stable without any sign of offense. Subaru disembarked from the carriage with Rem on his back, headed toward the mansion's front doorway along with Emilia.

"Come to think of it, I don't remember locking the door when we left. Could burglars get in?"

"Not that…it's her job, but I don't think we need to worry with Beatrice here. I wonder if she'd…come greet us at the door if we knocked?"

Without touching on the exchange with Otto, Emilia voiced a very un-Emilia-like joke.

It was rather difficult to picture *that* Beatrice greeting Subaru and Emilia at the door with a face full of joy, particularly considering the way she and Subaru had last parted.

Even so, there was no harm in trying.

"Maybe she'll rush out to set eyes on Puck…"

"It really would be odd of her, though."

Half-jokingly, Emilia smiled as she made the door knocker resound. The sharp, hard sound reverberated inside the mansion. Naturally, there was neither master nor servant in the mansion to repl—

"—Yes, please wait a moment."

"Eh?"

Subaru and Emilia were both dumbstruck by the reply that ought not to have existed. Then, before the pair could recover from being frozen stiff, the entry doors to the mansion slowly opened.

"Welcome back, Lady Emilia. I have been eagerly awaiting your arrival."

Standing on the other side of the open double doors was a woman greeting the pair with perfect courtesy.

She had long, gleaming blonde hair, and emerald eyes that seemed as transparent as gemstones.

Her tall figure was clad in a classical maid outfit; she carried herself in a splendidly tidy, feminine manner.

Her age was twenty years, more or less, and any way he looked at her, she was a maid through and through—the problem being, she was not either of the two maids who had been assigned to Roswaal Manor.

にかっ☆

NIKA
(GRIN)

Subaru was frozen solid at the sight of the unfamiliar maid. But his tension soon eased.

Emilia, standing stiff at Subaru's side, furled her refined eyebrows and said, "...Frederica?"

She knew the other party's name. When addressed, the woman replied once more.

"Yes," she said, and the woman—Frederica—released her hands from the hem of the skirt they had held as she said, "I am Frederica Baumann, returning to duty from leave granted by the master."

Slowly lifting her face, Frederica sent a warm, amiable smile the pair's way.

When that smile struck Subaru's eyes, he opened his mouth wide.

"You must be tired from your long journey. First, allow me to show you inside the mans—"

"Scary face—!!"

Subaru's very, very loud shout echoed across the sky of Roswaal Manor.

Frederica's smile was completely ruined by the bizarre fangs filling her mouth.

4

When looking at her as a maid, Subaru found the woman named Frederica to be perfect.

She dressed in a maid uniform that was not gaudy in any way, her words and gestures were exceedingly refined, and her behavior bore not a single trace of waste. Seeing her standing straight like it was natural made one's own body straighten up.

In all functional matters, she scored a perfect 100 as a maid—appearance-wise, too, that mouth excepted.

"Subaru, you idiot! You can't go saying that to a girl! Apologize properly!"

"P-please cease, Lady Emilia. It is fine. I am accustomed to people being surprised the first time they meet me. I do not mind it whatsoever."

"No, I will not! When you do something bad you need to apologize, especially when you've hurt someone. Isn't that right?"

Frederica, the aggrieved party, had a conflicted look on her face at Emilia's red, anger-filled expression. Emilia's point of view was good and proper, something Subaru deeply acknowledged when he went down on his knees on the entryway's floor.

Subaru proceeded to bow his head deeply toward Frederica to show he had reflected on the error of his ways.

"No, what Emilia-tan's saying is right. I was completely in the wrong just now."

"Err..."

"I'm sorry I said something terrible all of a sudden when meeting you for the first time. Boil me, fry me, do whatever you like...though I'd prefer it be as painless as possible."

Subaru apologized in a manner that was more effeminate than manly. After he'd said such rude words to a woman he'd just met, he couldn't blame Frederica for any reply she might wish to make.

"Um, Frederica, listen, Subaru's not a bad child. It's just, he has a bad habit of saying things without thinking from time to time..."

Emilia added her own words to bolster Subaru's apology. The oddly maternal words weighed on his mind, but Subaru was happy she'd spoken up nonetheless.

Frederica fell into silence at the look of the pair for a time, but—

"—Tee-hee. Lady Emilia, Master Subaru, you are both quite amusing..."

"Frederica?"

"I said I am not upset in the slightest, yet you did this anyway. And Lady Emilia, acting so maternal in making Master Subaru apologize like this... Oh, this has become so amusing."

Frederica forgave Subaru while hiding her mouth behind her sleeve as she smiled. Even with Subaru kneeling in proper Japanese fashion, she cut his feet right out from under him. "Besides," she continued, "I cannot put off asking about the circumstances forever. There is the reason I have been recalled, the absence of the master... and that girl, the spitting image of Ram."

"_____"

Frederica's gaze shifted toward a sofa—the sofa upon which Rem had been laid down to rest. The words she used—"Ram's spitting image"—proved that she had a prior association with both sisters, Ram and Rem.

"Oh, now I remember. There was a maid who quit a little before I came to the mansion."

"*Quit* is not quite accurate. I was given leave so as to attend to personal matters… It is just that I have ended up returning sooner than I expected."

"If it's before Subaru came to the mansion… Three months ago, then? I'm happy to see you again, though."

Emilia and Frederica smiled at one another, pleased to be reunited. Even then, Frederica hid her mouth behind her sleeve; maybe Subaru's rude words had given her something of a complex about it.

Subaru was even more ashamed of his slip of the tongue, but Frederica spoke nothing of it as she motioned to the mansion with a hand.

"After being called back, I found the mansion an empty shell… I was completely at a loss. Fortunately, I was able to grasp the situation from a letter in the master's office."

"Letter?"

"Yes, a letter penned by Ram. Even though she had called me back, this was the only word she left… Perhaps I am being too soft on her in saying it is just like her?"

Frederica gave a strained smile. From that smile, Subaru felt the weight of years of familiarity and trust between her and Ram. Likely, she'd had a similar relationship with Rem.

"And the reason Ram called you back, Frederica?"

Subaru brushed aside the budding sentiment in his chest as he prodded Frederica onward. That said, the question had an obvious answer. The mansion had been on high alert with the Witch Cult aimed straight at it only a few days ago.

In other words, Ram had called Frederica back as emergency reinforcements for battle.

"By the time I returned, the mansion's kitchen and garden were in a rather terrible state."

"There was a compelling reason for that! Right, Emilia-tan?!"

"Wait, Subaru. It's not like this is Ram's fault. It's just, an odd breeze seemed to blow through the mansion for some reason, more as time went on... I wanted to help, too, but..."

"A-ahh, that's okay, it wasn't anything you could have coped with, Emilia-tan..."

"Yeah... And Ram said, 'This is nothing. Leave it to me. I shall manage somehow.'"

"Man, she really isn't all she makes herself out to be! ...No, when she said she'd manage somehow, she meant to throw it all onto Frederica's shoulders from the start, didn't she?! Ram, not that your self-assessment is wrong, but geez, try, damn it!"

It was a decision so like her, Subaru could practically see her snorting "Ha!" in the back of his mind. Emilia gave a pained smile at Subaru's reaction and said, "But it's so strange. Ram should have been working hard all the time you were gone, Frederica. I wonder why she was all a mess for only those d— Ah..."

After speaking about it that far, Emilia found her own answer. She'd surmised what had been happening at the mansion during Frederica's absence.

That there was "someone" working with Ram to maintain the mansion.

"And without that, Ram couldn't keep the mansion going by herself, so she...asked Frederica for help?"

Subaru sadly accepted the natural conclusion. The very fact that Ram had gotten into contact with Frederica was proof she didn't remember Rem.

—No, he had more than enough reason to deduce as much. He didn't need direct confirmation.

"I'll take Rem to her room and explain to Frederica along the way. Emilia-tan, Otto's waiting outside... Can I get you to go invite him in?"

"Mm, understood… You'll be all right?"

"If Emilia-tan shows me a smiling face, I'll give even a Archbishop of the Seven Deadly Sins a butt kicking."

Emilia had a downtrodden expression on her, but Subaru spoke flippantly with a little smile. She proceeded to do as asked, heading out of the room to invite Otto, most likely waiting at the mansion's entrance, inside.

Watching her back as she left, Subaru said, "Now, then…" and turned back toward the sofa as he said, "This is Rem, Ram's little sister… You probably don't remember her, right?"

"Unfortunately, I do not. However, there really is no room for any doubt."

When Subaru, adjusting the sleeping Rem's position on his back, posed that question, Frederica drew in her chin. Subaru sighed at her reply, indicating the corridor with a motion of his chin.

"We'll talk on the way. I want to let Rem…sleep in her own room."

"I understand. This way, please."

Keeping her words to a minimum, Frederica opened the door as if to lead Subaru out. Together with her, Subaru headed to the mansion's east wing—toward Rem's bedroom.

"As far as I could tell, Rem and Ram are sisters that really get along…"

On the way to that room, Subaru told Frederica about facts lost to her: what kind of girl Rem was, what she'd been doing to that point in her life, just how lovely she was.

He spoke much like he had to Emilia on the road back to the mansion—

"_____"

As Subaru spoke to Frederica, he stated, and replied to, a number of thoughts inside his own head.

There had to have been a better way.

During the battle, he'd thought _I've done the best I can._ Somewhere, though, there had likely been a better, a more perfect outcome, one with the greatest possible results. And yet, Subaru had let it slip through his fingers.

If only he was smarter, surely Subaru would have noticed it.

As one example, the letter of goodwill that Crusch's envoy had brought to Emilia. Subaru had concluded that this letter, the root of much misunderstanding because it was blank, was a plot by the Witch Cult, but in that, he had been mistaken.

At that point the Witch Cult surely hadn't caught on to Subaru's actions, and no opportunity had presented itself to swap one letter of goodwill for another. In the first place, sleight of hand such as swapping missives wasn't the Witch Cult's style; it favored more direct acts of violence, something Subaru knew better than anyone.

In that case, there could only be a single truth behind the blank missive.

"The contents of the letter of goodwill were written by Rem. I'm the one who asked it to be sent, so if Crusch handed it to the messenger...only the fact that it was handed over stayed the same, and only the contents were erased."

That was the sloppy adjustment to the erasure of the memory of Rem from the world.

If only he'd noticed, if only he'd stopped to think more seriously about *why* the letter of goodwill was blank, if only he'd seen the truth behind it, he would have realized the tragedy that had befallen Rem.

Even if it was a tragedy occurring at a time when there was no turning back.

"That is a rather difficult story to believe."

He arrived at the usual answer to his own question at the same time that Frederica, having finished listening to his story, quietly spoke those words to him. The words held no ring of denial behind them. She looked around the area.

"So this is her...Rem's room. It is completely tidied up, but..."

When the two entered the room—Rem's bedroom—it looked like a guest room, with all personal possessions removed. It was the same sight Subaru had seen previously, on the go-around when he had returned powerless after the White Whale had stolen Rem from him.

That time, too, Rem's existence had been forgotten. Her bedroom had been just as clean and empty then as it had now become.

"Ram was probably dealing in her own way with the unnatural gap left by Rem being erased."

The faint hint of her breath and the warmth of her body were the only proof that she was alive. The symptoms of a Sleeping Princess were to require no food or water—simply to breathe and to sleep.

"Master Subaru, if she must be cared for in any way, I shall..."

"I want to do it. Let me do it. It's Rem's first return to the mansion like this, so I *have* to...no, I want to do it. Sorry to be so selfish."

Subaru put on a brave face and tucked Rem in bed, determined to do whatever he could for her. Subaru's words made Frederica pull back the outstretched hand she had offered him, narrowing her eyes.

"No, it is not selfish in the least. If anything, it makes my chest get a little tighter. For someone with eyes like a murderer, you are very kind, aren't you?"

"Hey, don't casually dis me like that, it really wounds my heart!"

When Frederica pointed out the look of Subaru's eyes, his voice went shrill as she smiled mischievously. He immediately realized that she was paying him back for the rude words he'd spoken to her earlier. In a true sense, the exchange just then had fulfilled the conditions for reconciliation between them.

"To begin with, you won't need to care for Rem. She doesn't need food or even baths... But please, pay her as much mind as you can. That's the only thing I ask."

"I shall take that to heart. If she is Ram's little sister, she might as well be my own. I wonder what kind of reaction the master and Ram shall have when they return?"

"I can't read Roswaal's... I don't really want to think about how Ram will react."

The sisters truly got along well. The older sister doted on the younger; the younger revered the older. It was a relationship filled with love.

He didn't want to see that scene fracture before his eyes, even if its fracturing was a fact from which there was ultimately no escape.

"I understand about the master and Ram. As for the reason for their absence from the mansion, if it was the Witch Cult going on the move due to Lady Emilia's entry into the royal selection...it is the natural decision to make."

"Did you hear about the royal selection stuff before you stopped working?"

"Lady Emilia came to the mansion about half a year ago. I was still here at the mansion at the time. My being given leave was related to it as well."

While Subaru put things in order at Rem's bedside, Frederica continued preparing everything besides the bed. Subaru knit his brows, sensing that something was off about the conversation he was having with her.

"What do you mean by, your stopping working and taking a leave of absence was related to the royal selection...?"

"My duty was essentially to tidy up the master's personal affairs for the royal selection."

"Personal affairs?"

"It was clear that nominating Lady Emilia, a half-elf, as a candidate would invite troubles. Before that, the master sent those around him away. Even here at the mansion, he left only Ram, capable of defending herself... Ram and most likely Rem, making two."

That answer accounted for the weird feeling Subaru had experienced upon first arriving at the mansion.

Considering the sheer size of Roswaal Manor, it would be nigh impossible to keep only the sisters Ram and Rem as servants. In actuality, Rem's skill kept the mansion afloat, but still.

"Upon the master's instructions, many servants were sent off to perform duties elsewhere. As a senior staff member, I assisted in this. In the end, I, too, left the mansion...though I ended up returning, as you can see."

"..."

Frederica's return to the mansion had been an effect of losing Rem. Subaru had already arrived at the answer to that question, but at the same time, hearing her words then and there made doubts sprout inside his chest.

Namely, Roswaal's steps to prepare for the royal selection had been a far cry from his actions ever since.

"Hey, Frederica. How much has he actually told you?"

"Master Subaru?"

"From what you're telling me, Roswaal made all kinds of preparations for the royal selection. It's common sense that half-elves and the Witch Cult are connected, so he had to know it'd be dangerous. In spite of that…"

There, Subaru's words trailed off as he continued to stare at Frederica.

"Where are his countermeasures against the Witch Cult, then? Rem and Crusch both said he had to have 'em. But I don't think he was relying on me. And if not, why'd it come to…"

The sights of the people of Earlham Village, slaughtered and tormented by the Witch Cult, and Rem and Ram, casualties in the battle against the cult, came rushing to the forefront of his mind—such was the tragedy that had befallen the Mathers domain.

Where were the countermeasures in those scenes? Roswaal wasn't anywhere to be found.

"If you know there was something, then…!"

"Unfortunately, I have no way to know the master's thinking in its entirety. There are most likely only two people in this world that he deems worthy of trust."

"Two people…? Who? Who are these two people Roswaal trusts?"

"—Ram, and the Great Spirit in the archive of forbidden books."

According to Frederica, as far as she knew, there were two people who might know Roswaal's intentions. He had no room to doubt the first. Ram, offering Roswaal her undivided fealty, was surely worthy of that trust.

However, the second possibility was a bolt out of the blue.

"The Great Spirit, in the archive of forbidden books…"

"A room inside this mansion separated from the rest via magic. Exactly how the Great Spirit separates the archive of forbidden books from the outside world via her own magic is…especially secret."

Frederica's respectful explanation left Subaru wide-eyed and at a loss for words. It was too far removed from his own recollections. But, unable to form any other reply—

"Her name is?"

With decisive certainty, Subaru posed that question to Frederica. Perhaps the reaction was not what she had expected, for Frederica seemed taken back for a moment. Finally, she replied:

"Lady Beatrice. That is the Great Spirit serving as the librarian of this mansion's archive of forbidden books."

5

The instant he turned the doorknob, somehow, he was sure.

As he walked around the mansion, his attention was abruptly drawn to the presence of the door. When he walked over and touched the doorknob, the suspicion that something was off about it instantly changed to certainty.

When he reacted to the open door that was simply "there," peering inside it—

"Heya. Been a while."

As Subaru lightly waved a hand, the archive of forbidden books spread before him, not changed whatsoever from before.

The large room packed with bookshelves was filled with the aroma particular to old books. Neither the thin gloom of the windowless room nor the serenity of the air had changed one iota. That applied not only to the room itself, but to the girl who guarded the archive as well.

The girl—Beatrice—sat on a stool instead of a chair, eyes lowered to the book resting on her lap.

"—Considering the ruckus in the mansion, is it from your return, I wonder?"

Beatrice glanced upward, beholding Subaru in her blue eyes as she murmured in apparent boredom. Then the girl seemed to lose interest, her eyes returning to the book once more.

"If you have returned, I should presume that the uproar of late has finally abated."

"Yeah, thanks to y— Or rather, you sure gave me a hard time. Do you have any idea how scared I was to have you not listen to me and run during the operation?!"

"Do I know or care, I wonder? I never asked you to worry about me in the first place."

"I'm pretty sure I said *I have a reason to worry about you*. I don't think I'm wrong, then or now."

Beatrice's words were unapologetic. Nor did Subaru retreat a single step with his reply.

When, on the eve of the Witch Cult's onslaught, Subaru's words urged Beatrice to evacuate, she had rejected them. As things turned out, the mansion had not incurred any damage, but going by that would be nothing more than argument by hindsight.

"A lot of people worried about you, Emilia and Ram in particular. You can do it later, but you should give them a proper apology."

"Apologize? Betty should apologize? Am I at pains to understand why it is necessary to do such a thing, and to whom?"

"Don't get all stubborn for nothing… If you're gonna be that stuck up about it, I'll go apologize to everyone in your place. I'll tell them you were bawling your eyes out with tears of gratitude when you told me to thank them."

"Do not speak such falsehoods! Do my tears truly flow for that long, I wonder?!"

His provocations with a flippant tongue raised the volume of Beatrice's voice, just like usual. Oddly, this filled his own chest with deep emotion, which made Subaru narrow his eyes.

There he was, exchanging words with Beatrice like that once more. Even after they'd parted ways in such a deeply meaningful manner, even though he still had a mountain of things he desired to ask her, things were as boisterous as before.

Exceedingly relieved by that fact, Subaru let out a listless sigh.

"You can dial back the drama a notch. It's not a bad thing to bawl your eyes out once in a while, you know?"

"Coming from a man who cried like a little baby on the lap of the woman he likes, those words do bear a certain weight."

"Can't you just forget about that already?!"

Once that had happened, when impassable hurdles piled higher and higher, sending his emotions crashing against a dam until they smashed apart. When he thought back to that time, his face burned so much he felt like it might catch on fire. All the same, though, the glow of the precious memory burned in his chest just as much.

Trying to paper over those complex emotions, Subaru loudly cleared his throat and changed the course of the conversation.

"...Anyway. I'm glad we're both safe and sound. Now is the time to come to an understanding."

"Understanding? Were you not the one to speak on your own, I wonder? Always so self-serving."

"Yeah, I suppose I always am self-serving. Most of the times I talk to you go like that. Do you remember? When we played tag here in the mansion, when we had the snow festival..."

Beatrice narrowed both eyes as Subaru began talking in a whimsical fashion. As her blue gaze shot through him, Subaru made various gestures as he reminisced out loud.

It was as if he was choosing his words with great care, diving deeper and deeper into their memories so that they touched upon the truth.

"It was like that during the demon beast uproar, too. Back then you helped me a ton when you lifted that curse."

"Stop it."

"As a result, I sucked up an even bigger curse, which backed me into a seriously bad corner. After that, to heal me it'd take going after the Urugarums in the forest, so—!"

Subaru's rapid-fire speech was powerfully cut off by an explosion of dry sound.

When he looked, he saw that the source of that sound was Beatrice's lap—or rather, the open book upon it she had so sternly closed.

Sensing Beatrice's irritation from that gesture, Subaru awkwardly pursed his lips.

With Subaru falling silent, Beatrice glared at him with a sharp glint in her eyes.

"Would you get to the point already, I wonder? Spineless coward."

"…Sure."

He couldn't summon a rebuke for the insult. That itself was proof the girl had judged him correctly.

He'd used this trick and that to prolong the conversation, keeping it lukewarm while putting off the conclusion, for which Subaru could only blame his weak heart.

He already had the words he ought to ask inside his chest. He required nothing more than the courage to put them on his tongue.

He closed his eyes, took a deep breath, and took pains to listen to his beating heart. After that, he opened his mouth.

"How much do you…do you and Roswaal know about what happened this time around?"

"…"

Upon receiving the question coming from Subaru's lips, Beatrice concealed her eyes under the edges of her long eyebrows.

The resulting silence weighed heavily. When it felt very long, Subaru exhaled as if he were breathing hard.

"…Beatrice."

She made no reply. Even as that fact burned him, Subaru realized his own hypocrisy.

What exactly did he want Beatrice to say? Even within himself, no answer was forthcoming.

Did he want her to be a mastermind with a grasp of everything? An ignorant girl who knew nothing about it? Someone who was neither of those things? Even he didn't know.

Finally—

"For the sake of argument…what reply do you desire from Betty?"

"Th-this ain't some what-if! Besides, it's got nothing to do with what I want you to say. What I want is an answer to my question. I want an answer deeper than just yes or no!"

The unexpected counterattack made Subaru unintentionally coarsen his voice. But Beatrice's cool demeanor toward Subaru did not falter.

"Betty finds it unfortunate you are so worked up, but perhaps she does not understand what you mean? Betty is not your instructor. If you expect her to politely educate you on every topic, you are sorely mistaken."

"Ugh…! Don't gloss this over! Someone told me that if I want to know what Roswaal's thinking, I should ask you. Sorry, but seeing the attitude you're giving me, I agree."

"Who said such a… Ahhh, you saw the half-beast girl who recently returned?"

When Beatrice spoke the word *half-beast*, a word he could not unhear, she made an adorable face as she clicked her tongue. The girl proceeded to close one eye, pointing a finger at Subaru.

"That girl's opinion might have some merit, I wonder? But though Betty and Roswaal are certainly connected, that has nothing to do with this latest affair. Might Betty know nothing of it at all, I wonder?"

"But he left you in the mansion. Here, in this mansion, alone, without any plan to deal with it."

"He left Betty because she is at least capable of protecting herself. Is that unrelated to Roswaal, I wonder? …But Betty does not think that he did so without a single thought."

Beatrice's reply made Subaru go over his memories once more. But when he thought back, he could not recall any countermeasures by Roswaal whatsoever during the battle.

Rem, Crusch, Frederica, Beatrice—they'd all said there must be some, yet he couldn't find any.

"It's not just that you, me, and everyone thinks too much of Roswaal? Everyone says a guy like that had to have a plan against the Witch Cult… Right, that's it!!"

That instant, he remembered something as if the very heavens had spoken. In accordance with his revelation, Subaru rummaged through his pocket in great haste, presenting to Beatrice the other thing he wanted to ask her about. And that was—

"Beatrice, here. Look at this."

—a black-bound book, its pages and contents sullied with blood.

Subaru had the worst history possible with its original owner. He figured that some kind of weird enchantment kept the contents illegible, making it little more than a paperweight unless the reader shared the owner's personality.

"This should be deeply connected to what that Witch Cult bunch is thinking. If you're not gonna show me what Roswaal's really thinking, at least you can tell me something about this b—"

"—A Gospel?"

Increasingly nervous about the lack of response, Subaru spoke rapidly until his words caught in his throat. Beatrice's dramatic reaction when she stared at the Gospel in Subaru's hand included a look of fright in her eyes.

Her lips trembled weakly, almost as if she could not believe her own eyes.

"...A war trophy I took from the ringleader of the Witch Cult bunch that had the mansion surrounded."

"And...the owner?"

"—He's dead. Crushed by a carriage wheel. I killed him."

When Beatrice posed that delicate question, Subaru spoke the truth firmly without averting his eyes.

Strictly speaking, Petelgeuse Romanée-Conti had not been a person. He had been an evil spirit employing the bodies of others as hosts under his control. Accordingly, the cause of death Subaru gave might not have been precisely accurate.

But it was Subaru who had dealt Petelgeuse the final blow, robbing him of life.

Knowing in his soul that nothing short of that would defeat him, Subaru had calculatingly killed him.

Petelgeuse Romanée-Conti was the first being Subaru had personally slain—

Subaru wouldn't claim he'd never hesitated, or that he had no regrets about sullying his hands. He had not bluffed about it to anyone else because he couldn't lie to himself.

The fact he had killed Petelgeuse and the fact he had been killed by Petelgeuse were engraved into his own heart, never to be forgotten.

"…"

However, though Subaru had poured many thoughts into those brief words, Beatrice had given him no reaction. Still staring at the book in Subaru's hand, she seemed to whisper to it instead of responding to his words.

"Geuse…have you also…left Betty behind, I wonder?"

"—? Who's that?"

"…No one at all. More importantly…if you killed him, what happened to the Archbishop of the Seven Deadly…to Sloth's Witch Factor?"

"Witch…Factor…?"

The words Beatrice mentioned meant it was Subaru's turn to show his incomprehension.

He remembered having heard the term *Witch Factor* several times to date. However, the term had come from Petelgeuse's mouth each time; he'd never thought it would retain any meaning after the man's death.

Subaru's bewilderment made Beatrice lower her face, confusion resting in her eyes once more.

"Hey, you can't just toss jargon onto a guy who doesn't understand the circumstances. What the heck is that Witch Factor stuff? Honestly, I have a feeling it's nothing good."

"You do not know? Could you truly not? If that is so, for what purpose did you kill Sloth…? Furthermore, what was Roswaal doing…?"

"All I did was smother the embers someone tossed my way! As for Roswaal, that bastard's in the Sanctuary! What's he thinking? That's what I wanna ask you, damn it!"

Subaru shouted, practically bellowing in impatience as they talked past each other. When his fierce emotion slammed into Beatrice, all emotion was instantly gone from her face. The resulting silence threw Subaru off.

Her expression was shorn of ferocious anger and sadness, and perhaps confusion and everything else. The sight made Subaru's breath catch as if he were out of air; Beatrice gave a long, deep sigh.

"—Are all the answers you seek...in the Sanctuary, I wonder?"

"What?"

"Roswaal's scheme, the meaning of the Gospel, even about the Witch Factor...if you desire answers to all these, go there. Will the half-beast girl show you the way, I wonder?"

"Wait a sec! What's this all of a sudden? You were acting so high and mighty all that time, what made you decide to talk all of a sudden? Besides, even without going to the Sanctuary, you could..."

"—Betty shall not speak of it. Betty has a right...not to speak of it."

The obstinate answer silenced Subaru. He remembered her adopting a stance of rejection like this previously. It was the exact same rejection she'd given him when she shook off the hand he offered when he wanted to lead her out of the mansion to safety.

In other words, the result was exactly the same.

"—?! You're planning to push me away again?! Again, just like before?!"

From behind, in the direction of the door to the archive, he felt a supernatural force twist the air to create wind pressure. The distortion became a wind that took Subaru into its grip, dragging his body toward the portal to shove him outside.

It was an exceedingly compelling use of the magic power known as Passage.

"The path to your answers has been made clear. Will Betty stop indulging you any further, I wonder? Your high-handed arrogance is truly irritating."

"Beako... Beatrice!!" he shouted, stretching out his hand. But, with rejection in her gaze and posture, Beatrice rebuffed the gesture.

The girl atop the stool closed her eyes, weakly shaking her head from side to side.

"Perhaps Betty is not a tool for your convenience."

"..."

"I am not such a convenient being...that is here to say what you want to hear, at a time you wish to hear it, in the manner that you prefer."

Beatrice seemed to wring her voice out. Subaru could not offer any denial or complaint.

It was not that her words had resoundingly hit the mark. What he felt was shock, as if he'd been smacked from a completely unanticipated direction.

The gaping hole in his thoughts robbed Subaru of his power to resist. He would soon be sucked into the door, hurled beyond, and locked out: from the door, from the archive of forbidden books—and from the heart of the girl known as Beatrice.

"Why…are you making that crying face again?"

Eyes lowered, there was no reply from Beatrice to Subaru's final question.

"—Daa!!" "Gyaah!!"

Shot out from the open door, Subaru spectacularly toppled backward. The place was a corridor in the mansion, the result of his having been indiscriminately teleported via Passage.

But this time it was not Subaru alone who was wrapped up in Passage, but—

"M-Mr. Natsuki, how did you come out of the washroom I just left…?!"

"_____"

"A-and how long do you intend to sit upon me?! Could you please move?!!"

Otto pleaded with a pathetic expression on his face as he lay on the floor with Subaru's butt upon him. However, the only thing in Subaru's head that moment was the final instant with Beatrice.

Why had she made such a sad face? Perhaps that answer, too, was—

"—If I go to the Sanctuary, will I find that out, too?"

"I do not know of what you speak, but I would truly like for you to move as soon as possible!!"

When Subaru murmured thoughtfully, Otto raised his voice from below, bitter at Subaru's continuing to ignore him.

6

"But really, why did you tumble out of the washroom? Please do not tell me something frightening like there is a hidden door or a hidden passage connected to it..."

"That's not it, you moron. It's a one-time miracle brought about by my wanting to do a two-man comedy routine with you."

"That's not an answer, though for a reply that is not an answer, it is quite frightening!"

Having been reunited with Otto via Passage, Subaru bit back his feelings of futility over the fruitless conversation with Beatrice as he engaged in suitable conversation with Otto on their way to the guest room. Just as Beatrice had said, she had made his path to arrive at answers clear.

Though the forceful manner in which she had done so had only added to his worries and misgivings.

"*Haa...* Grim prospects, huh?"

"What is with that sigh...? Is that sigh suggestive of good fortune slipping from your grasp?"

"Your prospects are just that grim. I'm sighing in your stead."

"Then it is *my* good fortune you have let slip?! Could you not do such things behind my back?!"

Unable to clear up the complexities inside his chest, Subaru's flippant tongue could still pull the wool over Otto's eyes just fine. At any rate, the pair arrived at the guest room over the course of such trivial conversation.

"Oh my, I see Master Subaru is with you. I shall immediately prepare tea."

Frederica, who had thought Otto alone would be returning, began pouring a fresh cup of tea when she noticed Subaru was with him. Subaru, making a sound with his nose at the warm aroma of the tea leaves, sat down beside Emilia on the sofa at the back of the room. He glanced sidelong toward her, just in time for their eyes to meet.

"Subaru, I see you were with Otto. You two really do get along."

"I keep having to say this, but you have it wrong. My relationship with him ends as soon as I fulfill my promise to buy up all his oil. So don't make anything more out of it!"

"What, you cannot remain forthright till the end, so you add an insult? What a futile performance."

Otto was tired and dispirited at Subaru's averting his face and engaging in tsundere comedy. During that time, Emilia brought the tea that had been poured for her to her mouth, taking a sip and giving Subaru a little smile.

"Subaru, you must be reeeally stubborn to act like this even though you became friends with Julius after everything that happened."

"Boys should be stubborn. I'm kind of old-fashioned about that. Also, allow me to point out, Julius and I are *not* friends. I will hate that guy *forever*."

"Yes, yes."

Subaru's lips tapered as a certain handsome young man arose in his mind's eye, but Emilia saw things differently. He grasped with a certain reluctance that the more he said about the matter, the deeper the misunderstanding became.

"Is it quaint to think that the more you argue, the closer you are?"

"No one says *quaint* anymore... Besides, I thought people who argue a lot get along poorly, with pretty much no exceptions?"

"Well, Subaru, when you and I had a big argument, did we end up getting along worse?"

"...Emilia-tan, you've gotten good at this."

Subaru had an awkward look on his face; Emilia had him dead to rights. Subaru's reaction made Emilia narrow her eyes, her voice practically a whisper as she continued.

"—So, were you able to speak properly with Beatrice?"

Emilia had not asked if he'd *met* her. She'd asked if they'd *spoken*.

She posed that question because she had no doubt Subaru had arrived at the archive of forbidden books. He wasn't sure he should call that trust, but one might say he would only respond to her trust halfway.

"I met her. I met Beatrice. But as for speaking properly with her... I'm not really sure."

"...I see. But you were able to meet her, Subaru. In the time I've been at the mansion, Ram and I hadn't managed to go meet Beatrice even once. I'm just a little miffed about that."

Emilia spoke it with the air of a pout, adorably sticking out her tongue. But the lack of strength in Subaru's voice had apparently conveyed something, because her violet eyes seemed hesitant about her continuing her words.

In place of Emilia, a response came in the form of the faint sound of ceramics.

"So you truly are able to enter Lady Beatrice's archive of forbidden books..."

"What, you doubted me?"

Subaru's shoulders sank as he acted just a little wounded at Frederica's deeply moved murmur. She shook her head.

"Considering the very few encounters I have had with Lady Beatrice during over ten years of service under the master, I could not but doubt. When you told me, 'I'm gonna go chitchat with Beako for a bit. I'll be back soon!' or the like and rushed off, I had no way to confirm for myself."

"Ahh, err, can't really excuse myself for putting it that way, huh?"

"To be honest, I thought it would take hours until you would be able to meet Lady Beatrice..."

Subaru, remembering how he'd given a threadbare explanation and rushed off, cringed and reflected on the matter. As Subaru did so, Frederica put significance behind the look she gave Emilia as she continued her words.

"However, afterward, Lady Emilia took the time to speak exhaustively about how reliable Master Subaru had become, so I awaited you half in expectation and half in concern."

"Huh?"

"Wait a— Frederica?!"

Frederica's unexpected statement left Subaru bewildered and

Emilia beside herself. Emilia jumped to her feet, cheeks red, vigorously waving a hand back and forth toward Subaru.

"Errr, it wasn't like that. Certainly I spoke to Frederica about you, Subaru, but she's blowing it out of all..."

"No, I heard her speak as well. To be honest, I was thinking *Mr. Natsuki, you lucky scoundrel...*"

"Even Otto now!"

Sold out not only by Frederica, but also by Otto, Emilia was red to the tips of her ears. Then she slapped her hands against her flushed cheeks, furtively glancing in Subaru's direction.

The reaction from Emilia, one she rarely permitted to be seen, made Subaru strongly clench his fist.

"Why don't you talk like that when I'm around...?"

"I can't talk like that in front of you, it's embarrassing... Sheesh, Frederica! Move on already!"

"Oh my, even though you glossed it over previously, that childlike charm of yours is falling by the wayside."

Frederica hid her mouth as she smiled, shifting her gaze from the eyebrow-twitching Emilia toward Subaru as she said, "Master Subaru, I heard plenty about you from Lady Emilia... No, more than plenty."

"*Fred—er—i—ca!!*"

"Yes, yes, I understand— So let us speak, Master Subaru, so that whether you found the archive of forbidden books or whether you did not, it does not become a roadblock."

"Become a...roadblock?"

Unable to get the gist of the mystery phrase, Subaru knotted his brows in incomprehension. As he did so, Emilia gently touched Subaru's shoulder, nodding as she continued.

"Subaru, we didn't doubt you'd meet Beatrice, but whether that girl would answer your questions is another matter, yes? I mean, both you and Beatrice are reeeally stubborn..."

"The excessively cute way you put that bothers me a little, but you have a point. So?"

"I made a promise to the villagers, and I have a lot of things I want to ask Roswaal about myself—so I asked Frederica to tell me about the Sanctuary."

"_____"

Subaru's throat caught over the fact that Emilia had acted for the sake of achieving their original objective.

The Sanctuary Emilia sought was the very same Beatrice had revealed as his path to answers. With such a sad face and voice, she had told him that the answers to all his misgivings were there in the Sanctuary.

So, too, had she said the "half-beast girl" would show him the way, namely—

"And did Frederica tell you about the Sanctuary?"

"I lost to Lady Emilia's persistence. I had been told to disclose as little about that as possible…but it seems strange to conceal it from the two of you."

"Um, I happen to be here as well…"

"It seems strange to conceal it from the two of you."

"Would you please correct that line?!"

Setting Frederica and Otto's remarks aside, Subaru was surprised the issue had moved forward in his absence. As he had the thought, Emilia kept her hand on Subaru's shoulder, lowering her brows.

"Subaru, was that all right? You're not upset I decided without you?"

"N-nah, I'm not upset at all. I whiffed it on my end, so if anything it's a huge help."

"Really? I'm so glad. So, Subaru, there's a favor I wanted to ask of you…"

Subaru was still off balance as Emilia looked relieved, lowering her eyes as she continued. When he heard the word *favor*, Subaru suddenly felt a bad premonition.

The word *favor* had precipitated something once before in precisely the same fashion—

"Wait! Don't tell me that favor is…me staying here at the mansion?"

"Eh?"

"If so, time out! Let's talk this over! Certainly, I can't call myself in tip-top physical condition, and Ferris stopped being my doctor, but it's not like I live a life of combat alone! If anything, fighting with the mind is where I really shine, well no, that's a little off, too, but...!"

Emilia's eyes went wide as Subaru desperately tried to make his case. But it was a place where such fervor was necessary. The situation certainly resembled when they'd headed to the royal capital for purposes of the royal selection. However, what was decisively different from then was the readiness in Subaru's heart.

He wasn't following Emilia without a plan or a care. This time was different from what had taken place before.

"Don't even try to stop me. I'm going with you. I can't let you just leave me..."

"Of course I'm not leaving you here. Come with me."

"If you tell me you're leaving me, just no, no way, no h— What did you say just now?"

As Subaru's ferocious emotions reduced the breadth of his vocabulary, her words seemed to slap his face, knocking him back to his senses. As that sank in, Emilia took the hand in contact with Subaru, touching it to her own breast as she spoke.

"I told you, come with me. I'd be worried sick on my own."

"..."

"Subaru, I'm...relying on you. Subaru, I...need your strength."

—Subaru could not put into words the impact of Emilia's quiet plea upon his own heart.

His mouth hung open. With Subaru unable to say a word, Emilia's expression clouded over with concern. Her violet eyes wavered as she stroked her own long, silver hair and said, "Err...did I say something strange?"

"...My motivational switch is all yours, Emilia-tan. Whether you're flipping it on or flipping it off, one word from you and everything's on auto. I seriously can't get enough of you."

Covering his face with his palms, Subaru extolled Emilia's graces with a deep sigh. "Eh? Eh?" went a confused Emilia, buffeted by the deeply meaningful statement, to which Subaru replied, "Back at you," sticking out his own tongue.

After all, Emilia was throwing Subaru for an even bigger loop than he was throwing her for.

"It would seem you have put your differences in order."

"Yeah, sorry for the lovey-dovey stuff. I just couldn't help myself."

"Lovey-dovey...?"

When Frederica tried to revisit the topic of conversation, Subaru turned to face her once more. Off to the side, Emilia seemed to have a question mark floating over her head, but she immediately regained her composure and gazed Frederica's way.

Frederica nodded toward their gazes, and her emerald eyes beheld the pair as she spoke.

"As has been conveyed to you, I have no objection to speaking about the route to take to the Sanctuary. It is just, a little time is necessary to prepare... Two days, perhaps?"

"Prepare... Ah, that figures, it'd be leaving the mansion empty. That shouldn't take..."

"No, I shall be remaining here at the mansion. It is Lady Emilia and Master Subaru's duty to head toward the Sanctuary. Managing the mansion is mine."

"Wait, you won't come with us?! How are we supposed to get to the Sanctuary, then?"

Subaru was taken aback, never having expected her to refuse to go with them.

Frederica's cooperation was limited to her telling them about the Sanctuary rather than actually leading them to it. Now he understood the source of Emilia's worry during the earlier exchange, but Subaru simultaneously noticed something else.

Namely, the sight of Otto Suwen leaning back, arms crossed, exceedingly confident, even cocksure.

"Hey, you over there, what's with that self-confident, puffed-up look? We're in the middle of an important conversation."

"Ho-ho-ho. You are a poor guesser, Mr. Natsuki. In the first place, should you not have wondered just why I am in attendance during such an important conversation?"

"You have a point. This isn't something an outsider should hear. Say, does this mansion have a dungeon?"

"Such statements are not where I meant to steer the conversation, you know?!"

"The mansion has a cell, yes. I can assure you that it is reasonably comfortable."

"Miss Frederica, could you please leave such questions unanswered?!"

Subaru had meant it as a joke, but it had brought the existence of a cell, and Roswaal Manor's dark underside, to light.

Either way, Otto's shoulders sank in dejection at his being tag-teamed when—

"Hey, cut it out, both of you. You mustn't treat Otto like some kind of outcast."

In Otto's stead, it was Emilia who rose to her feet in righteous indignation. Putting her hands on her hips, she glared at the comedic combo in question, Subaru and Frederica both.

"What a terrible thing to say to someone who went out of his way to offer his cooperation. And without Otto's help, it's going to be reeeally hard going to the Sanctuary, won't it?"

"Ohh...! Did you hear, Mr. Natsuki? Now *this* is how you should have reacted!"

"Ahhh, it's been a while since I've said E M D, so I'll say it now. E—M—D—!!"

"E, M...eh?"

When, in high spirits, Subaru invoked the old phrase, Otto registered the highest bewilderment score of that day. Setting his confusion aside, Subaru had grasped the circumstances from Emilia's statement.

"In other words, Otto said he'd go with us as far as the Sanctuary. To be blunt, I'd have had to leave all the dragon carriage driving to Patlash, so it's a huge help, but..."

"But what? That method of speaking implies something. Does my goodwill sit ill with you?"

"Sorry, the only merchant I expect freebies from is a guy with a fruit store and a scary face. That might be nicer on a human level, but it's a lot simpler to believe a merchant wants more than goodwill for collateral."

Cadmon, Anastasia, Russel—names and faces of merchants he'd come into contact with in the capital came to mind. In terms of personality, Otto was the closest to Cadmon, but in terms of mercantile tendencies, he was closer to the last—

"I can read your ulterior motive. The gist is, be cooperative with Emilia to get as close to her as possible and make a good impression on her backer Roswaal. Even more than getting your oil bought up, the point of coming with us is to get close to Roswaal, right?"

"Er, um, having my deepest secrets brought out into the light is a little..."

"Otto...is that true?"

"Lady Emilia's sincere eyes are painful, painful, painful! I am very sorry! It is for the most part exactly as he said! But believe me, I did not mean for any harm to come from it whatsoever, so please forgive me!!"

Though Otto tried to be defiant, he did not quite manage it, confessing as he conceded defeat to her sincerity. Subaru wearily shook his head at Otto's demeanor; this time it was his turn to pat Emilia on the shoulder.

"Well, let's not be too hard on Otto. You make it look easy, Emilia-tan, but it's really hard for people to act on someone else's behalf out of goodwill from the heart alone."

"I don't think I'm really such a good person...but doesn't that go for you, Subaru?"

"I exhaust all my efforts for Emilia-tan for my own personal reasons. Hmm, if it's one hundred percent impure, does that make it pure...?"

You want other people to think well of you. When you boiled things down, that was the starting point for actions taken in the course of interpersonal relations. That said, human life was not so dry that you could declare it an iron rule. It was merely a matter of degree.

Human beings were simply too complex to express in a single sentence.

"Even with your ulterior motive plain to see, we actually think pretty well of you. So relax already."

"That does not sound very reassuring coming from you, Mr. Natsuki, but..."

Subaru responded to the dejected Otto with a teasing smile before turning back toward Frederica.

"OK, Otto's helping. So the three of us get to hear you talk about the Sanctuary."

"Understood. Incidentally, has the master spoken to either of you about the Sanctuary?"

With Subaru & Co. sitting side by side on the sofa, ready to listen to her speak, Frederica posed them that question. Upon receiving it, Subaru and Emilia glanced at each other's faces as she said, "To be blunt, he said almost nothing about it to me. From the snippets I heard, it sounded like some kind of secret base several hours away... The fact that it was the first suggestion for evacuating people makes me think I wasn't wrong."

"Once...Roswaal told me that it was a place that would someday be...necessary for me..."

"Necessary for you someday...?"

The unexpected statement left Subaru looking toward Emilia with surprise in his eyes. That gaze sent Emilia apologetically lowering her own eyes. But before Subaru could ask a follow-up question:

"It sounds like something the master would say."

Frederica closed her eyes, her tone sounding faintly amused. Then she grasped the hem of her skirt, curtsying deeply. And then—

"I shall now speak of how to enter the place called the Sanctuary of Clemaldy. You must not speak a word of this to anyone else. Also, upon going to the Sanctuary, there is one name you must not forget."

"..."

"Garfiel. You must pay heed to the individual by that name. In the Sanctuary, that individual is the one you and Lady Emilia must approach only with the greatest of caution."

Complex emotions resided in Frederica's open emerald eyes as she put that name upon her lips.

# CHAPTER 2
## THE ROAD TO THE SANCTUARY

1

As a result of the conversation with Frederica, they set off for the Sanctuary in the morning two days after.

"To be honest, I'm gettin' restless just waiting around, but..."

Arms crossed, Subaru made a sound in his throat, the impatience in his heart unavoidable. But, according to Frederica, two days of preparation were necessary to get to the Sanctuary. Subaru could not dismiss her opinion.

*"The Sanctuary is protected by a special barrier...the Lost Woods of Clemaldy. The barrier keeps outside presences away by leading them astray, hence why it is called the Lost Woods. Two days of preparation are required to nullify that barrier."*

Thus had Frederica explained, intuitively calming Subaru so that he was not tempted to let haste make waste.

Though at first, Subaru found the talk of the "barrier" rather fishy, Frederica's explanation after the fact made him accept that it was the case.

"It's a place with a history of accepting demi-humans... Huh."

When he voiced the special way it had been expressed to him, Subaru vigorously scratched his own head.

It was something of an iron rule in fantasy worlds that there was friction between human and demi-human races. This world apparently was no exception. In the Kingdom of Lugunica, too, scorn against demi-humans was customary with many people. Subaru's experiences to date had led him to form a particular conclusion.

The prejudice and scorn toward demi-humans was likely an extension of the deep-rooted enmity toward half-elves.

Even so, perhaps due to some kind of conciliatory policy in the capital, he'd seen quite a few demi-humans in the Merchants' District and in the slums. However, he'd seen none in the Nobles' District—

"From what I read in a history book, they had this civil war called the Demi-human War in just the last century, too. Come to think of it, I heard a song related to that from Liliana, too, didn't I...?"

Liliana was a bard who had stopped by at Roswaal Manor during one of her journeys. He was certain that one of the songs she had sung during her stay at the mansion touched on that historical event.

"Kind of late to realize it, but...'The Ballad of the Sword Devil' sounds a lot like Wilhelm's nickname. Maybe that song's why he came to be called the Sword Devil in the first place..."

Subaru gave a satisfied nod as the manly sight of the swordsman he imagined melded with the heroic tale inside his head.

As a matter of fact, Wilhelm was indeed the main character of "The Ballad of the Sword Devil," but Subaru, petty man that he was, dismissed out of hand the idea that he personally knew a man whose name was recorded in the annals of history.

"Ah, Master Subaru, so you were indeed here."

Subaru was thrown off his train of thought when the door quietly opened and a voice spoke to him through it. When he looked back, he met the eyes of the girl peering in through the gap of the door.

The girl with reddish-brown hair and a ribbon on her head entered with an adorable smile as she addressed him.

"It's almost time to leave, so I thought if you weren't in your room, you might be here..."

"Servant lifestyle got me used to waking up bright and early... Wait, properly speaking, I still *am* a servant, so I'd better stop talkin' like *that*..."

"But I think... I *believe* those odd clothes suit you better than a servant's uniform, Master Subaru."

"You're payin' attention to your words, but you need a little more practice choosing them, I guess?"

The girl gave a pained smile as she quickly corrected her own words as Subaru rose from his chair and gave his back a stretch. The young girl in the servant's outfit—Petra Leyte—gazed at Subaru with her round eyes.

Petra was one of the children living in Earlham Village who'd long befriended Subaru. There was a reason she was dressed in a maid outfit that very moment.

"Gotta say, it's only two days since asking for maid applicants in the village, and only one since you've actually been in the mansion... I'm impressed you were able to find me without getting lost. That's almost too good for a girl your age away from your parents like this."

"I'm already twelve years old, plenty old enough to be a working g—I mean, an adult. Master Subaru, please treat me like a proper adult."

"I'll think about it when you master polite speech and get Frederica's stamp of approval. Until then, you're an apprentice maid in on-the-job-training, so I'm gonna treat you as cute as I feel like!"

Subaru shot the precocious Petra a smile as he mussed her hair with strokes of his hand. Petra gave an enjoyable *kya!* sound as she squatted, perhaps certain she was making a clean getaway.

Either way, it had been a simple process to get Petra into the mansion as a maid.

Frederica was keenly feeling the limits of a single person's power to manage the vast mansion. When she'd sought applicants from the village to help her, it was Petra who had responded.

At first, there was concern about her young age, but Petra's personality and suitability for the job had both proved exceptional.

*"Compared to you, Master Subaru, she is highly proficient, and her*

*future prospects are bright. She stands out among all the girls I have taught to date… Ah, Master Subaru, please sit down and relax."*

That was the assessment Frederica had given after instructing Petra over those last two days. As a matter of fact, it was difficult to recruit someone like Petra who could grasp the details of the mansion and its environs in such a short time.

It was enough for her to understand exactly where Subaru had unconsciously let his feet take him—

"You came to say goodbye to Miss Rem, right?"

"…Well, somethin' like that. I don't plan to be away that long, but I wanted to see her face. I'm countin' on you to take care of her while I'm gone, Petra."

Subaru conveyed his words in a joking tone as he gazed within the bedroom—and at Rem lying on the bed within. Her appearance never changed no matter how many times he came, or how many hours he spent at her side. Even so, he visited when he had time.

"…Master Subaru, it's almost time to set out, so…"

After Subaru fell silent, Petra tugged at his sleeve, indicating that it was time for him and Petra to part ways. Indulging in her generosity, Subaru said only one final thing:

"…Well, I'm off, then. Be a good girl and wait, 'kay?"

After saying goodbye to Rem's sleeping face, he brushed his hair back as he left the room.

"Master Subaru, it must be pretty hard for you, having so many people in your thoughts…"

"I feel that's like what people say to describe a playboy… Ah, well, it's not like I'm splitting my feelings into two prongs or something, but I have to admit…"

Subaru, heading for the rendezvous point at the mansion entryway, cringed under Petra's exasperated-sounding verbal assault, despite the fairly indirect way she put it.

That being said, Petra was not referring only to such things, but also to the context of the pair's current actions.

"I kinda figured I wouldn't find anything, but no luck here. You?"

"I checked every room, too... Is there really a mysterious room like that here? You're not playing some kind of trick on me?"

"I can't fault you for doubting me, but you know that Beatrice really exists, right? That's the loli in drills you were playing tag with in the mansion a while back."

"She was in a dress, not 'in drills'..."

Petra made a stern face toward Subaru's assertion as she closed the open door of the final room. With that, they had finished checking every door on that floor. Unfortunately, they had not found one that led to the archive of forbidden books.

"When she really wants to hide, it gets seriously rough... What's up with her, sheesh."

Looking like he was chewing a bitter insect, Subaru disparaged the girl who had not shown her face whatsoever.

Even though he and Emilia had decided to set off for the Sanctuary, Beatrice's demeanor in their last encounter was another matter altogether. Over the last couple of days, he'd gone around the mansion searching for her room as much as he could, but the results had not improved.

So he remained in the dark both about her relationship to the Sanctuary and about the truth behind the sad face she'd made—

"I can't talk to Rem. I can't meet Beatrice... What the hell have I been doing?"

"Master Subaru?"

"Well, keep an eye out for Beatrice for a bit, would you? Maybe you'll have a random encounter with her from opening one of these doors once in a while."

Naturally, even Petra grimaced at Subaru's unapologetic request. There were a lot of things for her to learn in a new environment. Subaru felt guilty about adding to her burdens, but...

"Sorry, I get it. But you're the only one I can count on, Petra. I'm really sorry about this."

"...I'm the only one you can count on?"

"Yeah, that's right."

Frederica was devoted to Rem, but having her pay extra attention to Beatrice was too much to ask. He couldn't help but think that she was an unsuitable person to entrust Beatrice to at the moment. But Petra seemed a similar age to Beatrice, so excess politeness ought not to be any barrier to contact.

Those were the various factors he'd taken into account when entrusting Beatrice to Petra, but—

"Tee-hee-hee. I guess it can't be helped... If you put it that way, just leave it to me."

"Oh, really? Seriously, big help. You're such a good, gooooood girl, Petra."

Petra's demeanor suddenly softened. Subaru stroked the smiling girl's head as he breathed a sigh of relief. Now no night would pass without anyone paying Beatrice any mind.

Though Subaru would truly have liked to have had a chance to exchange words with her one more time...

"Master Subaru, Petra. This way, please."

As they engaged in such conversation, Emilia and Frederica were already waiting at the entry hall ahead. When Frederica bowed, Petra hurried to her side.

"Petra, you did well to find Master Subaru. A job well done."

"Thank you, Miss Frederica. Anything about Master Subaru, please leave to me."

"My, she's reeeally full of confidence."

Petra proudly pushing out her chest made Emilia and Frederica look at each other's face with a smile. When Subaru immediately walked over, Emilia tilted her head a little and offered a greeting.

"Good morning, Subaru. Did you sleep properly?"

"I'm glad *you* didn't oversleep from having way too much fun on that picnic, Emilia-tan. Feels like the other guy might've done something that stupid, though..."

"Ah, you mean Otto? It's all right. Otto woke up a long time ago and has been preparing the dragon carriage in front of the mansion."

"The hell? Sorry I worried, then. But, oh yeah...his life is riding on this, too."

Talking business with Roswaal would make an enormous difference in Otto's life as a merchant, be it for good or ill. His drive was that of a man taking up the opportunity of a lifetime, and Subaru felt his high motivation reassuring.

"Plus, I'd better think up some words of consolation for when he's kicking himself at having come up short..."

"Could you *not* speak such awful things the moment I come back to call you?!"

Just that instant, Otto's eyes were wide as he returned, barging into the hall. Subaru listened to the pleasant sound of the morning breeze, taking a deep breath before he made a declaration.

"Well, now that we've had our clichéd banter, let's be off!"

"Do you not feel even a single shred of guilt?! Well, ahh, not that it really matters!"

Otto, splendidly swept up in the flow, was drawn along as everyone headed out to the mansion's courtyard. The dragon carriage was already parked in front of the entrance, with a jet-black land dragon and a blue land dragon perfectly in order.

In particular, the black land dragon—Patlash—stretched out the tip of her nose when she noticed Subaru.

"Just like usual, you really act all friendly toward me, huh?"

"However, it seems the lady concerned is merely saying, 'You may stroke me if you wish'..."

"Her breed's supposed to be really proud. Is that really the only thing left from her rearing...?"

Subaru put on a skeptical face at Otto's cross-species translation, an effect of his language blessing.

Everyone's lips treated Patlash as if she was temperamental, but in truth, from the time he'd first met her, Subaru hadn't felt any such thing, only great amiability. Even now, when he reached out his palm and rubbed her neck, the corners of her mouth were relaxed, and she was fond of people as far as he could tell.

"I really don't understand why. What, did I save you in a past life or something?"

Putting aside the notion of reincarnation, he was in a different world, so it wasn't likely a past life had anything to do with it. *It's probably just simple compatibility*, thought Subaru, and he left it at that. And that was one of the few strokes of good fortune that had bounced Subaru's way.

"Of course, to me, the number one stroke of good fortune was meeting Emilia-tan!"

"Eh? I'm sorry, I didn't hear quite right. Can you say that again?"

"It's pretty embarrassing, so I can't force it out a second time! I'll say it tomorrow!"

When Subaru hung his head, playing dumb as a defensive measure, Emilia went "Really?" with a mystified look. However, she immediately switched mental gears and turned to face Frederica.

"Well, please take care of the mansion...Rem, Petra, and Beatrice included."

"You can count on me, Lady Emilia. Please take care on your journey— Also, take this..."

Just as Subaru had done, Emilia freshly entrusted matters to Frederica. Frederica accepted the responsibility with a bow; finally, she offered something that came from her pocket.

This was a necklace—a necklace adorned with a glimmering, blue, transparent crystal.

"With this, you will be able to penetrate the forest barrier and enter the Sanctuary. After that, I have instructed the land dragons as to the location, so they shall surely lead the way."

"So that crystal is the condition for passing through the barrier, huh...? That's what took two days to arrange?"

Subaru peered at the glimmering crystal in Frederica's hand, twisting his neck slightly in artless skepticism. The crystal looked rare. She hadn't left in those two days, so how had she obtained it?

Frederica covered her mouth and laughed in response to Subaru's skepticism.

"Strictly speaking, the two days of preparation were not for this alone...but the two are not unrelated. At any rate, the place and qualifications are in order. The rest comes down to resolve and a strong will."

"Pretty exaggerated way of talking. Not that I mind...," Frederica said gravely.

"Mm, I understand that it's reeeally precious to you. I will take proper care not to lose...Frederica?" Emilia said, knitting her brows and nodding.

When Emilia's hand took the crystal offered to her, Frederica strongly grasped that hand.

"..."

Instantly, emerald and violet gazes intertwined, and Frederica's cheeks faintly stiffened. But she followed the impulse to harden her cheeks by closing her eyes, quietly letting go of Emilia's hand as she spoke.

"Lady Emilia, please take care of the Sanctuary. And do not forget about what we discussed."

"Y-yes, it's all right. Just what kind of place the Sanctuary is, and..."

"Please...be mindful of Garfiel."

"Mm, I get it. I'll give Garfiel my attention. Count on it."

Emilia gravely accepted the repeated warnings as she stuffed the crystal handed to her into a pocket. Subaru was watching the exchange to its conclusion, at which point they were just about ready to head out—

"Um! Master Subaru...could you take this with you?"

Red-faced, Petra held up a hand as she offered something to Subaru. She was trying to emulate Frederica as she offered a plain, white handkerchief with her hand.

Subaru, suspicious concerning Frederica's demeanor, went "Err?" as the gesture caught him completely by surprise.

"A white handkerchief to see you off on your journey. You can clean yourself with it along the way and return it when you get back—I understand it's not done much these days, but it's an old custom to wish for someone's safe return from a journey."

"Ohh, that sort of thing. Got it. Thanks, Petra. I'll bring this back to you safe and sound."

Having been taught the meaning of the handkerchief being given to him, Subaru wrapped it around his wrist. His reply made Petra lower her red face; she gracefully slipped behind Frederica's back.

"Ah? What's with that reaction all of a sudden? That difficult-age stuff's leaving me out on a limb here."

"From the looks of it, Lady Emilia, Master Subaru has no right to criticize you."

"Me? Did I say something strange?"

Frederica sighed deeply as both Subaru and Emilia twisted their necks, wondering what was amiss. In the end, they went without an answer to that question as Frederica stuffed the pair into the dragon carriage, all preparations to depart complete.

"Yes, yes. Both of you hurry along now. The Lost Woods of Clemaldy that the Sanctuary is in becomes a dangerous place when night falls."

"We get it, we get it, geez. On your end, take care of the villagers, 'kay? Also, make sure to dispose of the mayonnaise in storage before it goes bad."

"I really have to wonder about lining up those two issues in the same sentence..."

With an exasperated voice, she pushed on their backs, and Subaru and Emilia boarded the dragon carriage. When Subaru looked back out the window, two maids, short and tall, stood straight side by side as they looked up at the carriage.

"I pray for your safe return. Please give my best regards to the master and to Ram."

"Master Subaru, take good care of Big Sis, okay? Also, to the noisy person, good luck."

"Is that not a horrible assessment of me?!"

Heedless of Otto's reaction, Frederica and Petra quietly gestured, giving Subaru and the others a completely courteous send-off.

With that send-off pressed to their backs, the dragon carriage powerfully set off.

"Well, all aboard! Otto, we're counting on ya!"

"I really cannot approve of this treatment...!"

Otto left behind his lament at his treatment, poor to the bitter end, as they departed from the mansion.

2

"And just who taught you about that old custom?"

Right around when the departing dragon carriage vanished from sight, Frederica posed that question to Petra, still bowing right beside her.

The young girl's big eyes went round at the question as she bashfully said, "I heard about it from Mother. She said it was how she won over Father."

"So you get that tenacity from your mother, do you? However, it seems the man concerned did not realize its significance."

"It's fine. Even if he doesn't know, if he thinks of me when he looks down at his wrist..."

The reply was more forceful than expected. Frederica gave a strained smile at Petra's positivity. Truly, she was a precocious girl at a mere twelve years of age— It made Frederica think of Ram.

"She was a woman starting at a young age, too...in great contrast to her ability as a servant, however."

"Miss Frederica? Is something wrong?"

"Not at all. I was simply thinking of your senior. She should be at the Sanctuary right now, dealing with a particular problem child."

Thinking back to the girl who accompanied her liege, offering her life to him, Frederica exhaled in melancholic fashion. Her hand reflexively touched the breast pocket of her servant's uniform.

"Now then, even if Lady Emilia and others are absent, there is still Lady Beatrice here at the mansion. I will have you learn all the basics within a week's time."

"Yes! Ready and willing!"

"What a wonderful reply this girl gives..."

With an invigorated look, Petra raised her hand and happily ran into the mansion. Frederica smiled and observed her positive demeanor before finally turning in the direction of the dragon carriage one last time.

Frederica's beautiful emerald eyes faintly wavered, seemingly resisting the emotions filling her chest as her slender fingers took stationery out of her breast pocket. Then—

"With this, I have done as the master instructed. It all comes down to whether Lady Emilia can overcome the Sanctuary. There is nothing I can do now, save pray."

Her fingers traced the edges of the letter she had read many times over. Finally, those fingers turned toward her own neck. However, the sensation she sought was nowhere to be found…

"Please, Lady Emilia…be heedful of Garf."

3

"So that Puck guy really hasn't shown his face all this time?"

"…Yeah, that's right. I've called out to him over and over, and I can feel the link of the pact…but I'm reeeally worried. It's not often he doesn't show his face for a long time like this."

The interior of the dragon carriage racing toward the Sanctuary in good order echoed with Subaru and Emilia's conversation.

Thanks to the intervention of the wind repel blessing, neither loud sounds nor shaking were conveyed to the carriage interior. In that quiet atmosphere, they were not trading words about their enthusiasm at approaching the Sanctuary—rather, they were discussing an anomaly that had occurred during the last several days: Puck's absence.

In those several days, Subaru hadn't seen any sign of him, Emilia's contracted spirit and self-declared father figure. Beatrice's plan had been to conceal herself through the use of Passage; this was different.

"Come to mention it, I hadn't seen him before getting back to the mansion, either. Since we left Crusch's, maybe?"

"Mm…since we returned to the mansion, maybe. I really wanted to talk to him about the Sanctuary, but I don't feel like my voice is reaching him."

"Does Puck normally disappear from time to time?"

"Errr, it happened a lot before he and I formed our pact…but the frequency's reeeally gone down since then. Not meeting him for several days makes me a little concerned."

Subaru folded his arms as Emilia broached the subject of Puck prior to their pact.

It was obvious, but there *had* been a time before Emilia and Puck were linked. He'd always seen the two together, so imagining them acting separately really didn't seem right to Subaru, but—

"Do you know where Puck goes when he's not by your side?"

"I think he's probably doing something for the sake of world peace."

"Sounds like a little girl with fantasies about her dad's work, but if he ain't here, that's the least of our problems."

Setting Emilia's exaggerated expectations aside, she was the most precious thing to Puck in the entire world. The idea of him abandoning her to run off and do stuff somewhere sounded downright strange.

"Plus with Puck not here, I'm straight-up worried about our combat strength. Otto isn't exactly a master of the fighting arts, and my insides are all rattling around. Emilia-tan, it's tough for you without Puck here, right?"

"Subaru, it's reeeally hard to set aside hearing that your insides are rattling around, but…"

When Emilia gave him an exaggerated stare, Subaru gave a vague smile and waved her off with a hand.

"Goodness…! But relax. Even if Puck isn't with me, I have my contracts with the minor spirits. Those children can fight, too, so I'll protect you no matter what happens."

"Whoa, that's a real man's line…! Just wait, someday I'm gonna be able to say that with a straight face."

"I know. I'll wait, I'm reeeally looking forward to it."

She raised a finger, and faintly glowing minor spirits floated all around Emilia.

Subaru figured that, compared to Puck's, their power was like Earth compared to Heaven, but even so, they had fine combat strength on their own. All the same, it was pathetic to be relying on the only girl in the group, and the one he had his eye on, to do the fighting.

"As for 'no matter what happens'…Frederica warned us, didn't she?"

"About Garfiel, yes."

Emilia shared Subaru's concerns, lowering her voice as her lips spoke the name.

Garfiel was the name that they'd heard repeatedly from Frederica's lips over the last two days, the person they needed to be wary of. As a matter of fact, Subaru had heard the name itself several times before that.

"Bunch of times it came up that Roswaal was off to have a chat with the guy. On top of that, Ram spoke the name when the plan to evacuate to the Sanctuary came up, didn't she…?"

Ram had spoken the name as if he was someone she could trust. But the contradiction with Frederica's warnings made Subaru question his own judgment.

It wasn't simply a question of which one, Ram or Frederica, he wished to believe…

"I've been around Ram a lot longer, but her usual attitude makes me wanna shove that aside…!"

"I wish Frederica had told us about it in more detail, but…she said she was constrained by a vow not to speak about the Sanctuary, so it couldn't be helped."

"All the same, I sure have been hearing a lot about vows and stuff…"

Subaru leaned back in his seat as he made a sound of dissatisfaction in his throat.

In fact, Frederica hadn't really said much about the Sanctuary. What she'd conveyed to Subaru and the others had been limited to the special characteristics and dangers of the place, where it was located, and the name of a particularly dangerous individual. She'd helped them pass through the barrier, but her cooperation had ended at that.

"Compared to that, she sure said to watch out for Garfiel a lot, including right before we left… Do people at the mansion have some sort of quota for cryptic statements?"

"I don't think there's any such thing, but that was Frederica doing all she could. We should be grateful she warned us as much as she did without breaking her vow."

"I'd be even more grateful if she wasn't bound by that vow, though…"

"Don't sulk. A vow is a holy, inviolate pledge, not something one should breach for any reason. Vows, pacts, and covenants may bear different weight, but they should all be treated with equal respect."

Emilia wagged a finger left and right as she spoke those words, seemingly for Subaru's benefit.

It went without saying that Emilia was obstinate when it came to oaths of any kind. To Subaru, vows, pacts, and covenants were simple wordplay; the two appreciated their importance in very divergent ways.

"I'm not saying you should break pledges every which way, but… there's a time and a place for everything, right?"

"Absolutely not. Oaths…promises are very important. Properly speaking, there's nothing forcing you to uphold a promise, but people uphold their promises anyway. They work hard to uphold them, don't they? Even if no one's watching, even if no one notices, they do it, because the other party believes they will do so."

Emilia touched her chest, staring at Subaru in dismay at his words. Her tone of voice was gentle, with no hint whatsoever of reproach. The words hurt all the more for it.

"It's because people believe in you that you strive to uphold the promises you've made. A promise is like a ritual tying two people together through mutual trust, isn't it?"

Subaru crept onto the carriage's seemingly rock-steady floor and bowed his head straight down. When he apologetically touched his forehead to the floor, Emilia went "Ah," touching a hand to her own lips. "Um, I'm not trying to criticize you, Subaru. Certainly, you didn't uphold your promise with me, and if you do it again I'll be rather annoyed, but…"

"The pain, the pain, my ears hurt!!"

"Also, I've reflected on being too emotional about it. I needed to make up with you right away, Subaru, but I was being stubborn. Sorry."

"The pain, the pain, my chest hurts!!"

"Hey, um, I am a spirit mage, so oaths hit reeeally close to home with me. To a spirit mage, pacts with spirits are extremely important, so…yes, promises are really important. Subaru, you should reflect on that more, after all."

"The pain, the pain, my heart hurts!!"

As Emilia began to sulk, perhaps from the deep melancholy of the time coming back, Subaru lay prostrate before her.

At that moment, he could truly appreciate why Emilia had flown into such a rage in the waiting room at the royal palace: unaware of just how insensitive he was being, Subaru had been trampling on the most important parts of Emilia's psyche.

"You've reflected on the error of your ways?"

"I've reflected. Deeper than the sea, taller than the mountains, wider than the sky, vaster than outer space."

"Then it is fine. I forgive you… I'm not sure what you mean by *outer space*, though."

As Subaru wore a pathetic look on his face, Emilia nodded toward him and smiled pleasantly as she touched a finger to her own lips. The charming smile bore no hint of anger; the adorable gesture made the look on Subaru's face crumble.

He was deeply grateful to Emilia for smiling and forgiving him for the way they'd parted ways in the capital. At the same time, he thought anew that she was not the only one he needed to apologize to for his behavior that day.

"It seems that we've entered the forest."

As Subaru immersed himself in thought, Emilia's voice suddenly pulled him back. Her eyes were turned toward the window; the change in the landscape had apparently told her they were nearing their destination.

The Sanctuary was said to be protected by a special barrier well within the deep-green forest.

There, in that place, were Rem and Roswaal, two other parties to whom Subaru needed to apologize.

"Well, setting Ram aside, I might have a duty to apologize, but I think I have just as much of a right to smack Roswaal in the side of the face."

"...Yeah, I suppose so."

"I'll start with 'Do you have any idea what I had to go through because you weren't around?!' And then, I'll make him spill his guts about everything! I have a right to that much, don't I?"

"...Yeah, I suppose so."

"—? Emilia-tan, the side of your face is cute when you're thinking. Can I give you a hug?"

"...Yeah, I suppose so."

Subaru didn't have the courage to go "I'll help myself, then," at her cut-and-pasted reply. The stiffness of Emilia's cheeks and the stress in her eyes drew his attention.

"Emilia-tan, are you nervous by any chance?"

"—! That's amazing, how could you tell?"

"I'd love to say I can tell everything about you, but I think anyone could in this case."

Emilia's look of surprise brought a strained smile out of Subaru as he prodded his own cheek with a finger. Emilia followed suit by touching her own cheek, whereupon she realized just how tense her own expression was.

"Sorry to worry you. I was thinking, we'll be in the Sanctuary soon...a village only for demi-humans."

"...Ahh, that so? I'm sorry, too. I hadn't thought about that."

When Emilia divulged the reason for her nervousness, Subaru felt pathetic for not realizing it himself.

According to Frederica's explanation, the Sanctuary was not merely a settlement for demi-human races. It was a settlement where "demi-humans in particular circumstances" came to settle. So it was possible that—

*There might be half-elves who went through the same stuff Emilia did...*

"…I've…never met any half-elves besides myself. I hadn't really… thought about it very much. But in the Sanctuary, it might be possible…"

Emilia's voice trembled with nervousness. But he couldn't tell if that nervousness was from worry or hope. Emilia probably couldn't tell, either.

The only way to get a solid answer was to go to the Sanctuary and see. But—

"—! Emilia?!"

"Eh, ah… What's this…?!"

The next moment, Subaru and Emilia simultaneously raised their voices at the strange occurrence inside the carriage.

The source of the occurrence was none other than Emilia, herself quite nervous. A blue radiance was welling up from inside her chest, instantly tinting the interior of the dragon carriage with a bluish glow.

Startled by the light, Emilia thrust a hand into her pocket—and pulled out the shining blue crystal emitting that light.

"The crystal's shining… Subaru!"

"The hell… I have a really bad feelin' about this! Emilia, I'm borrowing that!"

Thinking that the ferociously shining blue crystal looked much like a magic crystal on the verge of exploding, Subaru instantly snatched the crystal away from Emilia. Then he rushed to the dragon carriage's window—

"If it's nothing we'll pick it up later! For now, I'll toss it outs—wait, wha—?!"

"—aa…"

Just as he was about to throw the dangerous object away, the faint moan made Subaru look back, aghast.

"Emilia?!"

When he looked back, his gaze was met by the sight of Emilia listlessly collapsed onto the dragon carriage's floor. Emilia was prone, limbs spread out and unconscious. It had happened suddenly without any forewarning—

"No, the forewarning was this?! Shit, Emilia, are you all ri—?!"

For an instant, Subaru hesitated in deciding whether to prioritize Emilia or the crystal. Prioritizing Emilia's safety, he was attempting to rush to her side when—

"—Ah? Hey?!"

The instant he stepped forward, the blue, shining crystal emitted an even stronger light that enveloped Subaru's entire body.

He had no time to regret his choice of priorities. The next instant, the world vanished.

"Emilia—!"

He stretched out a hand and shouted.

However, neither his voice nor his arm reached the fallen girl before the air connecting him to her was severed.

"———"

It was over in an instant. Feeling the shine of the light, Subaru swiveled his head, but he couldn't see a thing.

The world had been erased—no, rather, it had been temporarily blotted out by being bathed in a light too strong for his sense of sight. Blinking repeatedly, he finally realized that contours were gradually forming within his indistinct vision.

But regaining his sense of vision did not put his confusion to rest. After all…

"…Where is this?"

He was not in the dragon carriage's interior, where he should have been. Rather, Subaru was standing in an unfamiliar forest, alone.

4

"—! Not the time to say that! Where's Emilia?!"

Setting aside his momentary daze, Subaru surveyed the area, desperately striving to grasp the situation.

Trees suggestive of being deep in a forest stood left, right, and center around him. Moss and grasses stretched unhindered at his feet, without the faintest trace of human passage.

"Cheek… Ow, it hurts when I pinch! Meaning this isn't a dream…!"

Ruling out the choice of avoiding reality, Subaru largely grasped just what had happened to him.

It was the shining crystal in his hand. The powerful light that had shone until just prior had already vanished, but there was no way it was unrelated to his circumstance. It was probably the blue, shining crystal that was the cause to begin with.

"—Teleportation. Kinda like Beatrice's Passage."

The mechanism was unclear, but Subaru, having been shifted by similar incantations in the past, made an educated guess. He'd experienced Passage a number of times during his dealings with Beatrice.

The problems were the reason and purpose behind the shift, and how to rendezvous with Emilia and the others.

"Plus, Emilia was on the floor when I left. I've gotta get back ASAP...!"

If the shift was from something similar to Passage, Subaru's jump couldn't have been that far. At the very least, it ought not to have been to some far-flung place on a map of the world. At the very least, he must be in the same forest.

"I mean, it was all Beatrice could do to send me as far as Earlham Village. There's no way this rock has enough power to send me farther than that."

Coming to that conclusion, Subaru smoldered with impatience as he gazed down at the crystal in his palm.

The crystal had been the cause of the shift. Having momentarily hesitated to throw it away, he'd ended up stuffing it in a pocket instead. Though walking around with it was dangerous, he was scared of throwing it away in case he might need it later.

Besides, he didn't know Frederica's intentions in handing them the crystal.

—Or even whether Frederica was related to the shift.

"Shit! Right now, gotta save the thinking for later. If I can at least figure out direction from the location of the sun..."

Brushing excessive thoughts aside, Subaru racked his brain to raise his chances of a rendezvous by any extent he could manage.

Then, when he was about to begin walking in search of any clearing in the forest—

"...aa?"

The next moment, Subaru lifted his head, coming eye to eye with the figure appearing right before him.

"_____"

The unexpected jolt of meeting the unemotional eyes brought Subaru's thought process to a complete halt. If the other party had intended him harm, the opening would have proved fatal.

But, fortunately, the opponent made no reaction. Save for backing away slowly, Subaru was the same.

"And you...are?"

When Subaru took a step back, the other person's entire body entered his field of vision, and he comprehended this was a girl.

The young girl had long, rose-colored hair and looked like she was in her early teens. Her visage had almond-shaped eyes and a long, refined nose; her skin had a pale, fleeting look, as if it would break apart the moment you touched it. In height, she did not even reach halfway up Subaru's chest. Her small body was clothed only in a white, poncho-like garment.

A doll—that was the impression he received, not from her beautiful appearance, but from the air hovering all about her. She had emotionless eyes, an emotionless, unchanging face, with a muted presence and so little apparent willpower that it felt insufficient for a person.

But she had one feature that strongly tugged at his attention. Namely—

"Those long ears... Are you an elf?"

"..."

When Subaru asked the question, the girl's doll-like expression remained intact as she said nothing. However, the tapered ears, longer than those of a normal human, poking out of her rose-colored hair told Subaru that the answer to his question was, without doubt, a yes.

Subaru had been speaking to Emilia about the possibility of

encountering half-elves besides her just moments before. Subaru's thoughts were exceedingly thrown off by the surprise of encountering an elf in the flesh so very quickly. Furthermore—

"Aa...! W-wait! Where do you think you're going?!"

Moving like an apparition, the girl turned her back on Subaru and ran off. It was so sudden that Subaru reacted late, and began pursuing the girl in great haste as she widened the distance.

"Wait! Please, wait...! Are you...are you someone from the Sanctuary...?"

The agile girl practically flew as she raced into the overgrown woods. Subaru, desperately pursuing her over bad and unfamiliar footing, felt pain rising as his breath rapidly grew louder.

"S-shit... Damn it all!"

How was the forest related to the Sanctuary, and to begin with, who was that girl—?

Knowing that asking would only deplete his endurance, Subaru gritted his teeth and focused his strength into his legs.

For several minutes, Subaru proceeded to chase the girl's fleeting back as if his life depended on it. Then his field of vision suddenly widened.

"—! I got through the woods...but where the heck is this?"

Coming to a stop in the clearing, Subaru bent his knees as he breathed raggedly over and over. He wiped off the sweat coursing down his brow. When he raised his agonized, grimacing face, Subaru found a strange structure ahead of him.

The structure, constructed from stones piled onto one another, was a ruin of particularly primitive architecture.

Most of the outer facing was covered in green moss and vines; the few exposed portions of the rock face were spectacularly cracked. It was unclear how many centuries had passed since its construction, but, considering that the structure was half-overrun by the forest, it hadn't been buried to start with, making it at least several centuries old.

The ruin, standing in the tranquil forest air, seemed like a temple, or perhaps—

"It kinda feels like a tomb. For a sec, I thought it was a pyramid... Hey, wait a...!"

Thrusting his admiration for the ruin aside, Subaru hastily looked for any sign of the girl he was pursuing. He'd arrived by following the girl there; she was the real priority.

But however much he surveyed the area, the girl who ought to have been there was nowhere to be found. Her presence, her lingering scent, and even her footsteps were absent. It was clear as day that he'd lost track of her.

"This is the worst... After I get teleported, I let my only lead get away...!"

Roughly scratching his head, Subaru despaired from the bottom of his heart at his own ineptitude. But he had no time to be down in the dumps. Even if the girl, his one lead, had vanished—

"Maybe I can hope for something from this ruin...? It kinda feels like a temple, so I can't call it unrelated to someplace called the Sanctuary..."

Wishful thinking though it might be, Subaru cautiously began walking toward the ruin. Even when he saw it up close, his initial impression of the stone structure didn't change all that much.

There was no sign whatsoever of human presence, of human handiwork, or any sense that a living soul dwelled there.

"Heyyy, is anyone here? If this is the Sanctuary, someone answer, please—!"

Though he called out to the ruin and the surrounding forest in a loud voice, it echoed fruitlessly in the air. Sighing deeply when he did not get the hoped-for response, Subaru grudgingly walked around the ruin—

"—Well, there's an entrance..."

About halfway around the ruin, Subaru spotted a set of moss-covered stairs. When he climbed the stairs, careful not to slip, he found an opening with a dimly lit passage within—no doubt continuing into the ruin. He'd found his entrance.

Naturally, the interior of the ruin was not lit, and the corridor he saw from the entrance continued into darkness. Even when he timidly called out, he heard nothing but the lonely echo of his own voice.

Put bluntly, he didn't have a good premonition in the slightest, but it is said that one can only get a tiger cub by going into a tiger's den.

"Not that I really want a tiger cub…but if it's the girl who brought me here earlier, turning back now would be giving up the store."

Having come that far, Subaru did not doubt that the girl and the ruin were related. If the teleportation via the crystal was related to the girl as well, the ruin had to be related to the Sanctuary.

In the first place, it should have been Emilia, the one possessing the crystal, who was teleported.

"Then it being me instead of Emilia wasn't part of the plan… Whether snake or Oni, only way to know is to see what pops out…"

The very fact that he'd been teleported had already limited their options. With no clear way to rendezvous with Emilia, Subaru decided it was best to accept the invitation and play along for the moment.

"…"

Breathing deep, Subaru clenched his teeth and stepped into the ruin.

He employed the trick of keeping his right hand constantly against a wall to never lose his way in the dark. The sensation against his hand was less of a stone wall than of the slender, delicate vines covering it. The vines had overgrown the passage so thickly that it was hard to tell where the original wall stood, and it felt more like the artery of a living entity—the bizarre atmosphere of the ruin itself made him feel like he was entering the body of some giant creature.

"…"

The only things he could hear in the darkness were his own breathing, his loudly beating heart, and his shoes.

He had lost his sense of sight due to lack of light, and the cold, serene air robbed him of all use of his nose. His sense of hearing loomed large in his mind, but at some point, he'd lost track of the wall that he'd been touching.

The feeling on his tongue was that of air mixed with sand and dust. Tasting nothing despite the sensation, Subaru relied more and more on his sense of hearing. The sounds of his shoes, his heartbeats, and his breathing were the only things he could depend on.

These things proved to him that he was connected to the world, not adrift for all eternity.

His sweating increased, his heart quickened, and his soul raged, pleading for release.

Where he was, what he was doing, whom he sought—these things grew vague.

But he was seized by a powerful drive not to stand still. Someone kept pleading with him not to stop, to grit his teeth and bear the weight he carried on his shoulders. At some point, his mind became churned.

The still-echoing voice, the warmth of a touch, an earnest plea, all mingled together when—

"I see. This is the desire that drives you. How curious, I must say."

Amid the darkness, Subaru Natsuki heard the amused voice of a Witch.

5

Returning to the moment in the story when Subaru found himself facing the Witch on top of a hill...

"_____"

A faint wind tickled the back of Subaru's neck, rekindling the chill that traveled up his spine. His back was moist from a great deal of cold sweat, and the overwhelming pressure he was under had not abated at all.

He stood opposite the girl—Echidna—as she sat in a white chair, doing nothing besides tilting her teacup.

"It hurts to see you so on guard. However I seem to you, am I not but a single, innocent maiden?"

"...Sorry, but lowering my guard for a girl I just met declaring herself the Witch of Greed is seriously not happening."

"Ah, I see. Certainly, that was another oversight on my part."

Echidna touched the back of her hand to her lips as she giggled and smiled in an amused fashion. The sight of the nonchalant girl did not drain the tension from Subaru, who remained ready to rush her at any moment. He opened and closed his sweat-drenched hands, as prepared as he could be to instantly overwhelm his opponent.

The problem was that such preparations, full or not, were likely futile before Echidna.

"There are a mountain of things you wish to ask. However, you do not know what may cause me to take offense. Therefore, you watch how your opponent moves in silence... The demeanor of a bird watching its prey, is it not?"

"_____"

"And you ignore me? Goodness, that wounds me on a fundamental level. As you can see, I am nothing more than an innocent maiden. I cannot help but wonder when a boy gazes at me with such eyes."

"You being a maiden on the inside is like a piece of paper with *death flag* written on the backside. Just so you know, my internal danger alarm is ringing like crazy."

Having experienced death repeatedly since arriving in that world, Subaru had an acute nose for danger. It hadn't diminished the number of his deaths at all, but it at least allowed his mind to keep functioning.

According to his senses, the danger posed by the girl before him rivaled that of the White Whale and Sloth—no, it exceeded them.

"It is natural for you to be on guard, but a coward like you can do nothing to me, can you? At the very least, I would like you to sit before the tea goes cold."

Speaking these words, Echidna offered Subaru the empty seat opposite her. On the white table between the two rested a cup of steaming tea, likely poured for Subaru's benefit.

Sit down, drink her tea, speak with her—that was what Echidna requested.

Nothing would improve even if he refused. Indeed, the odds

things would get worse were higher that way. Subaru had virtually no choice but to accept.

"Let me ask you one thing… I was inside a ruin that was completely dark. Where is this, and when did I get teleported here?"

"Teleport… Ah, you mean that Dark spell. Unfortunately, you have misunderstood. What you experienced was not physical movement through space. I simply invited you into my castle for tea."

"Into your castle…for tea…?"

Subaru knitted his brows at Echidna's words, turning his eyes to the hill's surroundings once more.

The hill stood at the center of grassland rustled by the wind that seemed to continue infinitely. In all four directions, the world was completely flat with no obstacles to be seen, full of a sense of liberation. It was downright surreal.

The fact that this didn't seem like a real place lent weight to Echidna's claim that he hadn't been teleported.

"But there's no castle here. If this is your territory, did some debt collector walk off with everything except two chairs and a table?"

"Tee-hee-hee. You are amusing. Except for fellow Witches, I cannot even count on my hands the number of those who would speak with such impudence before me. I never thought the number would increase after my own death."

With a lighthearted laugh, Echidna counted the memories on her fingers, delighted with Subaru's reply.

Subaru grimaced. He couldn't simply ignore her demeanor, nor the significance of *after my own death*.

In the first place, he had to consider her self-declared title. When he combined it with the current supernatural circumstance, he had no reason to doubt Echidna's identity or her power.

"Aw, shit! All right, all right already! I'll sit! I'll drink your tea!"

With no way to advance or retreat, Subaru did the only thing he could out of visible despair, sitting across from Echidna and practically snatching the steaming cup from the table, draining its contents all at once.

It was neither water, nor green tea, nor black. The drink had a mysterious flavor that wasn't unpleasant.

For the first time, Echidna's eyes went wide in apparent surprise at Subaru's disdainful actions.

"To drink something offered by a Witch in one gulp... You are quite a brave soul."

"Hah?! Like chickening out at this point is gonna do me any good. For starters, if you wanted to kill me, you'll probably turn me to ash the next instant. No point being on my guard about one cup of tea."

Subaru waved off the smiling Echidna's words, saying "Thank you for the drink" as he put the teacup down.

"It wasn't particularly good- or bad-tasting. What kind of tea is this...?"

"It is generated from my castle. I suppose you could call it my body fluids."

"Damn it, why'd you make me drink *that*?!"

Subaru leaped from the chair to his feet, then went down onto his knees in what seemed to be an attempt to vomit what he had just imbibed. Echidna giggled and smiled at Subaru's exaggerated reaction.

"You wound me. When I examine my appearance, I do not think I seem quite that evil."

"No matter how beautiful the girl, I don't wanna drink anyone's fluids without being ready for it! Wait, I can't drink anything called body fluids, prepared or not!! I'm not a damn pervert!!"

At the very least Subaru didn't *think* he was inclined toward becoming aroused by secret ingredients like saliva and sweat.

"Shit, can't vomit it out...! Hey, this isn't gonna make me sick, is it?!"

"You may rest at ease. They are body fluids, after all, and thus readily absorbed by the flesh."

"That isn't exactly good news, so quit it with that face!"

Echidna's demeanor came off as proud for some reason, which made Subaru wince. Echidna carried on.

"Putting that aside, you are indeed a mysterious individual. The fact that you can stand unaffected before me like this is proof enough."

"What? Are you so beautiful that people normally shut their eyes when they see you? Just to make it clear, my eyes are fed a steady diet of the most beautiful girl around as far as I'm concerned. When I look at you, I can only go 'Wow, she's cute' so many times."

"No, a normal person in my presence would vomit. Amusing, isn't it?"

"What's amusing about that?!"

These exchanges, filled with concerning thoughts since the beginning of their time together, made Subaru feel exhausted in body and spirit as he slumped into his chair. He took another glance at the Witch before his eyes.

She had white, seemingly bleached hair, and a black dress that seemed like something a person would wear at a funeral. Somehow, she seemed at once fickle and baby-faced, yet also mysteriously seductive. She certainly possessed a face that stirred the heart.

But he felt pressure from her that was wholly undiluted, marking her as no normal being.

"Now then, while I am most pleased to have a fresh conversation partner like this, that is not the case for you, is it? You have things you wish to ask me, yes?"

"...That, that's right! I got swallowed up by the mood, but that's right. You're... No, before that, where is this place? I should be in some weird ruin. How'd I end up in your castle?"

After the teleportation, Subaru had entered the ruin in search of clues about the Sanctuary. Somehow, he'd blindly stumbled into Echidna's castle—the realm of the Witch of Greed.

"In the first place...are you really a Witch? According to what I'd heard, aside from the Witch of Jealousy, every other Witch in the world had been killed..."

"Whatever doubts you might harbor, you are not mistaken in that assessment. Jealousy destroyed the other six Witches, and I am no exception. This is merely my tomb."

"Tomb… You mean I'm inside your grave?"

Echidna's collected reply made Subaru recall the sense he'd had before entering the ruin—that the solemn atmosphere was suggestive of a temple, or a tomb.

His gut feeling had been right. The ruin was, properly speaking, a tomb. But it was the tomb of a Witch.

"After my death, my soul became a captive of this place, the Witches' Tomb. It is not my body but my spirit that has invited you into my castle. Put one way, you are inside my dream."

"Just the spirit, is that even possible? Meaning my body's sleeping outside somewhere?"

"Why is it not possible? You know of a space similar to this, do you not?"

"_____"

Echidna's probing question caused Subaru's breath to catch, a reaction even he found suspicious.

Nothing came to mind. Yet, why was there a strange hesitance in his heart?

"…I don't know what you're referring to, but what you're saying isn't wrong."

Echidna's words were not lies. However, nor was Subaru's answer any kind of deceit.

When told that he was inside a dream, Subaru was both surprised and quick to accept…as if his heart alone instantly understood the impression that world gave off.

As to why he thought so, he could not find the reason anywhere within his memories, but…

"I get that this is inside a dream and inside of your tomb. So how do I get out of here?"

"The method of awakening from a dream is simple. You must either strongly will yourself to awaken, or be awoken from the outside. Though it must be said, mine is a special dream. You might not be able to awaken unless I will it to be so."

"—! Then don't tell me you…!"

Subaru's gaze sharpened as Echidna's emotionless statement shocked him.

The words *inside a dream* and *Witch's castle* suddenly weighed heavier in his mind. If Subaru's spirit was a prisoner there, both Subaru's flesh and his soul were in the palm of her hand.

"You don't intend to let me escape, then…?"

"Ah, it's not really like that. If you really want to go back, I'll send you back. I mean, it's not that I called you here. You intruded all on your own, you know."

"Can't you do something about my sense of tension? Mr. Serious can't breathe like this, okay?"

"That is because, unlike you, Mr. Serious is not standing before me. Perhaps he is vomiting behind a tree?"

Mentally exhausted from Echidna smoothly spewing poison, Subaru was completely thrown off his stride. In the end, he still wondered just why Echidna had made contact with him.

Or was it really nothing more than the Witch responding to the arrival of a guest—

"You said you didn't call me. In other words, the elf who was outside isn't involved in this? Or this crystal?"

Subaru rummaged in his pocket, locating the blue crystal with his hand. Since she'd told him he was invited in spirit only, he was worried about what he was carrying, but Subaru had apparently arrived with everything he'd had on him.

However, when Echidna received Subaru's question, she put an elbow to the table.

"Unfortunately, though my complexion is in good order, I am quite dead. I know little of the happenings outside of my tomb. Therefore, I am not related either to the elf you speak of or to that blue crystal. Are you satisfied?"

"I'm unsatisfied 'cause it means everything's still a big mystery. But that's the stuff I wanted to ask."

Subaru nodded at Echidna's reply, returning the crystal to his pocket as he rose to his feet. He was unsure whether the crystal's teleportation was truly unrelated to the Witch or not, but he had no reason to stay there any longer.

Staying and chatting over tea left his primary objective, rendez-vousing with Emilia, unaccomplished.

"At any rate, if you're gonna send me back, then send me. I'm super-worried about the girl I got split off from on the outside. If I've got the time to drink your body fluids, I wanna meet back up with her at the earliest second possible."

"I do not mind, but are you really fine with that?"

"With what…?"

"Leaving my little tea party—others wishing to speak with the Witch of Greed rarely have the opportunity, even if you do."

When she said it, Subaru realized it for the first time.

He realized the true nature of the malaise he'd felt from the being called Echidna since arriving in that place—the strange oppressive feeling that continued without any hint of gradually abating.

"_____"

Echidna's deep, black, bottomless eyes had a suspicious glint to them, as if they knew everything about Subaru.

The true nature of that ill feeling was Echidna's inexhaustible curiosity.

It was her deep interest in the existence before her eyes that made her scrutinizing gaze feel so oppressive.

"What are you? …Do you know the things I want to know?"

"And so you ask *me* the nature of my knowledge— Truly, you are an amusing one."

Subaru made his rapidly drying mouth move, wringing out his voice for the question he tossed her way. The words made Echidna giggle and smile, and Subaru's entire body was wrenched by a sense of oppression even greater than before.

"There is no need to reflect deeply upon it. All that is required for questions and answers is for two beings to be present."

That instant, the air warped, and the landscape—the vast, blue sky and the grassland—suddenly began to fall apart. The sky cracked, the grassland melted, and the horizon of the world was smashed into tiny pieces.

As the world crumbled without a sound, Subaru touched the table, seemingly clinging to the one certain thing left. The table, too, crumbled into dust, and Subaru closed his eyes, seemingly girding himself against a nonexistent tremor.

"All we need are words. Your curiosity, your hunger to know—I acknowledge your *greed*."

Then he realized it: All that remained of the castle of dreams was the hill, and chairs for the two of them.

Subaru gingerly opened his eyes and sat in the opposite chair as he gazed at the Witch. Aside from her and the white chair, the world had been stripped down to its barest essentials, with nothing but gloomy, stagnant darkness spread over where the grassland had been. The one thing he was certain of was if he fell into it, there would be no coming back.

That sent a chill running up Subaru's spine as Echidna, in high spirits, joyfully clapped her hands toward him.

"Now, what do you wish to ask about? Daphne, the Witch of Gluttony, creator of beasts in defiance of the will of Heaven to save the world from starvation? Camilla, the Witch of Lust, filled with love for the world, granter of emotions to they that are inhuman? Minerva, the Witch of Wrath, who, lamenting a world filled with conflict, sets people straight through her fists? Sekhmet, the Witch of Sloth, who, wanting a moment's peace, drove the dragons beyond the Great Waterfalls for that reason alone? Or Typhon, the Witch of Pride, the young, innocent, merciless one who continued to render judgment onto sinners?"

He'd never heard of these—no, these were lost vestiges of history unrecorded in the present world.

Hearing her speak the name of one Witch after another, Subaru was speechless. Echidna smiled all the more as she continued.

"Or perhaps Echidna, the Witch of Greed, the embodiment of craving for knowledge, whose search for any and all wisdom lingers even after unto the afterlife?"

Touching a hand to her own breast, Echidna said the words in a self-deprecating fashion. "Or perhaps," she continued, "the Witch of Jealousy, the abominable woman who destroyed and consumed the other six, and made the whole world her enemy?"

6

Subaru Natsuki felt a powerful aura of death in the form of the girl seated before his eyes.

That was the desolate insight Subaru had gained about Echidna, proven by her own witchy ways.

She was a being nothing like him. It had nothing whatsoever to do with her enmity, or lack thereof.

In the face of truly inescapable terror, it was easy for a person's emotional responses to go on lockdown.

"Awww. It seems I have intimidated you too greatly. It has always been thus; my lips grow too loose when I become interested in something. A Witch's nature is truly a troublesome thing."

With Subaru cowed into silence, Echidna remained seated as she voiced words of self-reflection. However, there was not a single trace of *actual* reflection. The wall separating the two remained absolute.

The true nature of the malaise he'd subconsciously ignored until he realized its presence was laid bare a second time.

"Knowing that makes me feel rather lonely. But you should begin to adjust to it soon. I hope that this circumstance, where you cannot even look directly at my face, changes somewhat…"

Echidna's bizarre statement made Subaru grimace; the fear he tasted froze him stiff. But Echidna tilted her head, the black eyes she trained upon the uncomprehending Subaru indicating anticipation of some kind.

Her white, bleached, beautiful hair fell down onto her shoulders. As Subaru gazed at it, he felt as if the agonizing seconds would extend for all eternity—but this came to a sudden halt.

"*Haaa—ah?*"

"Mm, faster than I thought. That is a compatible person for you. It is helpful that you acclimated so quickly."

"What…are you…talking about?"

As Echidna nodded and smiled in satisfaction, Subaru broke out in a cold sweat and restrained his chest with a hand. His heart was loud, as if it had forgotten how to beat for a while, and his painfully numb limbs pleaded for mercy.

However, he had escaped the fear that had held him in its grip until a moment before. It had vanished like magic.

"You drank my tea, yes? That activated your Witch Factor and strengthened your resistance. Now you and I can speak. My, my, a very good thing for both of us, is it not?"

"Wait, wait, wait... I've heard that term before... I can't just let it go. What did those body fluids from before do? What did you to do my body?"

"Please do not misunderstand... I did not have you drink it with ill intent. If anything, I think rather fondly of you... That is a little embarrassing to say out loud."

Echidna's cheeks reddened a bit, and she looked shy at having spoken so affectionately of him. But at that point Subaru was well past reacting to her games. What he wanted was her true intent.

"You have killed someone possessing Witch Factor in the last several days, yes? Upon his death, the Witch Factor selected you as its new bearer. It is thanks to this that you were able to safely enter my tomb."

"So you're saying...the Witch Factor is the condition for being invited into this castle of dreams?"

"No, it is merely what qualified you to enter the tomb itself. You are an exception among exceptions. To begin with, you seem to have leaped quite a bit ahead of schedule—by rights, you should be aware of far more than you are...about me, about the tomb, and about the Sanctuary."

"—! You know about the Sanctuary?!"

Pouncing on the term lobbed his way, Subaru closed the distance and grasped Echidna's shoulders. When Subaru touched her slender shoulders and drew his face near, the beautiful Witch averted her gaze.

"...I have little experience in such matters, so I cannot decide if you are brave or simply brazen."

"Don't make light of this! If you know about the Sanctuary, that makes this simple! Is this…no, do you know about the forest outside of the ruin? Should I think of that as the Sanctuary?"

"You're so cold. But you asked, so I shall answer: It is so. As you hoped, the area outside the ruin is the Sanctuary. Properly speaking, the Sanctuary is the name given to the place that protects this tomb."

"Then…!"

If he got out of the castle of dreams, raced out of the ruin, and cut through the forest, he could rendezvous with Emilia and the others. Even if he didn't meet Emilia, he ought to be able to meet those dwelling in the Sanctuary and get out of his predicament.

All that meant the elf who'd led him there was indeed a resident of the Sanctuary.

"All of a sudden, I wanna go outside even more. You said you'd send me there, right?"

"Eh? Ahh, I guarantee it… I guarantee it, but I would be very lonely if you simply rushed off like that. Um, is there nothing else you wish to ask me?"

"Sorry, but Emilia should be outside. I wanna link up with her more than I wanna talk with you. Besides…"

Echidna furled her brows in dismay, her words causing Subaru to scratch the tip of his nose as he carried on.

"You don't know about things on the outside, right? It's tough saying this after all that sound and fury, but to be honest, there's not really anything I want to ask you…"

"…Eh? You're kidding, right? That cannot be. I mean, I am the Witch of Greed, you know? People all over the world seek me to grasp at my knowledge: knights, people of privilege. You sit before me, permitted to ask anything to wish, and you say *that*?"

Taken back as she was by the unexpected reply, Echidna's expression distinctly faltered for the first time. The Witch flailed about as she exhausted all the words she could to prevent Subaru from leaving.

"Calm down, let us speak. Certainly, I am ill versed regarding the present era. But in turn, I possess vast knowledge about the older era, to the point I can boast there is nothing I do not know about it. I possess historical truth no one remembers, undiminished after four centuries…and you possess an opportunity to gain that knowledge."

"But I'm not all that interested in Witches. Even if we talk about them, they're all dead, and there's a lot of other things besides that I need to think about…"

"Ehhh…!"

As he made his farewells in earnest, the unsatisfied Echidna's eyes grew tearful. Their positions had been completely reversed, with Subaru shrugging off the Witch who had felt so oppressive before.

The image of the Witch of Greed had thus been ruined. Without malice, it seemed she was just an ordinary girl.

Certainly, there was no lack of information he wanted to know. He'd like to know about the Witch Factor she'd spoken of, or the Sanctuary there to protect her tomb. Or perhaps, perhaps, perhaps—

"For example, that. Do you know details about the Witch Cult's Archbishops of the Seven Deadly Sins?"

"Archbishops of the Seven Deadly Sins? Hmm, unfortunately, I do not know the term. Could you tell me about them in more detail?"

"Our positions really are reversed, sheesh… Well, if you don't know, that's fine."

A smile came over Subaru at the sight of Echidna being thrown off—it hid the pain in his chest.

"Yeah, it's fine."

He'd hoped. But those hopes had been easily dashed. So there was no point staying there any longer.

If she knew nothing of the archbishops, she knew nothing of their Authorities, the damage they did, or ways to repair it.

—Meaning she didn't know how he could save Rem.

"Can you send me out already? I'll come chat with you over tea another time, okay?"

"Is that really a promise you can easily make with a dead person, and a Witch at that…?"

With Subaru in a hurry to make his escape, his words made Echidna sigh, all poison seemingly drawn out of her. Then, in a resigned fashion, she waved an arm, and Subaru felt wind behind him.

When he looked back, a single door had appeared in the world of bottomless darkness and a broken sky.

"Pass through that door, and you shall awaken outside. Goodness, I have never had a tea party such as this."

"Sorry for not indulging in your hospitality. Incidentally, about this ruin... Can I ask, when I leave the tomb, where should I go to head toward the residents of the Sanctuary?"

"I told you before. I know little about the outside. Quite naturally, I do not know the location of the settlement, either."

"Man, for a calm, collected know-it-all character, you really come up short..."

He meant to needle her, but Subaru's shoulders sank at how Echidna amply puffed out her quite average breasts. After that, he raised a hand toward her in lieu of words of departure, thus announcing he was taking his leave.

Though he had been fiercely on guard at the beginning, it was a surprisingly gentle way to end a tea party with a Wit—

"—Now then, since you are heading back from a tea party with a Witch, it is about time I take the compensation due."

Most improperly, it was a demand tossed toward him at the very, very end.

Subaru, feeling horror as the echo of her words terribly clawed at his spirit, turned his head alone toward her.

Echidna, the Witch, said not in malice, but with nothing more than a quiet, gentle smile—

"...It bears mentioning that I'm a pauper up there with the best of 'em. A Witch's compensation is not paid in coin. What I seek from you is a pact. My terms are that you are forbidden from speaking to others about what took place at this tea party. You are bound by a similar pact, so it is a simple matter for you, is it not?"

"A similar pact…"

What Echidna described—facts known to him that he was forbidden to divulge to others—it was almost as if she was talking about Return by Death.

"The invitation to the tea party, the Witch Factor taking root… Considering my good fortune in getting to know someone deeply interesting such as yourself, I too have gained greatly. That's right, I shall grant you one final souvenir…"

Stroking her white hair, Echidna stood up and stretched a pale finger toward Subaru's chest. For some reason, Subaru found himself gazing at her slow movement, unable to budge an inch.

To a bizarre extent, he could neither reject nor rebuff the finger that seemed to glide toward him.

"I grant thee the qualification to challenge the trial of this Sanctuary."

"The trial of…the Sanctuary?"

"Even if you do not understand now, you will realize the value this place holds. I wonder what emotions you will bear toward me when that time comes… I very much look forward to finding out."

Pulling back the finger touching his chest, Echidna gently licked its tip. The gesture was seductive enough to give Subaru a chill, reconfirming in his mind her witchy nature.

However amiable her behavior toward him, however teenage her smiling face, what was before his eyes was—

"You really are a Witch, huh?"

"Yes, it is so. I am a very bad magic user, you see?"

Along with those words, Echidna used that finger to give Subaru's forehead a very light nudge.

Subaru seemed to fall back, tumbling downward; the next moment, the open door swallowed him whole.

"_____"

He fell into the darkness. Then the darkness vanished within the light.

Cast out of the dream, the being called Subaru Natsuki floated upward—and outside, his consciousness awakened.

7

The instant Subaru awoke, the first thing he felt was a hard sensation against his cheek.

"…aa, uu…"

Moaning with a half-asleep voice, Subaru became aware that he was lying prone. He blinked several times, and reality poured into his vision, awakening him over the course of several seconds.

Pressing his arms to the ground, he slowly lifted himself up—

"This, is… errr…?"

He brushed off the dirt on his cheek with his fingers and squinted into the darkness. When he looked, Subaru saw that he had fallen inside an old ruin—to be precise, several tens of meters into the corridor leading into it.

To his back was the entrance to the tomb, and it was from there that light entered into his eyes. Thanks to that, his escape route was plain to see, but it made for a pretty crummy ruin exploration.

"Anyway, I'd better get out and hook back up with Emilia and Otto…"

Shaking his heavy head, he placed a hand against the wall, wobbly as he rose to his feet. He had no business inside the ruin. The Sanctuary lay outside. Having gone astray, he needed to be outside to rendezvous with Emilia.

He couldn't quite put his finger on why he was so certain of that, but—

"I feel like, someone said that to me…"

"Yo. Ya sure got some guts, comin' straight out from a place like that, outsider."

"Ah…?"

As he exited the ruin with fragmented thoughts, a voice called out to him the instant his eyes narrowed from the light.

His vision, accustomed to the dark, was hazy. As it gradually adjusted, Subaru found himself looking down at the surrounding landscape from the modestly elevated ruin.

In front of the ruin was a single dragon carriage, and a young male driver with a most pitiable look on his face.

"M-Mr. Natsuki…"

"Otto? What are you doing in a place like… No, before that, where's Emilia?!"

"Inside the dragon carriage! I-it has been most terrible since that moment! I-I…!!"

When Subaru raised his voice at the unexpected reunion, Otto shouted back even louder. But thanks to that, Subaru was able to confirm Emilia's presence, and this made his shoulders sink in relief. Otto was pleading about something, but that concern could wait. The immediate problem was—

"Hey, forget the whiny guy. *I* come first here, damn it!"

The individual standing right beside the dragon carriage spoke to Subaru with a voice that issued seemingly through clenched teeth. Turning his face toward the speaker, Subaru shrugged.

"What a coincidence. I was just thinking the same thing."

"Hah! That's 'ganglion before you think' for ya!"

"Gangl… Ah?"

As Subaru knotted his brows at the mystery phrase mixed in with the reply, the other party took a step forward. With a coarse manner of speech and a hostile glint in his eyes, the speaker's external appearance in no way betrayed Subaru's first, ferocious impression of him.

He had short, combed-back blond hair and a highly visible white scar on his forehead. There was ferocity in his sharp green eyes, and he was dressed in crude clothing Subaru could only call that of a country bumpkin. For a man, he was fairly short, especially in a stooped posture, but the dense, ghastly aura coursing from his entire body made certain others would not underestimate him due to his small stature.

More than any of those things, the individual had one external feature that set him apart. And that was—

"Hey, are ya shakin'? Well, yer luck definitely ran out. Here ya are in a place ya shouldn't be, and now *I* caught ya!"

As the man spoke, his eyes narrowed, and he laughed—with a mouth full of sharp, extremely distinctive fangs.

Subaru had déjà vu. He'd seen a smiling face just like that extremely recently.

"Well, if yer gonna curse yer bad luck, do like 'Bazomazo swept away right and left'!"

"Wait! Hey, you, listen to us bef—"

"'Tear and tear but Kalran's skin's still blue'… I ain't listenin'!"

Lending no ear to the voice urging him to stop, the fanged man stepped forward; the next instant, he vanished from sight.

An impact made Subaru's breath catch. Before he realized it, he had been caught by his collar. When he turned his head to the side in surprise, the man's ferocious glare was right beside him, close enough to share a breath—and his own feet were rising into the air.

"Oowaa—!!"

His view of the world was flipped upside down as he was hit by a powerful sense of floating, from which he understood that he had been hurled. Subaru proceeded to soar toward the dragon carriage in a powerful straight line. If he was to collide with it, he would suffer injury, be it light or heavy, but—

"You're kidding—?!" "Da, huu—!"

The voice of utter shock was not that of Subaru, but that of Otto as he watched through the fingers of the hands with which he covered his own face.

With no way to stop it, Subaru thought he'd collide with the dragon carriage, breaking every bone in his body. But, by seemingly miraculous coincidence—no, it was an inevitable reaction that rescued him from peril—

"Patlash is simply too incredible!"

The pitch-black land dragon neighed proudly as Otto's voice praised her exploits.

It was none other than Patlash's benevolent decision that had saved Subaru from crashing into the dragon carriage. The land dragon had adeptly set the dragon carriage in motion on her own, thus ensuring that Subaru crashed into the door of the carriage proper. As a result, Subaru punched through the carriage door, sailing in only to have a seat bring him safely to a halt.

"Shit. That one was a little too... Hey, Patlash, wait!"

Tumbling out of the seat, Subaru looked out of the carriage to see the land dragon roaring and charging the man. With a twist of her body, Patlash had unhitched herself from the dragon carriage, seemingly consumed with rage toward the man who had injured Subaru, baring her fangs to bring them to his neck.

"Ha! That decision gave me chills. Yer a good land dragon...nah, a good woman."

However, the land dragon's biting attack missed its mark, and the left arm the man thrust out stopped her in her tracks. Even so, Patlash put strength into her jaw, moving her head as if to bite the man's arm off.

But that head, and that jaw, stopped cold, her power inferior to the man's simple brawn.

"I won't hurt ya. Just put ya to sleep a bit."

As the land dragon's pupils contracted in fright, the man proudly made that statement. Then, with the land dragon still biting his arm, he tucked a hand under her broad head and hurled her huge body. With a softness that belied the heroic image, he tossed down her large frame, quietly rendering the land dragon powerless.

"He threw Patlash...?!"

"H-his skill is no joke... Eh?!"

Subaru and Otto doubted their own eyes as the man before the pair leaped very high, onto the driver's seat of the dragon carriage. With the assailant so close, Otto adopted a combative pose in great haste.

"D-do not underestimate me! I may not look it, but I too am a merchant! I have ways to deal with midjourney violence! Fear the power of Suwen School violence repulsion ar—*dahuu!*"

"Shut up, amateur. Thanks to your land dragon, I'll settle for half killin' ya. Go to sleep."

Otto was in a worked-up pose, but fainted in anguish as soon as the man flicked his forehead with a finger. It was less of a finger strike than a forehead poke, but its might was such that Otto went down in the blink of an eye without so much as a groan.

Now that he was past Patlash and now Otto, no obstacles remained between him and the dragon carriage.

"—Ugh!"

Biting his lip, Subaru looked back inside the dragon carriage. Where one section of seating had been removed in favor of the simplified bed used to carry Rem, right then a different girl—Emilia—slept upon it.

Otto must have laid her there after Subaru teleported. Even now, Emilia had yet to return to consciousness. Subaru had to protect her no matter what it took.

"Thank yer land dragon for fightin' so hard. I'll half kill ya and toss ya outside the forest. After I make ya swear that ya won't tell anyone else about this place, ya hear me?!"

Just as Subaru hardened his resolve, the man bared his fangs and boarded the carriage. The sharp glint of his fangs at the tip of his upward swinging arm cleanly robbed his declaration about half-killing of all its persuasiveness.

Before the man's wicked deeds, Subaru raised both arms wide to shield Emilia and shouted.

"Wait! You're Frederica's... You're involved with Roswaal and his people, right?!"

"—! Huhhh?"

With a loud voice and a scowl on his face, the man stopped his blow right before it connected with the tip of Subaru's nose. From there, the man gazed at Subaru for a while, surprise and anger residing in his eyes in equal measure.

"...What the hell is that name doin' comin' outta your mouth?"

"Hmm, I wonder why? Think about it nice and hard."

"Already did. I dunno. I'll think about it more after I smash your face in!"

"Cut it out with that nasty way of thinking!! We're with Roswaal, geez!!"

When his opponent took a step toward him in earnest, Subaru

hastily raised both hands high and pleaded his case. His words made the man's sharp fangs audibly clench. After thinking it over for a while, he said:

"Aah? Wait, you're sayin' the one sleepin' is that Lady Emilia chick?"

"You know...Emilia's name?"

This time, it was Subaru's turn to be surprised, because the man had referred to the sleeping Emilia as *Lady*. His reaction made the man cross his arms, nodding with a smug face as he answered.

"Oh yeah, heard all 'bout her. The silver-haired half-demon that bastard Roswaal's taken in, right?"

"She's a *half-elf*. Don't call her that in front of her ever again."

"Hah! Well lookie here, guess you can put some backbone into your voice."

The man gave Subaru a sharp, scornful gaze before making a sound through his fangs and turning his back. Then, when he left the dragon carriage, Subaru suddenly rushed over, gripping the door and forcing it closed.

The man's shoulders jumped at Subaru's violent action. He shrugged, looking back.

"Relax already. I ain't worked up no more. I don't wanna have Ram yellin' at me."

"I really relate to how you feel about that, but...that doesn't answer my first question, you know?"

"Ahh?"

Though the man spread both arms wide, asserting that he had no intention of fighting, Subaru did not lower his guard. Such behavior made the man sink into thought briefly, finally making an *ahhh* noise and nodding as if he finally understood before he spoke.

"—Me, I'm Garfiel. Haven't you heard of me?"

"So you're Garfiel...!"

*Garfiel* was the name of the individual he'd been told over and over again to be wary of back at the mansion. Subaru's brow furled at the gobsmacking development of having encountered the man himself so soon.

His reaction made Garfiel click his tongue, then stare intently at Subaru.

"I've got somethin' to ask you, then. How'd you know I'm related to Frederica?"

"…You're…seriously asking me that?"

When Subaru batted the question back, Garfiel audibly bared his fangs in visible displeasure. Taking his silence as a yes, Subaru felt energy draining from him as he scratched his face and replied.

"Anyone could tell just by looking at your face, sheesh."

The shape of his fang-filled face was undoubtable proof that he was related to Frederica by blood.

# CHAPTER 3
## A LONG-AWAITED REUNION

1

"I have been thoroughly molested. Where, exactly, should I direct my anger?!"

"Oh, shut up, coachman. It's just a little bump, so whatever. I apologized, right?"

"When did you apologize? Surely, you cannot mean your earlier statement of 'Sorry for smackin' ya, I got ahead o' myself'? That was more abuse, not an apology. Am I wrong?"

With the dragon carriage resuming its trot, Otto stubbornly vented at Garfiel from the driver's seat. Perhaps Otto's change in demeanor after having undergone such a painful experience so recently revealed he was surprisingly tough.

Though Subaru was deeply impressed, Otto disregarded this as he gazed up at the heavens and lamented.

"There was a flash of light inside the dragon carriage, and Lady Emilia collapsed, with Mr. Natsuki nowhere to be found! Do you understand how terrible I felt when I was at the end of my wits?! And then to be captured by a man dressed like a brigand!"

"I'm really sorry about that. You were a huge help. Emilia's safe thanks to you. I'm really thankful."

"R-right... Ah, well, if you feel properly thankful, all is well, really..."

"Super easy to please, wow..."

With Otto telling his tale of woe from right after they were separated, Subaru spoke respect infused with pure thankfulness.

In point of fact, it wasn't hard at all to imagine Otto's panic at being attacked. That he had protected Emilia afterward, keeping her safe pending Subaru's meeting up with them again, had earned Subaru's thanks—and enormous gratitude.

"Waaait, what's this brigand thing, you don't mean *me*, do ya?"

"Whom else could I be referring to?! You forced the dragon carriage to a stop, bullied me with your claws, and forced us to proceed with you until we reached Mr. Natsuki..."

"Right, I was wondering about that. How the heck did you end up where I was?"

Considering how he had been teleported via the power of the crystal, Subaru had assumed it was difficult to discern where he was located. Subaru didn't remember sending up any smoke signals, so how had they met up with him at the ruin?

Subaru's question made Garfiel, riding in the dragon carriage with them, rub his own nose with a finger.

"Me, I just caught the scent of an outsider. Didn't think you'd snuck in all the way to the tomb, though. I'm tellin' ya, I was pretty nervous."

"—My scent, you reached me following your nose? A special scent?"

Subaru lowered his voice a little, unable to let the remark slip by.

Subaru had a special scent wafting around him—the strange physical condition that had been pegged as the lingering scent of the Witch. Rem and the Witch Cultists had been able to sense it, so if Garfiel could sense it as well...

However, Subaru's suspicions were belied by Garfiel's shaking his head and the words that followed.

"It ain't good or bad. The scent comin' from ya is just plain normal. I found ya 'cause it ain't a scent I've smelled before, that's all. It's like, 'Sometimes, even Meimei is busy.'"

"…Sorry, I think there's a bug in the translation between you and me from time to time."

Subaru tilted his head as the enigmatic phrase flew right over it, his nose crinkling as he wondered just what Garfiel was saying. There'd always been words that didn't mesh well from both sides, but he felt like he'd suddenly hit the limits of otherworldly translation.

Either way, Garfiel's nose apparently had not caught what Subaru suspected. That being the case, his next question would have concerned either the ruin or the teleportation—but then something changed inside the carriage.

"—a, huu—"

With a faint exhalation, the girl sleeping on the simplified bed awoke.

"Ah…Emilia!"

Emilia sat up in bed, velvet eyes blinking. Subaru hastened to her side and took her hand, as if to check Emilia's body temperature to make sure she was real.

"I'm glad you're all right. Man, you really had me going for a while there…"

"Su…baru…? Er…"

Emilia looked up at the relieved Subaru, looking like she had no idea what had happened. But when she looked around the interior of the dragon carriage, she noticed the presence of an unfamiliar man and leaped to her feet.

Then she stood opposite Garfiel, shielding Subaru behind her.

"—Who?! I'll say this once, you won't lay a single finger on Subaru!"

"Wait, wait, Emilia-tan! I'm happy, but it's really complicated, everything's all right, so just…!"

"Hah, quite some lip for someone who was sleepin' all this time. Interestin'…!"

"Hey, don't you get all worked up, too! Calm down! Let's talk this through!"

Emilia, taking an unusually aggressive, worked-up stance, triggered

Garfiel's combative spirit in turn. Subaru wedged himself between them, grasping Emilia's shoulders.

"Please, Emilia-tan, just relax. Some stuff happened while you were asleep, but it's been worked out already. He's Garfiel. You get it now, right?"

"Garfiel… Wait, you mean the one Frederica talked about?"

Blinking several times over at the name, Emilia looked at Garfiel. When she did so, he puffed out his chest and answered.

"Yeah, that's me—Garfiel. The world's strongest man."

"Right, right, the world's strongest… Huh? What did you say just now? You said world's strongest? With a straight face?"

"I said it, yeah. What's so strange about that…?"

He meant it as an explanation to Emilia, but the unexpectedly grandiose statement surprised even Subaru. Garfiel crinkled his nose, seemingly offended by their reactions.

"You've heard my name, so you heard about all that from Roswaal, right…?"

"I heard your name with the nuance that you were a powerful person, but…that didn't mean physical power, did it…?"

If it meant martial might, the term *powerful* was being used in an unusual way. But, given the present circumstances, the chances of that seemed rather high, and they still had no certain proof he was an ally.

Subaru had never thought Frederica's telling them to be wary of him would come to fruition like that.

"I'll ask this again, but you're Garfiel who lives in the Sanctuary. You've got a relationship to Roswaal, and right now Ram and the people from Earlham Village are here, too. We can believe you on that?"

"You're free to doubt me, but either way, you've crossed the barrier. It's not like you can turn back now, right?"

"Eh? We crossed the barrier? Since when?"

Emilia's eyes widened in shock at the surreal fact. Incidentally, Subaru was just as surprised as she was. "Hey, hey," said Garfiel toward them, and continued his words:

"Gimme a break. In the first place, didn't you fall asleep when you got close to the barrier?"

"I slept because of the barrier...? Now that you mention it, the crystal got bright then, too..."

"The timing was the same. Meaning they were both reactions to the barrier!"

Subaru snapped his fingers. The crystal's radiating light inside the dragon carriage matched up with the facts. Subaru got the crystal out of his pocket and rolled it on his palm; Emilia nodded deeply as well. Then—

"—? What is it, Garfiel?"

Hearing Emilia pose the question all of a sudden, Subaru followed suit, lifting his face. When he did, he followed her gaze to find Garfiel staring at the crystal with a conflicted look on his face.

He looked like the blue glow made him recall some kind of painful memory.

"Something about this? You probably went through some scary stuff on account of this rock. Besides, I'm kinda wondering why the barrier that made Emilia-tan collapse didn't do anything to Otto or me."

"The rock's nothin' to me. And of course the barrier reacted to Lady Emilia. The barrier's a test that reacts to dirty blood."

"—!"

"Hey, Garfiel. What's this business about dirty blood?"

Garfiel's statement sent pain running across Emilia's cheeks. Angry at that fact, Subaru probed to determine the true meaning behind Garfiel's words.

"Don't make me repeat myself. She's a half-elf. Get it into your..."

"Hah, don't get bent out of shape about it. I'm not tryin' to single out Lady Emilia by sayin' it. *Dirty blood* don't mean just half-elves. It applies to me, the others... She ain't no exception... She's mixed, just like we are."

"Mixed...mixed blood, you mean?"

Without a word, Garfiel indicated *yes* to Emilia's question. Receiving his answer, Subaru realized just why he'd heard the Sanctuary was special beforehand—and what was meant by "particular" demi-humans.

"In other words, the Sanctuary is where demi-human people with mixed blood live…"

"Correct… Gotta say, though, you came to the Sanctuary without Frederica even tellin' you that much…?"

"She kept saying she *couldn't* tell us the details. Within what she could say, she kept saying to watch out, but…because of some vow, she couldn't say much more than your name."

"Vow this, vow that… Huh? Ha, excuses from head to toe. Just like her master, huh?"

Clicking his tongue, Garfiel gave an answer that was closer to a cursing than an expression of malice.

There was no doubting he was related by blood to Frederica, but it was no atmosphere for asking anything him about it. Maybe Frederica refused to speak of him because—

"You don't really get along well with Frederica?"

"Emilia-tan?!"

"If you're gonna ask if we get along well or not, we don't. Besides, everythin' from here on don't concern her. Everythin' from here is about us, and you people who came through the barrier, nothin' else."

Emilia's straight-to-the-point question took Subaru by surprise, but Garfiel replied in a surprisingly calm fashion, sinking his hips deeper into his seat as he indicated the outside of the dragon carriage with his chin.

Subaru understood what his gesture meant: They would soon arrive at their destination, the Sanctuary.

"We welcome you, Lady Emilia and her two servants."

The words of welcome had a title of respect attached, but there was not a shred of respect or warmth in them. Having spoken them, Garfiel replied to Subaru's and Emilia's suspicious gazes with an audible clenching of his fangs.

With that, he spread his arms very wide, indicating the entire area.

"For whatever reason, Roswaal calls this the Sanctuary, but…it ain't a place suited for pretty-sounding words like that. It's a place where rejects gather and live together, a dead-end laboratory."

"Laboratory…?"

"Rejects."

Subaru and Emilia knit their brows as different words tugged at their respective minds. For his part, Garfiel laughed, not concealing his mouth like Frederica did.

"As for me, I think it's more accurate to call it the tomb of the Witch of Greed!"

"The Witch of Greed?!"

As Garfiel continued, Subaru tilted his head at the never-before-heard statement; in his stead, it was Otto, overhearing the discussion inside the dragon carriage, who had an exaggerated reaction.

In a fierce panic, Otto peered into the carriage from the driver's seat and said, "Um, ah, er, excuse me… You don't mean to say this is genuinely related to the Witch of Greed, yes…?"

"Wait, wait, WAIT! 'Cause you got super surprised I'm reacting late, but what's the Witch of Greed to begin with? When people say Witch, they mean the Witch of Jealousy, right…?"

The Witch of Jealousy had plunged the world into the lowest depths of terror; even in the present, she was feared as the most awful of calamities.

Subaru knew only of the Witch bearing the title of Jealousy. He'd never heard of any others. Despite that, the term beyond his expectations sailed overhead, bringing the worst of possibilities rushing to the forefront of his mind.

"Don't tell me the Witch Cult has one Witch for each of them? Seven Witches, so seven archbishops in total?! How hard do you think it was defeating even one of them?!" Subaru exclaimed.

"Having to defeat all of them would be an especially harrowing prospect, but there is fortunately no concern about *that*. It is just that for a Witch besides Jealousy to become an issue is a very, very great problem in itself…"

Subaru was relieved to have his worst imagination rebutted, but Otto's concern had not been wiped away. Subaru found himself suspicious when Emilia, sitting beside him, took up where Otto had left off.

"Well, you see, a reeeally long time ago, and this would be four hundred years ago…there were six Witches other than the Witch of Jealousy. But the Witch of Jealousy killed them all, supposedly…"

"Seems like she ate 'em. Matter of fact, there ain't much for records left of the Witches the Witch of Jealousy killed. But there's exceptions to that."

"So you're saying this is one exception? There's something odd about the names of other Witches?"

With Garfiel bolstering Emilia's words, Subaru pulled what was left of his question back toward Otto, who sighed as he continued, seeming to detest even speaking the words.

"It is not a topic I enjoy speaking of, but it concerns the traits of Witch Cultists. As you already know, they are adherents of the Witch of Jealousy, but…they do not acknowledge the existence of other Witches. Even merely hearing the name of one is enough to drive them into terrible rampages."

"That's awfully oversensitive…"

"In the Volakia Empire to the south, rumors spread of the name of a Witch besides the Witch of Jealousy. A metia supposedly related to the Witch emerged, but there is no telling whether it was true or false."

The empire to the south, and the Witch Cult—those two elements coalesced in Subaru's memory. He remembered a story Julius had relayed to him while they were traveling together at the height of the campaign to subdue Petelgeuse.

"You mean the story that a single Archbishop of the Seven Deadly Sins wiped out a city?"

"That is the one. Perhaps the rumor of a metia was fact, or perhaps it was merely a convenient scapegoat after the fact… Either way, the cost was the downfall of an entire city. Speaking about Witches has been strictly prohibited everywhere since."

With Otto concluding his harrowing tale, Subaru nodded in

sympathy. Subaru hated the Witch Cult and everything surrounding it, but the current conversation had added one more reason to hate it.

"Isn't it dangerous to spread around scary trivia like that?"

"It's not like it's gonna leak outside. But the old hag says it's the tomb of the Witch of Greed, so there ain't no mistake. It's just like, 'Peromio festered from the point he heard it.'"

"Not that I'm really interested in *what* was festering, but I take it you don't know the fine details?"

"If you wanna know details, pry 'em outta Roswaal— At the moment, I ain't sure you even could, though."

"—? What do you mean by that? Has something happened to Roswa—"

"I'm sorry. We seem to have arrived at the vill—is this a village? The settlement. Shall we enter?"

Emilia probed deeper to discern Garfiel's meaning, but before she could get anywhere, Otto announced from the driver's seat that they had arrived at their destination. His words made her look outside, whereupon she said...

"So this is the Sanctuary..."

Emilia's whisper-like tone made Subaru let out a similar breath as he narrowed his eyes.

There, after taking so long to cut through deep forest, was cleared space, with a lonely settlement lying within. When it was compared to the image given by the name Sanctuary, it was impossible to wipe away the impression of an undignified, dirt-poor habitation.

Stone towers at the settlement's entrance lay fallen and mossed over. They could see stonework pillars in the distance, all of great age, covered in moss and vines so far as they could tell.

The impression was much like that given off by the ruin, but the settlement gave off a fragment of that only, something Subaru could only call...

"Feels like a pretty run-down place..."

"Just to say it, the people are pretty run-down, too, okay? They're all wrinkled hags and old men. It's got that 'Man or Kegelmo, we all grow old' feel to it."

"That's the first time I understand what one of your sayings means, but man, you aren't pulling any punches."

Garfiel's words about the settlement he himself lived in were absolutely merciless. Some people liked to talk poorly of their homelands out of modesty, but Subaru didn't sense a shred of that from his voice.

It seemed to be a fact that he was alienated from this place, the Sanctuary. Either way—

"Let's keep going until we find a good spot to park the dragon carriage..."

"I see you're back, Garf. You certainly took your sweet time."

"Yeah."

Putting everyone's impressions of the Sanctuary on the back burner, they made the dragon carriage run to the center of the settlement, where Subaru was surprised to hear a familiar voice.

It was tossed their way from the center of the settlement, right along the route the dragon carriage was following.

There, a lone girl revealed herself, her demeanor cool as she stood tall. The sight of the girl made Garfiel dash right out of the dragon carriage; he leaped down, waving a hand with a smile.

"Yo. Pretty rare for you to come out and welcome me back like this. Did the bastard finally kick the bucket?"

"If that were the case, Ram would be turning this entire place into a sea of flames. You should be most grateful to Master Roswaal that it is not so."

"I don't know what ya mean, but geez, that's some thinkin'!"

Garfiel approached her, seeming very amused by the abuse from the girl in the familiar-looking servant's outfit. As he watched from a distance, Subaru's lips slackened in visible relief.

"Hmmm, so that is the older sister of the girl whom you were speaking of. I see... It is quite obvious, but she looks just like the sleeping Miss Rem, yes."

Otto, laying eyes upon the girl for the first time, was deeply moved as he murmured. Just as he'd said, in appearance she and Rem were two peas in a pod, but the individuals on the inside were completely different.

Subaru was reuniting with Ram, the nonworking servant of Roswaal Manor, after several days of separation.

"Ram!"

Ram noticed Subaru leaning out of the dragon carriage and waving toward her. Her pink eyes narrowed slightly, followed by an easy-to-understand sinking of her shoulders.

"I know not where you were, Barusu, but I am disappointed at your late arrival. If only you had noticed something was wrong and come running... Ah, I was a fool to expect such a thing."

"If you don't know where I've been, then follow that part to the end, damn it! Also, this goes mainly for Roswaal, but it's hard to figure out what you people are up to. Also, I need to talk to the man himself face-to-face!"

When Subaru rebutted, Ram replied with a "Ha!" that was the same as it had ever been. From there, her gaze turned toward Emilia, who was right at Subaru's side.

"Lady Emilia, I bid you a warm welcome. As Master Roswaal is awaiting you within, I shall escort you to him. Garf, please guide the dragon carriage and coachman to a suitable place."

"Man, you're rough with people! That's fine, though. Hey, driver bastard. Come with me, I'll show ya in."

"Do you mean me by that?! That is the worst thing you have called me to date, you know!"

Even though he'd introduced himself by name, it was "driver bastard" now. On top of that, the prospect of being all alone with Garfiel made Otto look toward Subaru and Emilia in search of salvation.

Subaru responded to his clingy gaze with a deep, knowing nod.

"I'll bury your bones later!"

"Those are not words *ever* used with a good connotation, are they?!"

Leaving that lament behind, Otto was led off by the overbearing Garfiel, dragon carriage and all.

Upon their separation, Subaru gave Patlash a concerned rub of her nose, but Otto was no doubt safe under her protection. Perhaps it was strange to entrust a human being to a land dragon, but oh well.

"That Patlash, she's reeeally trustworthy and dependable, isn't she?"

"Plus, where Otto's concerned, I feel like there'll always be uncertain elements no matter how much I'd worry about him."

Watching driver and dragon carriage depart, Subaru said, "Well, then," and turned Ram's way. Having gazed in silence at the previous exchange, she turned her face away from Subaru's gaze with a neutral look and said, "What?"

"…Nothing, I've just been wondering if you were all right. I mean, given how we parted ways, and not being in touch with you at all after, to be honest, I was really nervous."

"I suppose you were. As you can see, today Ram is as robust and adorable as ever. No harm has come to pass for the villagers evacuating to the Sanctuary with me. You may rest easy about that."

"That so? That's, yeah, I'm relieved to hear it… That's comforting."

"—?"

Subaru's shoulders sank with relief, but the odd wording at the end of Subaru's sentence made Ram look at him suspiciously. Her reaction made Subaru grit his teeth, locking down the emotions that had surged as far as his throat before he made them into words.

"…"

"Ah, Ram. It's odd for us to just stand here and talk like this, right? Could you show us in?"

With Subaru sinking into silence, unable to immediately speak, Emilia spoke those words to Ram in his place. Ram slightly knitted her brows at the words, but she immediately said, "As you wish," bowed, and turned her back.

Not probing any further and immediately marching off was very Ram-like, but…

"Subaru, are you all right? You're not angry I butted in?"

"Nah, it's fine. I was just being pathetic… I was just scared of asking Ram about Rem right this moment, you see."

Subaru listlessly shook his head, giving a pained smile at Emilia's consideration for him.

He was afraid to be certain. Several times over, he'd already experienced a sense of loss through Emilia, Petra, and others—but it wasn't something he'd gotten used to. For that matter, hearing it from Ram would probably have the greatest weight of all.

The fact she hadn't asked about Rem's whereabouts under those circumstances was more than enough proof that she had forgotten her younger sister.

"Emilia?"

"It's natural for you to be afraid. I don't think that is pathetic at all, so..."

As Subaru hung his head, Emilia took hold of Subaru's hand, meeting his eyes as she spoke those words in a sincere voice. Floating in her purple eyes were deep worry and a great deal of affection—those feelings gave him some consolation.

Gathering the scraps of his nearly lost courage, he thought he just might be able to find the words to ask her next time.

"Let's go and make everything better. Rem, and lots of other things, too."

"...Roger that. Whatever happens, I'll protect you as your meat shield, Emilia-tan."

Subaru and Emilia were still holding hands as they walked behind Ram, going deeper into the Sanctuary.

—Subaru did not realize that it was he alone who gained courage from it.

2

The house was the most intact structure in the Sanctuary.

The residence formed of stone material was about the same size as an average stand-alone house from Subaru's world. The interior was divided into simple corridors and rooms, feeling like a reasonably comfortable place to live.

Between Roswaal Manor and the Nobles' District in the capital, Subaru had seen extravagant structures, but one of this size felt much closer to home. But ignoring Subaru's impressions—

"Myyy, Lady Emilia and our good Subaru. It feeeels like it has been quite a loooong time since I have seen you."

Roswaal waved to the pair with a fishy smile, something that felt out of place to the extreme.

His eccentric clown makeup, his exaggerated words and gestures, and the very aura of his presence were so unbefitting an ordinary person, it simply felt *wrong* for him to be inside an ordinary house such as that.

However, now that they were before him, feelings of things being wrong or out of place were trifling affairs.

"First, it is good that you are saaaafe and sound, Lady Emilia. I heard the circumstances from Ram, but it would be difficult to liiiive with myself if anything should have happened to you."

"If you really think so, you could cough up a more proper reaction to… No, more importantly, what the heck happened to you?"

Roswaal expressed relief at Emilia's safety, but Subaru and Emilia were left as perplexed as before.

As for why, Roswaal was a painful sight while greeting the pair, lying in bed and wrapped in bandages stained with blood coming from his own body. His unclothed upper body lacked a single space unwrapped by bandages; he had multiple deep wounds and was in a grave condition. That the makeup on his face was unmarred felt like a sign less of robustness than of a bizarre level of obsession.

But he did not give off the slightest hint of being injured, acting completely normal.

"My myyyy, you ask me that? I, too, am but a man. It truly pains me to be seen in such a shameful state. I suppose you are not so geeentle as to refrain from asking why?"

"As if I could! Truly, Roswaal, what happened? To get hurt this badly… And on top of that, you're…"

His flippant tone about something impossible to gloss over put the genuinely angry Emilia in a bind. Indeed, the wounds were so grave she hesitated to press the point. She wanted to ask, but she didn't want to force the issue.

Roswaal responded to the discord with Emilia by closing one of his differently colored eyes, specifically the blue one.

"I wonder where I should begin the taaale? In regards to my wounds...perhaps I should call them a baaadge of honor, or the unavoidable consequences of my actions."

"Please do not paper over things like that. I am asking a serious question. I want a serious answer from you."

"Hmmm... It would seem Lady Emilia is not in good humor, either. Considering the place, I do not believe that can be...helped."

It felt wrong to Subaru that Emilia was taking an interrogatory tone. When Roswaal, apparently agreeing with him, pointed out that very thing, Emilia exhaled with an air of resignation.

"Since I came here—no, since I came in contact with the barrier, I think—my chest has been astir. I can't calm down. What is this place? Even though it's called the Sanctuary, it doesn't feel like any such thing to me. If anything, it's the opposite..."

"Perhaps you can accept that the tombs of Witches have aaaalways been referred to thus?"

"—!!"

Emilia's breath caught strongly when Roswaal invoked the other name of the Sanctuary.

Hearing the term from a mouth other than Garfiel's lent it greater weight. However, since that only added to the information they needed to ask him about—

"Wait, let's put what we want to ask about in proper order. I feel like we're just gonna be running around in circles at this rate. We need to get to a conclusion."

"Myyyy, a most sound suggestion. It seems that our good Subaru's mental state has changed since last I saw him."

"That story's gonna get seriously long, so I'll brag properly about it later... Ah, one thing, though."

As Roswaal prodded him, trying to make light of the matter, Subaru stared straight at him before continuing.

"I succeeded in forming an alliance with Crusch. Satisfied with the results of leaving me there now?"

"Ahh, I am most saaatisfied. Truly, truly, you have acquired something difficult and long yearned for."

"…That so."

The affirmation felt more sincere than Subaru had expected. While surprised, he accepted it in good grace.

He'd expected as much for a while, but Roswaal really had left Subaru in the royal capital with the expectation that he'd fight hard. Roswaal's having used that to his own advantage wasn't amusing to Subaru.

The fact that his countermeasures against the Witch Cult had been conspicuously inadequate amused him even less.

Setting aside that dissatisfaction for the moment, Subaru ordered the more immediate questions in his mind before starting.

"First, the people of Earlham Village. Ram said they were safe and sound, but is that really true?"

"Please rest at ease. The state of my body may make that diiiifficult to believe, but I aaaam a lord, after all. I negotiated earnestly upon their behalf and had the cathedral opened to give them shelter."

"Cathedral, huh? I'll ask for more details about that later. Next…"

"Tell us what you meant by 'Witch's Tomb' earlier."

As Subaru moved ahead, Emilia intervened, choosing the next topic for herself.

It was one of the issues on Subaru's list, so he had no objection. But Subaru didn't think the hard voice and the way she asked felt very Emilia-like.

Roswaal responded to the tense Emilia's question with a wry smile and closed one eye.

"It means exactly what it says. This is the final resting place of the Witch named Echidna, once known as the Witch of Greed—and to me, these grounds are holy."

"The Witch Echidna…"

The tone with which Roswaal replied to the question, and put the name to his lips, made Subaru's breath catch.

His reply was quiet and gentle, yet filled with sharpness that clawed at the mind. There was no echo of his normal clownish demeanor; what filled his voice was emotion that pounded hard into Subaru's chest.

The instant Roswaal invoked Echidna's name, his expression looked softer for what might have been the very first time.

"..."

Seeing the side of his face, Ram, attending at his bedside, gently lowered her eyes. Subaru did not notice her reaction; rather, he touched a hand to his own chest.

For some reason, the name Echidna—a name he shouldn't have known—strangely churned within him.

"Subaru, are you all right? Is something wrong?"

"Nah, I'm fine... More importantly, we know this is the place a Witch died. But, Roswaal, why are you safekeeping a place with a history like that? Do you have some kind of connection with this Witch?"

"The reason is simple. This land has been under the care of the Mathers family, passed down from generation to generation. It began under the lord of this house at the time...the Roswaal from which I inherit this name. In other words, it is from this Roswaal in history that this Sanctuary has been passed down."

When Subaru broached the issue of his relationship to the Witch, Roswaal followed suit, filling in the blanks. The explanation left Emilia touching her own lips, knitting her refined eyebrows.

"'In history'... Then the Mathers family has been involved with the Witch of Greed since long..."

"—Echidna."

"Eh?"

Emilia's eyes opened wide when the name alone was abruptly slipped in. Roswaal trained his eyes toward Emilia. "Echidna," he repeated, making certain she heard him.

"Pleaaaase, employ her name when referring to her. Calling her the Witch of Greed implies all sorts of nefaaarious things, does it not? And it is somewhat looooong."

"Errr, I understand. Then can I take this to mean...this is Echidna's final resting place, and the Mathers family has taken care of it because it was involved with her for a reeeally long time?"

"Yes, that is correct. Having said that, 'taken care of it' is somewhat exaggerated. Echidna's barrier means that outsiders cannot pass through the Lost Woods without the proper formalities. On top of that, the barrier has a special effect on those whose blood fulfills a particular condition. You have experienced this as well, Lady Emilia?"

"It's true, I lost consciousness when I came into contact with the barrier. But, according to Garfiel, the barrier only causes trouble when half-bloods like me come into contact with it. It didn't do anything to Subaru, right?"

"Er, actually, I can't really say it did nothing to me..."

"Eh? What do you mean by that?"

When Subaru scratched his cheek and murmured, Emilia lifted her face in surprise.

She didn't know that once the barrier had knocked her out, Subaru had been teleported while she slept. Along the way, Subaru hadn't found a good time to bring it up, but also, he had hesitated greatly to do so.

After all, he couldn't discuss it without discussing its connection to Frederica's crystal.

If Frederica had conveyed that Garfiel was a dangerous person, entrusted Emilia with the crystal, and on top of that, plotted to have that crystal teleport her, he wondered what objective Frederica had in doing so.

"Subaru, if something happened, tell me. We decided we'd discuss important things, didn't we?"

"We did, but this is..."

"Subaru."

The earnest gaze and the plea of her voice made Subaru's shoulders sink in resignation. From there, he took the blue crystal out of his pocket and explained the circumstances to all present.

He explained that the crystal had reacted to the barrier, teleporting Subaru alone to a different location in the Sanctuary. There he'd met a girl, been led to the ruin, and lost consciousness while inside. Later, he'd been caught by Garfiel and brought along, bringing them back to the present.

"Frederica handed over this crystal before we left the mansion.

There's no question it reacted to the barrier and made the teleport happen. Emilia was the one carrying the crystal to begin with, so..."

"Barusu, what you are trying to say is that Lady Emilia must have been the target?"

As Subaru spoke of the circumstances, Ram summarized the last part in his stead. Her assertion made Subaru draw in his chin. The image of the young girl he'd met in the forest came back to him.

The girl had been emotionless, doll-like. She had done Subaru no harm, leading him to the ruin and running away—and he had to wonder, had that been intended for Emilia instead?

"If that is true, it was Lady Emilia who would have been teleported by the crystal during the time the barrier had robbed her of consciousness. If so, it is most fortuuuitous it was Subaru who was sent in her place."

"And then I hooked back up safe and sound. Body doesn't have... anything special wrong with it."

Subaru rotated a wrist, smiling at Emilia as he asserted his robustness of health. But, as he smiled at Emilia, she lowered her head and gingerly posed a question to Roswaal.

"Frederica said the crystal was necessary to pass through the barrier, and why she was giving it to me... Was that true?"

"...Unfortunately, the proper formalities for passing through the barrier do not involve an object. I suppose that is proof Frederica was up to some kind of scheeeeme."

Roswaal's reply made Emilia's words catch in her throat as her listless shoulders sank. Of course they did. The talk just then had established Frederica's infidelity as a virtual certainty.

"Frederica's worked for you a long time, right? Over ten years is what I heard."

"...Yes, that girl was still veeeery young when I first employed her. She is a very capable girl, and not once has she acted in defiiiiance of my will..."

When Subaru posed a question in Emilia's stead, Roswaal shook his head in apparent dismay. Then he glanced meaningfully toward the edge of his vision, whereupon Ram accepted his gaze with a solemn nod.

"And so Frederica's scheme has ended in tears... That just now was a joke."

"Was it really a joke? It sounded pretty serious to me..."

"It was. But the punishment will not be—now we know that Frederica is deeply related to the present circumstance here in the Sanctuary."

To Ram, Frederica was a coworker of particularly long standing. Knowing her coworker had been unfaithful, she nonetheless spoke calmly, her face betraying no unrest concerning that fact.

"What do you mean by the circumstances in the Sanctuary? What is happening here right now?"

"Lady Emilia, did you not think it strange? That Ram and I, and the villagers fleeing to the Sanctuary, remained in this place rather than return to the mansion?" he asked.

"Eh? That's... I thought it must be because of your wounds, Roswaal," she answered.

In point of fact, Roswaal, lying on the bed, bore wounds that were quite deep. Even if he was to return to the mansion for treatment, he couldn't be moved without having recovered to at least some minimal degree.

But Roswaal shook his head, seemingly telling her that was not the reason.

And then—

"Currently, all present fiiiiind ourselves imprisoned in the Sanctuary... Ram, the villagers, and myself... Ah, now that you have entered, that includes the two of you as well."

"Huh?"

Subaru and Emilia were both dumbstruck at the casual yet explosive statement.

3

"...Imprisoned? That doesn't, well, have a very nice ring to it."

Somehow, Subaru managed to recover from the initial shock and wring out those words. Emilia managed to swallow down her own surprise, giving the injured Roswaal a painful stare as she said, "Then, Roswaal, don't tell me that those wounds were from…"

Emilia was in shock as she combined the sight of him wounded with his earlier statement. Neither could Subaru, having arrived at the same thought, conceal his own shock.

"There's someone in this village who can overpower Roswaal, hurt him this much, and keep him captive? That's no laughing matter."

Subaru touched a hand to his chin, nervously pondering a foe powerful far beyond his expectations.

Roswaal was the kingdom's preeminent magic user; the demon beast disturbance had proven that in earnest. Subaru could not believe that anyone could easily put Roswaal through this much pain and suffering.

Who in the world had done this to—

"Wha—? You're still doin' chitchat? You shouldn't push a wounded guy too much. 'Make a mottled Kuchibashi run and it turns black,' you know?"

"—!"

Surprised by the sudden voice, Subaru turned around in a hurry. At the end of his gaze was Garfiel, who'd appeared at the entrance to the room. He took a look around the room and whistled toward Emilia.

"Hey now, what's this greeting all of a sudden? Wha—? Are you *that* ticked off with me?"

"I'm being on the safe side, since the earlier conversation made me think the most dangerous person here is you."

Garfiel audibly clenched his teeth in amusement. Emilia stood on guard with Subaru and Roswaal at her back, seemingly to shield them from him.

Being shielded by Emilia was a thing in itself, but Subaru blinked hard at a separate issue. Namely—

"Hey, what'd you do with Otto? He was with you, right?"

"Ahh? What, that noisy guy? Him, well… You get it, don't ya?"

Garfiel nodded defiantly, and his sharp gaze turned even sharper. Subaru, sensing bottomless hostility from his statement, felt the hairs on his back stand up.

Emilia lowered her stance, as if she had the same sense from Garfiel as he.

—The atmosphere grew strained. At the drop of a pin, combat between the two would become unavoidable.

"Ha! Fine, if you want a piece of me, I'll be happy to... Daaah?!"

"It is not fine at all. Know your place, stupid Garf."

But the atmosphere primed to explode was smashed apart by the powerful impact sound of an iron tray.

Circling around his back during the exchange, it was Ram who had brought Garfiel down with a single, merciless blow. As Garfiel writhed in agony, Ram looked down at him, sighing as she addressed the others.

"Lady Emilia, Subaru, it is equally unsightly of you to jump to conclusions so quickly. Garf has nothing to do with Master Roswaal's injuries... He may look like a simpleton, but he is not quite that thoughtless."

"...Is that so?"

"Yes, Lady Emilia, he had nooothing to do with it. I was about to say so that very moment."

Roswaal's utterly shameless exaggeration left Emilia lowering her arms, astonished. Then she rushed over to Garfiel, kneeling upon the floor, in great haste.

"I-I'm very sorry! I completely misunderstood... I was certain you'd eaten Otto or something...!"

"Wow, Emilia-tan, your ideas are really something! Even I didn't think he'd gone that far!"

Though it was certainly true Subaru suspected Otto's life had been in danger, he hadn't suspected Garfiel of doing such a thing.

Following in the flustered Emilia's footsteps, Subaru checked to see how Garfiel was doing. Garfiel, shaking the head Ram had struck with that hearty blow, opened his mouth wide at the pair's assertions.

"As if I'd munch on a guy like that. He's noisy, and he says stuff a guy ain't emotionally prepared for, so I ditched him back at the dragon carriage."

"You're being pretty vague there, and you kick up a ruckus even without Otto..."

His suggestive demeanor had caused a misunderstanding that had nearly led to a great disaster. That disaster had been averted by Ram.

"Thanks a bundle, Ram. Don't want any unnecessary bloodshe— Hold on, your tray's all bent out of shape!"

"A necessary loss to stop Garf. Next time, it would seem I should use the corner, not the flat of the tray."

Ram took inspiration from the bent tray for how she would deal with him next time.

Setting Ram's demeanor aside, Garfiel, the victim of her pummeling, plopped himself into a chair in a corner of the room. Then he rubbed his head as he looked at Ram and said, "Ram, if you feel sorry 'bout that at all, how 'bout some tea?"

"Please wait while I head out briefly to gather fallen leaves."

Making a sound from her nose at the grandiose request, Ram really did head out of the house. Subaru had to wonder just what she intended to do with fallen leaves. Though that tugged at his mind, what also tugged at it was the ardor with which Garfiel watched Ram's back as she departed.

"I was wondering this from the exchange at the village entrance too...but what? You have a thing for Ram?"

"She's a fine woman, ain't she? Ain't exactly weird for males to be attracted to strong, capable females."

"We're not dividing chicks by male and female, so stop chirping about that, sheesh..."

Garfiel had replied openly to Subaru's question, but his road to romance was treacherous. Ram's affection for Roswaal ran deep, hanging over his prospects almost like a curse—

That was an unmistakable side of romance in any world, but—

"Well, then. Based on that reaction, you don't look like ya talked about the important stuff yet. You're free to turn into pieces of garbage if ya want, but...you should talk 'bout it to Lady Emilia, at least."

"To me?"

With Ram absent from the room, Garfiel tapped his foot as he refocused the conversation.

Emilia was surprised that her own name was in his statement, but Garfiel paid her surprise no heed, sending his dangerous look stabbing right through Roswaal.

"The fact she got past the barrier means she's wrapped up in our business. What the hell's with this peaceful, pleasant conversation? You people playin' around or somethin'?!"

"I'm not sure why you have a bee in your bonnet, but…this business we're wrapped up in doesn't sound unrelated to this whole imprisoned business."

Garfiel, as snippy as ever, narrowed his eyes at Subaru's assertion. Feeling as if he was facing off against a fierce, overbearing beast, Subaru put the conversation to that point in order in his head and said:

"According to Roswaal, this isn't imprisonment by brute force. Regardless of how you look and act, you can't be short-tempered and violent enough to…"

For an instant, being hurled by Garfiel reemerged in his memories.

"…to do that kind of thing."

"Subaru, you seemed reeeally unsure just now…"

Subaru, on the receiving end of a rare quip from Emilia, looked straight at Garfiel. Receiving his gaze, Garfiel said, "Go on," urging Subaru to continue. "I'll listen. If you ain't the dirt stuck to a half-demon's foot, that is."

"Half-elf. Next time I'll get Roswaal to light your butt on fire."

Garfiel lowered his head as Subaru shamelessly proclaimed he would borrow another's power for his retribution. At his reaction, Subaru lifted a finger, turning that finger to indicate the Sanctuary outside.

"I'll continue. Now that imprisonment by force has been crossed off the list, what other way can I think of? To be honest, I don't have much information to go on…but there's one thing that sticks out in my mind."

"…You mean the barrier?"

"That's right. You're so smart, Emilia-tan."

Coming up with the answer on her own, Emilia had sounded unsure in her answer, but her view was in line with Subaru's own.

If neither Garfiel's brawn nor Roswaal's injuries was responsible for the imprisonment in the Sanctuary, it left the barrier as the only possibility—the barrier with a special effect originally meant to protect the Sanctuary.

If it had been a simple barrier, Subaru might not have come to such a farfetched idea, but at any rate...

"When she came in contact with the barrier, Emilia fainted. According to Garfiel, that's not an effect limited to Emilia—it's like that for most of the people living in this Sanctuary, he said."

"In other words, Subaru...you think that it's the barrier's effect that's keeping Roswaal and the others in here and preventing them from returning to the mansion?"

"There you go again! Exactly. Wow, Emilia-tan and I are in perfect sync today!"

Elated that they were thinking along the same lines, Subaru went for a high five. But, when Emilia tilted her head rather than play along, Subaru gently eased his hand down and looked at Garfiel.

"So, that's what I was thinking, but...am I right?"

"...Sorry, I've gotta drop my assessment of ya. Three steps down from a piece of mud."

"That assessment is pretty out there, but, mm, I'll aim to gradually raise it back up."

Taking that as a roundabout way of saying yes, Subaru nodded and looked over to Roswaal. As he did so, Roswaal closed one eye at Subaru's and Emilia's thought processes, amusement resting in his yellow eye.

"My myyyy, there truly has been quite a change in the span of several days. The optimism in both Subaru and Lady Emilia is quite reassuring. It was well worth making my heart that of an Oni and letting matters be."

"I have a mountain of things to say to you later about that 'letting matters be' part. Keep in mind, if you weren't wounded, the iron fist of my anger wouldn't be a soft thing."

"Myyyy, how frightening."

With Roswaal in such high spirits, Subaru brandished a clenched fist. Whether he'd have seriously let Roswaal have it was another matter, but his irritation at the previous statement was no act.

He'd give the man a tongue-lashing later for his lack of counter-measures against the Witch Cult's attack during his absence.

"But right now, talking about the barrier comes first. Is that reaction the cause of the imprisonment?"

"I cannot call it correct in the strictest sense. However, it is not far off from the truth. It is a fact that the cause of our being hindered here in the Sanctuary is a circumstance involving that barrier."

The barrier had the power to rob mixed people of their conscious-ness and make intruders get lost in the forest. But it did no harm to those of mixed blood already inside—it lacked the power to hinder Roswaal and the others on its own.

"So the fact you've been stuck here anyway means..."

"That's 'cause the people under the barrier's effect are gettin' in their way."

The answer to his question was bluntly revealed from the mouth of one of the people concerned. When he turned toward the speaker of that ferocious declaration, the sharp, green eyes of the golden-haired man of mixed blood glared back at Subaru and the others.

"Garfiel..."

"Way I see it, it's a simple story. As long as the barrier's up, we can't get out of the Sanctuary. The barrier's got nothing to do with ya... but that ain't very fair, is it?"

"...Then because you want to get out but can't, you're holding Roswaal and the others captive? Even to the point someone gets hurt like this?"

Subaru, feeling like the issue had just become very petty, felt anger toward the short-tempered act. However, when he pressed the issue, Garfiel grimaced unpleasantly.

"Say whatever you want about it. But it's not like it don't have any-thing to do with ya?"

"...So, for the same reason, you don't intend to let us go, either?"

"No, no! It ain't that, it's way simpler! Your precious little princess can't get out of the Sanctuary for the same reason me and the grannies can't, damn it!!"

"Ah…"

Subaru gaped when Garfiel laughed loudly and pointed at Emilia as he made the statement.

Truly, he was fed up with himself for not having realized such an obvious possibility. It was exactly as Garfiel had said. It was already proven beyond doubt the barrier's effect was active upon Emilia; she, too, was a prisoner of the Sanctuary.

"Can't anything be done about that? Like… Right! If the barrier knocks people out when they touch it, how about having them carried out by people not under its effect…"

"Ah, Subaru, amazing! We could use that method to get people o—"

"An amusing suggestion, but 'tis best avoided. If you do not seek to leave us as soulless husks, at least."

Yet again, a third party intervened in Subaru's conversation that day.

The intervention of an unfamiliar voice caused Subaru to turn toward the entrance. Just like Garfiel had done earlier, a small figure was standing there—whereupon Subaru let out an "Eh?"

She had long, pink hair, doll-like beauty, and pointed ears, all things he had seen before. The features were without doubt those of the elfin girl Subaru had encountered in the forest—

"You're that… Agh—hot-hot-hot-hot-hot?!"

"Here, Barusu. Tea, as requested."

Subaru, surprised by their reunion, instantly began to speak, but the sudden feeling of a hot, steaming drink pressed against his cheek made Subaru yell from the burning pain, tumbling onto the room's floor.

The clumsy servant having returned, Ram gazed down at Subaru's state with a look of scorn.

"Such a big fuss. How unsightly for a man."

"That has nothing to do with being a man or not! You burned my cheek, you know?! What were you thinking?"

Sitting up in the face of heartless, merciless abuse, Subaru vented his grudges with tearful eyes. It was hardly Ram's first act of violence toward him, but this was the least logical of them all.

Subaru was enraged at the high-handedness toward him. "Goodness," said Ram, and pressed a damp cloth to Subaru's cheek as she said, "Please keep quiet about the elf from before."

"Huh?" Subaru said, dumbfounded and wide-eyed as Ram was so close that she was practically touching his ear.

However, Ram said nothing about that and handed a different steaming cup to Garfiel and said, "The very essence of crude tea."

"Ain't that usually said with more, oh, modesty?"

"It is the juice from fallen leaves. You should be grateful it was poured by Ram's hands and drink it to the bottom."

Subaru put his own thoughts aside as he watched the terrible treatment she gave the man.

"Subaru, are you all right? Should I cool your cheek with ice?"

"A-ahh, it's okay, I'm all right. I'm used to Ram doing crazy stuff. It's like an everyday ritual."

"I-is that so… When did things become like that while my back was turned?"

That prompted Subaru to reminisce about the tragedies of his life as a servant. But it was not that upon which Subaru's mind was focused; rather, it was Ram's whisper into his ear.

She'd told him to keep quiet about the elf. But his questions about that were soon answered.

"I'd heard Young Gar brought in humans from the outside again… Quite a rambunctious youngster."

Speaking those words, the elf concerned lowered her eyelids. The voice, the expression, the emotions lacking from the earlier individual—they felt as if they came from someone very old, something that threw Subaru off.

"Err, and you are…?"

"I apologize for my late introduction, Lady Emilia. I am Ryuzu Bilma. I suppose you might call me this village's representative. As you can see, I am a tottering old woman."

"R-right… You are as old as you look…"

When the girl calling herself Ryuzu bowed and named herself, her declaration made Emilia seem conflicted.

Subaru's reaction was the same as hers. Apparently, he wasn't the only one thrown for a loop at Ryuzu, who looked like a young girl, declaring herself a tottering old woman.

On the outside, she looked like an adorable early teen. She was dressed only in a white robe, one that made it impossible to see her limbs past her cuffs and hem. Furthermore, her words and actions from her years of maturity clashed with her appearance—

"It's a loli hag in the flesh…! I thought I might see that stereotype here someday…"

"To think I would be called 'hag' upon a first meeting. The youngster is ruder than even Young Gar and Young Ros…"

"When you add *loli* to the pejorative *hag*, it goes from an insult to a badge of honor. It is a status highly esteemed back in my homeland. No, I'm serious."

Replying with appropriate flippancy, Subaru tried to somehow put a lid on the chaos inside his own mind.

Ryuzu was the spitting image of the girl in the forest, but the air she gave off was clearly different. And Ram had forbidden him from speaking of the other girl's existence.

*Something's goin' on here*, said Subaru's instincts, ringing like an alarm bell, but…

"Hmm… Very well, then. So you must be Barusu… Young Su, in other words."

"Paired with the 'Young Gar' thing, calling me that makes it sound like we'll start getting treated as brothers, but that's fine. Just please at least remember that my proper name is Subaru Natsuki."

Subaru introduced himself to nip the mistaken name, obtained via Rem, in the bud. His line caused Ryuzu to slap her hip, saying, "I get it, I get it," in an elderly fashion before she said, "Now, Young Gar, would you be a sensible boy and yield your chair to me?"

"Ya get ticked off when I treat ya like a hag, but you turn into a tottering old woman when it's convenient, damn it…"

"Did you say something?"

"Nuttin'…"

Garfiel clicked his tongue and yielded the chair in which he sat to Ryuzu. As he did, he brushed some dust off the chair and, in deeply devoted fashion, lent Ryuzu a hand so that she could sit in it more easily.

"Somehow you seem like some hick from the countryside whose rudeness is all mouth…"

"Oh, shut up, third rate! What are you comparin' me t—? Whoa! This tea's *awful*! It tastes like grass!!" Garfiel grimaced spectacularly at the fallen leaf tea Ram had poured for him.

Subaru took advantage of that interlude to get the topic back on track again as he said, "So, now that Ryuzu is with us, let's get back to the earlier topic… What's your basis for saying my idea's bad?"

"Earlier, Miss Ryuzu said something reeeally scary sounding, but…" Emilia glanced sidelong at Ryuzu. Subaru nodded at her words.

"She said 'soulless husks,' right? What did you mean by that?"

"I meant exactly what I said. When the mixed come into contact with the barrier, they lose consciousness. But I cannot call that impression quite correct. The souls of the mixed are repelled by the barrier, it is more correct to say."

"The souls are repelled…? Err?"

Emilia didn't seem to quite get that explanation for the mechanism by which the barrier knocked people out. Subaru gawked at Ryuzu, somehow managing to digest her words.

"In other words, if the mixed force their way across the barrier, body and soul will be separated from each other? And that'll leave the soul inside the barrier without a body… That's how I should interpret 'husk'?"

"Ho-ho, the boy understands rather quickly. That is the long and short of it."

When Subaru replied with his own interpretation, the impressed Ryuzu smiled. After she saw that smile, Emilia's eyes were still wide with surprise when she looked at Roswaal.

"B-but how is that related to Roswaal's injuries? If the barrier's power does not function for anyone except those of mixed blood, someone else inflicted those wounds on Roswaal...and it wasn't Garfiel, right?" Emilia asked.

Roswaal's shoulders sank. "As Ram said earlier, he is not quite thaaat thoughtless of a man— Though I do not denyyy that Garfiel is capable of inflicting such pain upon me."

"Serious...?" Subaru was aghast.

"He is serious."

Ram's brief words affirmed they were true. It meant a great deal coming from Ram, both a realist and someone placing Roswaal at the summit of her mental pyramid. Apparently, Garfiel had the might to back up his claim to the title of world's strongest man.

The exchange was another way of saying, *There is no escaping this imprisonment by force.*

"Me, I feel like I should be kind of insulted by the way you're talkin', th— Ram, don't make a scary face like that! Anyway, it wasn't me. He got hurt like that 'cause the trial rejected 'im."

Whether he knew the depth of their surprise or not, Garfiel violently dragged the conversation forward. Subaru gaped and gulped, calming his mind down somewhat as he voiced his thoughts.

"...First the Sanctuary has a barrier from a Witch, and now there's a trial. Just gets better and better."

New problems only added to the number of topics. When Subaru scowled at that fact, Roswaal replied, "I suppose soooo," and stroked the bandages over his chest as he continued. "Howeeeever, this is most likely the final piece of information to be added. Those who are qualified obtain the right to take the trial to lift the barrier. My wounds are proof of what happens when that precondition is disregaaarded."

"Disregarded the precondition? For the trial...?"

"The precondition is to have blood affected by the barrier—in other words, to have mixed blood. If anyone else undertakes the trial, their flesh is repelled and shredded."

"—!"

Subaru and Emilia simultaneously gasped in surprise. So that was the cause of Roswaal's own body being bandaged to such an extent. Were it not for the bloodstained bandages, Roswaal's wounded body would be naked—such was the cruel state he was in.

Countless lacerations ran across his upper body, almost like a bomb had exploded inside him, with blood oozing out that very moment. It seemed like perhaps healing magic had little effect, or perhaps something was continuing to wound him afresh—

"So let me get straight to issuin' ya our demands."

Speaking those words, Garfiel pointed straight toward the shocked Subaru—no, toward Emilia. He seemed to be saying that Emilia was needed to resolve the circumstances involving the Sanctuary.

With Emilia's breath catching as she gazed at that finger, Garfiel continued, saying, "Lift the barrier around this Sanctuary. To do that, take the trial. Until that's lifted, no one leaves—not that you personally can leave anyway."

4

The instant Subaru stepped into the place called the Cathedral, he felt a change in the air.

It was not a bad change. Surprise registered where, until that moment, a quiet atmosphere without conversation had reigned, followed by a cascade of attention—and the onrush of joy.

"Master Subaru!" "Ohh, thank goodness you are safe!" "Is everyone else all right?!"

The ones welcoming Subaru when he showed himself were the people lodging in the Cathedral—the people of Earlham Village who had evacuated, fleeing from the Witch Cult to the Sanctuary together with Ram.

They looked happy to see Subaru, but their situation was little different from when they had left the village. Subaru was relieved that they had not been treated poorly in the Sanctuary, though.

"I'm the one who told you to take refuge here, after all. I'm glad you're all safe."

"Master Subaru, it is we who are glad you are safe... How is the village, and the others?"

"Yeah, relax about that, okay? We drove off the dangerous folks, and the people evacuating to the royal capital are back in the village. No one's hurt, they're all in great shape."

"Ohh—!"

When Subaru pounded his chest, giving the villagers his meta-phorical stamp of approval, all the villagers' faces brightened.

Subaru responded to their reactions with a smile as he finally took a look around the Cathedral. The stonework structure had a high ceiling, and was filled with a solemn, serene air that lived up to the name.

So far as Subaru knew, the atmosphere was probably close to that of the chapel of a church. Because the temple site was fairly large, it was able to comfortably accommodate the fifty-odd residents who had evacuated.

Put frankly, there had to be many inconveniences involved, and they did raise such dissatisfactions with Subaru as they said, "We're worried about the fields and livestock we left behind. Besides, we're separated from our children, too, so..."

"But are the lord's injuries all right? Such terrible wounds, for our sakes..."

Their statements, showing less concern about the disorder in their daily lives than pure concern for the future, hurt Subaru's heart.

Here they were, far from their families, with their own lord bearing wounds. The seeds of their anxieties were inexhaustible. But Subaru's feet had brought him there to bring an end to their situation.

For that reason, among others, Subaru loudly cleared his throat, drawing all eyes of the villagers upon him.

"Err, listen to me, everyone! As you know, the dangerous elements threatening the village have been driven off! The other group that evacuated has returned to the village, and they're waiting for you to return as we speak!"

The moment Subaru reached "waiting for you to return," shadows of anxiety came over the villagers' faces. Naturally, they too knew why they remained in the Sanctuary.

They also knew Roswaal had sustained his wounds with the aim of liberating them.

However—

"Looks like you all know that getting out of here won't be easy. But it's all right! After all, there's a girl right here to undertake the trial to free everyone!"

"Master Subaru...you can't mean?!"

"Whoa, whoa... Nah, it isn't me. If I could, I'd do it in a heartbeat, but..."

Subaru scratched his head with a pained smile at the reaction from the freshly enthused villagers.

His words were no lie. If he could be the challenger, he'd take the trial without a moment's hesitation. But Subaru did not fulfill the conditions to challenge the barrier. Accordingly, the one who would undertake the trial would be—

"I'm sure you all know her—the royal candidate, Emilia. She's facing the trial."

"_____"

Subaru's declaration sent the villagers gasping once more. Nodding back at their reactions, Subaru reached a beckoning hand toward the entrance to the temple—and the girl waiting there for him.

After a moment's hesitation, Emilia slowly revealed herself, silver hair flowing behind her. Her cheeks were stiff from tension as Subaru stood at her side and surveyed the villagers.

Those gazes had rejected her once before. Now, she had the courage to face them without the "identification scrambler" robe. Even so, Emilia bit her lip, bowing her head deeply then and there.

"I—I am sorry to have made you wait. In place of your lord, Roswaal L. Mathers, I shall undertake the trial of this Sanctuary.

I may not seem very formidable...but I'm sure I will overcome and liberate everyone from this barrier."

At first, she was timid, with little confidence, but by the end, she was speaking more quickly and fluently.

Emilia's proclamation left the villagers perplexed as they looked at one another's faces. Once before, Emilia had extended her hand to them only to be rebuffed. That rupture had hardly been repaired. All Subaru had done was slam a lid on top of it so that you couldn't see the cracks and punt the can down the road. As far as the villagers were concerned, Emilia was stuck in their stereotypes of half-elves.

"..."

Emilia kept her head lowered as she awaited the villagers' response. Her lips were tightly pursed, and on her face, Subaru saw resolve, and a hint of fear, about the prospect of rejection.

But a figure walked closer to Emilia—the old woman who was both the head of Earlham Village and someone who had often touched Subaru's butt. Sensing her presence, Emilia lifted her head; the old woman nodded and spoke.

"A few days ago, you lowered your head to us, and we rejected your assistance. In spite of this, you reach your hand out to us once more. Why? For the sake of the royal selection?"

"..."

"To maintain the support of the populace, you lower your head and say that you shall save us. That is natural. I have no complaint about this, if that is indeed the case. But what we find frightening... is that we do not understand the reason why."

"You don't understand the reason why...?" Emilia asked, eyes shaking in bewilderment at the old woman.

"We rejected you because you are a half-elf. We do not understand the reason why you, a half-elf, would do this again despite that. That is what we wish to know."

"And that you are not a Witch beyond our ability to comprehend."

Emilia was surprised. She was being compared to a Witch to her face, and yet, she'd been asked to deny she was one. It was probably something she was experiencing for the first time. No doubt Emilia had been always tormented by discrimination that permitted no rebuttal, the conclusion simply forced upon her.

"..."

For an instant, Emilia shifted her eyes toward Subaru, who was standing by her side. Her gaze clung to him, apparently in search of an answer. Subaru tucked in his chin, nudging her forward without a word.

It was Emilia's own words they were seeking. Borrowed words would be meaningless.

"I...have no confidence that I can give an eloquent reply to your question. Right now, I do not have any reeeally convincing words to make you all accept what I say."

Reluctantly, and with Subaru's affirming nod pressing her onward, Emilia began to speak. With her own clumsy words, she sought to explain why she wanted to do this.

"It's just... It may have been a short time, but I spent the last several days with the family members who aren't here with you. So I thought all over again...families need to be together."

Emilia touched her own chest as if looking for something, stroking the dim crystal hanging from her neck. Inside it was surely sleeping family of her own, family she could not speak with at the moment for reasons unclear.

However, believing that her feelings about family were not different from theirs, Emilia surveyed everyone's face.

"I want to return you to your families. That is...not a promise I made in that village, but it is something I swore to myself. That is what I want to fulfill. That's all."

"..."

"I haven't really thought much about...maintaining your support and so on. But, if possible, I'd like everyone to...no, err, rather, I want to...get along with all of you."

At the very, very end, Emilia's words weakened, and the pace of her speech slowed. Once she had spoken her piece, she and the villagers were mutually silent. The silence continued for seconds, perhaps tens of seconds...

"Lady Emilia."

"...Y-yes?"

"We know this is very selfish of us to say—however, please take good care of us."

For a moment, Emilia looked like her thought process had ground to a halt, unable to digest the meaning of those words. But when she saw the old woman's head bowing before her, she finally grasped their meaning.

"Ah...I—I may be a greenhorn, but please bear with me!"

"No one says *greenhorn* anymore."

Subaru gave a pained smile, instantly tossing his own quip on top of the obsolete language sailing out. Emilia had no time to deal with it, for she was busy dealing with other villagers' follow-up comments, engaging in scattered conversation.

Satisfied at the turn of events, Subaru distanced himself from the throng and headed to the entrance of the Cathedral. And there stood—

"Lady Emilia seems to have...changed somewhat. Did you put her up to this, Barusu?"

"This is something she came up with on her own. You shouldn't go crediting someone's determination to someone else, you know."

"...I suppose not. Ram is at fault this time."

Ram apologized for the somewhat cold impression she gave from the entrance concerning the exchanges taking place at that moment. The apology, rare coming from her, surprised Subaru, which made Ram narrow her pink eyes.

"What? Even Ram apologizes when she feels she has done wrong. It simply does not happen very often."

"From time to time, I'm seriously envious of that brimming-with-confidence attitude you have."

"It is not a matter of confidence whatsoever. It is natural providence that Ram is correct so often."

The way Ram crossed her arms in self-affirmation grander than mere overconfidence ever could be made Subaru's shoulders sink.

"With this, Lady Emilia shall undertake the trial. She has received voices of support from the villagers...just as Master Roswaal wished."

"Hey, stop saying it like that. Emilia doesn't calculate things like that, you know."

"And you intend to shoulder the burden of the dirty work yourself, Barusu? How heroic."

Ram's slender lips eased up a little as she bantered with Subaru in sarcastic fashion. But Subaru didn't feel genuine scorn for him from either her eyes or the tenor of her voice. Perhaps what he sensed was distress.

He couldn't say *That's not like her*. Ram's kindness just happened to be difficult to see on the surface.

"So you're worried about Emilia, too, huh? I'm a little surprised."

"...Ram is the epitome of kindness and benevolence. Besides, if Lady Emilia can perform as Master Roswaal hopes, there will be meaning to his body's having been whittled down like that. Of course I am concerned."

"Roswaal went pretty far, putting his own body on the line..."

Ram's morose statement put a pained face on Subaru as he let those words trickle out. As to what Roswaal's true intentions regarding the Sanctuary were, Subaru could only sigh.

Roswaal, lacking the proper qualifications, had undertaken the trial only to be rejected by the enchantment, suffering grave wounds that left him at death's door. Such a reckless challenge could only have calculations bordering on madness behind it, things no normal person could even conceive of.

Passing the trial was unavoidable if the barrier of the Sanctuary was to be lifted—and, faced with this fact, Roswaal had taken the initiative, sustaining wounds as a result. That even Roswaal, in an attempt to fulfill his duties as lord, was unable to succeed in the trial had established to all his people the difficulty of the matter.

He had acted without hesitation before his people, wounding his name, reputation, and even body in the process—

"And here comes Emilia out of the blue, galloping in to undertake the trial and liberate the Sanctuary..."

"The residents of this Sanctuary and the refugees held captive... Either way, they shall have a great deal for which to thank Lady Emilia. It would be good if they thought of her being a half-elf as a trifling matter..."

"People's hearts don't dance in your palm that much... Besides, Emilia doesn't weigh things like that. You and I both need to have that fact sink in."

Subaru watched from a distance as the villagers interacted with Emilia at the center of the Cathedral with hard, smiling faces.

He understood Roswaal's thinking. This was a necessary challenge if she was to make it to the end of the royal selection ahead. He could appreciate the true intent behind Roswaal's telling Emilia this place would, at some point, be necessary to her.

But he could not raise both hands high in approval. This was Subaru's stubbornness at work.

"Incidentally, Barusu...there really is nothing wrong with your body?"

"Ah, yeah, no problem. I wasn't lying when I said as much when I talked about the teleport. Even though Roswaal got all beat up like that, I only fainted... Dunno what to say."

"I suppose you should be grateful to have such a puny Gate."

"It's the truth, so I can't argue, but geez...!"

Raising his voice at the very blunt remark, Subaru gave his hips a big twist on the spot before continuing.

"Um, I was surprised that the ruin I teleported to was the place for the trial. Plus, there's the thing about bad stuff happening to unqualified people trying to get in... Totally a trap that kills on first sight."

"You saw from Master Roswaal's wounds, right? Even someone blessed with only an average Gate should receive a rather stiff punishment. There is no telling what would have happened to Lady Emilia if she'd entered unawares, either."

"...You think Frederica planned it like that?" Subaru lowered his voice and aired the suspicion he'd been harboring for a while.

Ram sank into thought for a brief moment, then closed one eye as she said, "I wonder. The circumstantial evidence suggests Frederica planned something. In point of fact, Lady Emilia only avoided such a fate by a hairbreadth, escaping by Barusu's noble...relatively noble sacrifice."

"Hey, don't correct *that*. Well, I don't mind you correcting the 'sacrifice' part because I got through it fine, but if I had sacrificed myself, call it noble even if it's a lie!"

"I shall take it under advisement. In regards to Frederica, there is something I ought to tell you, Barusu."

Following that preamble, Ram confirmed the state of the area around her with a sharp gaze. It was as if she wanted to be careful that no one overheard their conversation— No, it was not "as if" at all.

Ram approached a half-step closer to Subaru, her voice a whisper as she spoke.

"Not everyone living in the Sanctuary supports being liberated from it."

"—! What do you mean by that?"

"There is also the matter of the elf being hidden from Miss Ryuzu and Garf, as well as Frederica's actions...but Miss Ryuzu is only the titular leader, guiding the militants like Garf. Among the residents, there are also those who do not desire liberation from the Sanctuary and who choose to remain sheltered within the barrier."

"Sheltered inside the barrier... What's up with that?"

Subaru, knitting his brows at Ram's warning, indicated incomprehension toward the behind-the-scenes maneuvering. If all was according to Garfiel's explanation, everyone living in the Sanctuary was of mixed blood. Naturally, that meant they were affected by the barrier and unable to leave...so long as the barrier existed, at least.

"They're fine with this. To those who wish to stay, the current state, with minimal interaction with the outside, is ideal. And thus, to break this state is…highly troublesome to them."

"You think Frederica's working with folks like that?"

"It is possible. At present, it is mere supposition based on the available information."

With Ram's subtext sounding like *Do not even suggest I am being emotional*, Subaru backed off and dropped the subject. However, the words left Subaru twisting his lips, his internal nervousness undiminished.

Reflexively, his hand touched the white handkerchief tied around his own neck.

"And that is? A rather old-fashioned protective charm, yes?"

"Petra… Ah, a cute girl in the village. She gave this to me before I left. She was hired as a new maid to help Frederica out at the mansion… That's why I'm worried."

If Frederica was operating from a position of malice, it was quite possible she'd take Petra hostage. He'd never forgive himself if something happened to the girl who'd offered her cooperation in such good faith.

Even more than that, Rem was back at the mansion. He'd spoken exhaustively to Frederica about just how important the girl was, both to him and to the other people at the mansion.

But Ram exhaled and said, "Ah, that," in reply to Subaru's misgivings, then continued. "Rest at ease. Frederica would never do ill to a new worker at the mansion. She has surely not fallen into heresy such as that. You need not be concerned for the girl."

"…Do you trust Frederica, or do you not trust Frederica? Which is it…?"

"I know not what she schemes. But that Frederica is indeed Frederica, I do not doubt."

Having asserted the point with such force, Ram averted her gaze from Subaru's face. She folded her slender arms and motioned with her chin—indicating Emilia at the center of the Cathedral.

"Be careful, Barusu. The most certain means for those opposed to liberating the Sanctuary to achieve their aims is to cause Lady Emilia harm. We do not know who our enemies are. Remain ever vigilant."

"So this is secret from Ryuzu and Garfiel, too, huh…? Those two being opposed to liberation is too far-fetched, I suppose?"

"Even if those two are not involved, someone related to them might be. It is best that as few people know as possible…even if one of them has very loose lips, yes?"

Subaru couldn't even manage a groan as she drove the implication in like a nail, making it painfully clear just whom she meant.

Either way, now that he was in the Sanctuary, Ram's warning was exceptionally important. In particular, he'd never have known there was an antiliberation faction if she hadn't told him.

"Man, that girl really did look just like Ryuzu…"

Ryuzu herself might disagree, but he couldn't imagine they were unrelated. There was a mountain of things he wanted to ask her about, not least of which was her own lineage.

However, this was not the time to question her about his various misgivings.

"Master Roswaal made time for you this evening. Be satisfied with that."

"After seeing those wounds I'm not gonna complain… I still feel like suspecting that was part of his scheme, though."

"That is even more farfetched. Garf came to see how Master Roswaal was doing… Does he look like the kind of man who would cooperate with Master Roswaal's plans?"

"You're pretty harsh with the guy who's fallen for you!"

"Even though he knows it is hopeless."

That last comment was the harshest of all, enough to make Subaru sympathize with the absent Garfiel.

"This evening, huh?"

Once his sympathy ran its course, he murmured to himself about the time pledged to them for conversation.

Unlike during the day, when they had been able to ask little about the circumstances surrounding the Sanctuary, Roswaal had set time aside so that they could speak about those matters.

However, the time promised to them would come after Emilia undertook the trial.

"It would seem the sun is finally setting."

Ram murmured as she turned her head outside the temple, looking up as the sky of the setting sun was repainted in the colors of the night.

Night was coming.

A night when people would be tested by the trial so as to set the Sanctuary free.

5

The atmosphere of the Sanctuary underwent a great change after sunset.

The settlement had been little more than a lonely, destitute village to begin with. It had only the minimum lighting necessary to ward off the darkness of the night; except for the weak lighting coming from houses, there was no aid for a nighttime stroll save the light of the stars.

That was why a bonfire had been lit in the center of the settlement to illuminate the path toward the tomb, making that night an exception.

"Thanks to that, we were able to hook up safe and sound. Thank goodness for fire! Right, Otto?"

"Look me in the eye once and try saying that one more time! Damn it all!"

There in the Sanctuary, in the clearing illuminated by the bonfire, Otto's face was red with anger as his outraged voice echoed. He stamped the ground with his foot, thrusting a shaking finger at Subaru as he ranted.

"Do you think this is something that can be papered over with a little light conversation?! You completely left me behind at the dragon carriage, unable to move away from it, since morning, you understand?!"

"Having said that, you're the one who told Garfiel you'd stay with the dragon carriage, right? Patlash, my fave dragon, was here, too, so you shouldn't have been lonely... Well, it's a fact that I forgot you, though."

"That fact sinks deeply into my empty stomach!"

Subaru's brazen reply left Otto fuming amid the bonfire light breaching the darkness of night.

After arriving in the Sanctuary, he'd been on the same page when stabling the dragon carriage was left to him, but, having been completely forgotten over the course of furious conversation, had only just reunited with Subaru under his own power.

Incidentally, it was already the dead of night, with supper at the Cathedral long over.

"I can't really call it an awesome-tasting meal, but beggars can't be choosers."

"So I am not only a chooser, but a beggar as well?! I really am holding a grudge over this!"

"My bad, my bad. I'll apologize properly later... Right now, I've gotta focus over here."

When Otto drew close, Subaru nudged his forehead back, giving a pained smile as his gaze shifted elsewhere. When Otto followed suit, he narrowed his eyes, gazing at the girl at the center of the clearing surrounded by faint points of light.

"Lady Emilia and minor spirits, yes? Just how many difficult issues arose while I was unaware?"

"'Difficult issues'... Don't say it like anything and everything's all troublesome stuff we've got on our shoulders."

"Am I wrong to call these issues difficult, then?"

"They're difficult issues. Ultradifficult. On top of that, Emilia has to take 'em on all by herself."

Humphing at the knowing look on Otto's face, Subaru proceeded to walk over to Emilia. With her eyes closed as she received the blessings of the minor spirits, she sensed his presence, lifting her face and pursing her lips.

"Get enough cheers of support from the minor spirits to satisfy you?"

"Mm, it's all right. But I suppose I do want one final push."

"May I?"

"If you want to, Subaru. Please."

"Good luck, don't lose! E M D—!!"

Emilia let out a little laugh at Subaru's enthusiastic cheer, briefly adding "Thank you" before shifting her gaze toward the tomb she was to challenge.

Standing beside her, Subaru licked his lips and looked up at the ruin, which gave off a very different impression compared to during the day.

"It is a tomb, so it's waaaaay creepier at night than daytime. You're all right, Emilia-tan?"

"I'm a little worried, but it's nothing. This is something I have to do."

Clenching a pale fist, Emilia took a deep breath infused with plenty of vigor. At the same time, Subaru began to worry that she looked a little too worked up.

"Hah! Well, she's full of pep. Ya'd better be, not that I'm expectin' anything from ya!"

"Garfiel and Ryuzu."

Turning toward the voice, Subaru saw two short figures walking through the entrance to the clearing—one a young-looking girl, and the other a teenage boy. Though very different people, the pair without doubt represented the Sanctuary.

In addition, Ram came in, following in Garfiel and Ryuzu's footsteps. It seemed they were the only ones who would be watching Emilia undertake the trial.

"It's a little lonely having this be the entire audience."

"The humans of Earlham Village have been forbidden from venturing out at night. There is no proper lighting for them at this hour, after all…"

"Besides, we do not want to kick up an unnecessary ruckus. The elderly are very sensitive at night."

"Ya sure wake up bright and early in the mornin', though!"

Ram and the others replied to Subaru's musing in sequence as they lined up before the tomb in good order.

Ram was a proxy for the injured Roswaal; Garfiel and Ryuzu represented the interests of the Sanctuary. Subaru, Emilia's retainer, and the outsider Otto filled out the roster.

Otto was the only one whose presence seemed tentative and not strictly necessary, but setting that aside…

"I'll watch you take up the challenge in place of the people from the village. I'm sure they really wanted to cheer you on."

"Mm, thank you. I'll work hard to fulfill your expectations, those of the villagers…and everyone else watching."

"—?"

It was only when Emilia added the part at the very end that her gaze shifted beyond the clearing. Subaru wondered what her gesture meant, but he had no time to pursue the matter.

Emilia exhaled briefly and turned back toward the tomb, walking toward the stairway at the entrance.

The next moment, there was—

"A light, from the tomb…"

It was Otto who murmured it, but his surprise was shared by everyone present.

The five watched as the surface of the ruin Emilia was to challenge glowed with a faint light, seemingly welcoming the challenger, illuminating the Witch's final resting place with a green, phosphorescent glow that seemed to sink into the darkness.

"This is proof that the tomb recognizes Lady Emilia as being qualified to undertake the trial."

Ryuzu looked up at the phosphorescent light surrounding the tomb, putting into words the reason for the beautiful scene. Subaru and the others were speechless as they stared at it, with only Emilia unhesitant as she climbed the stairs.

Then, when she reached the top of the stairs, she was greeted by the entrance to the deep, dark ruin biding its time.

"—I am off."

Subaru felt like he heard her speak those words in a little voice.

He watched Emilia proceed into the tomb's corridor until he

could no longer see her back. The entire ruin remained enveloped in the phosphorescent light; the trial had surely begun.

The ruin had rent Roswaal's body into tatters and had caused Subaru to faint and lose consciousness. When Emilia stepped within, worry welled in Subaru, almost as if someone were grasping his beating heart—

"Do not be concerned, Young Su. The tomb has firmly welcomed Lady Emilia into it. The light you see is proof of that. You need not worry that she will bounce off like Young Ros."

"The image of him bouncing off is bouncing right off of me... Er, sorry. You're just being concerned for me..."

"Ho-ho. I do not get upset when someone apologizes. Perhaps that is why I was too soft in raising Young Gar."

Subaru put on a strained smile, struck by the great contrast between her little-girl appearance and the elderly smiling face she presented. As Ryuzu spoke, she glanced sidelong at Garfiel, watching over the tomb some distance away.

He crossed his arms, audibly clenched his fangs, and kept scraping the ground with the tips of his toes, unable to calm down.

"I was just thinking..."

"Mm? About what?"

"The trial of this tomb—only those of mixed blood affected by the barrier can take it, right? Now that I think about it, Ryuzu, have you or Garfiel done it already?"

"Logically, it is possible to merely undergo the trial. However, we cannot liberate the Sanctuary. This is because of the never-ending pact that binds us residents to this place."

"...Another pact, huh?"

Subaru's distasteful tone and the bitter look on his face made Ryuzu raise an eyebrow.

"Ohh? Young Su, you dislike pacts?"

"I don't have a good impression of them. I have bad memories of trials over the last few weeks, too. The guy I hate most in this whole world talked about them a bunch."

"My, my, what a poor impression indeed. It must cause the spirit-user girl no small amount of trouble."

Spirit mages took all oaths very seriously. Ryuzu's words were proof this was a publicly known fact.

As a matter of fact, pacts and oaths were among the reasons Subaru and Emilia had once split up. It went almost without saying that Subaru had internally concluded it was his own fault. All the same—

"Accepting it and liking it are two different things. I'll keep putting a red line through them in my lexicon going forward."

"Obstinate, aren't you...? Well, a little stubbornness in a young one like you is adorable, too..."

It was really hard to wrap his head around the *young one* part. At the same time, Subaru saw a whiff of chagrin rising onto the side of Ryuzu's face. Perhaps it was nothing more than her having been robbed of the opportunity to challenge the trial for herself and having to rely on an outsider to lift the barrier. She might have quietly felt powerless on the inside.

Thinking along those lines, he could understand Garfiel's irritation, too. Considering the grasp of his personality Subaru had arrived at in a short time, there was no doubt he was the type who'd rather die than leave his problems for someone else to solve.

"..."

From there, time proceeded to flow. Subaru did nothing and said nothing as he waited for Emilia to return.

There was no visible change in Garfiel. Ryuzu continued to stand beside Subaru in silence. When he shifted his gaze a little, he was surprised to see pleasant-looking conversation passing between Ram and Otto.

To Subaru, who had experienced little *pleasant* conversation with Ram, this was an alarming development. He was about to think fruitless things, such as *I'll have to get him to spill conversation tips for Ram later*—but something happened first.

"Ah?"

When the change met the eyes of all others present, they instantly gasped as one.

Reflexively, Subaru blinked and looked back, by which time the source of light over all that time had already been lost. In other words, the almost dazzling phosphorescent glow surrounding the tomb...had been extinguished.

"The light's gone?! Hey, is everything all right?!"

"The light of the tomb should not cease so long as the trial continues..."

"Meaning something went wrong?! Emilia!"

Raising his voice at the sudden disaster, Subaru raced toward the tomb without a first or second thought. Ryuzu reached toward his back, shouting with urgency in her voice.

"W-wait, Young Su! You are not qualified to enter the t—!"

"Aaah? What the hell?!"

Ryuzu's voice trailed off in shock, leaving a bewildered Garfiel to send spittle flying as he picked up where she'd left off. Ram and Otto were just as surprised; even Subaru's breath faintly caught.

The tomb lit up the instant Subaru's foot hit the steps, beginning to radiate a green, phosphorescent light.

"The same as Lady Emilia... Er, Mr. Natsuki!"

"If I can get in, it's the answer to my prayers! Everyone stay outside! I'll call if anything happens!"

"Barusu!!"

Shrugging off the voices trying to stop him, Subaru raced up the stairs and dived into the tomb.

The ruin's air was cold and dry. The corridor in which his steps echoed was enveloped by the same green, phosphorescent light covering the outer walls, giving him a pretty good view of the moss- and vine-covered interior.

The strange sensation accompanying each and every step clawed at his chest. The scene, the location somehow seemed familiar to him, the inside of his head anguished as if being violated by some unknown memory.

"Of course I know this place... I came here before, in the dayt—!!"

Deciding that his memory from that time was the culprit, he impulsively stomped on the thought in his head with a shoe as he dived deeper.

The air deep in the ruin was stagnant, invading his nostrils with a dusty scent. He felt his lungs worsen with each and every breath. He shook his head as he went deeper, deeper, deeper—

"A room?"

When he finally reached the end of the corridor, Subaru beheld a door before his eyes that led into a small room. The grimy stone door was already open, having abandoned its duty of warding off intruders, so Subaru slipped in without resistance.

"…"

He raced into the room, a cramped chamber surrounded by stone walls. Strangely, the vines and moss had not encroached upon it, and it had deteriorated only insofar as the ruin's age would suggest. In back of the not-particularly-large stone room was another closed door that likely led deeper still, and in front of it—

"—Emilia!!"

A silver-haired girl was spread out on the floor, seemingly having sprawled her limbs when she collapsed upon it.

Unable to see her face from the entrance, Subaru desperately ran to her side.

He didn't know what had happened. All he knew was that he had to pick her up and escape from the tomb as soon as poss—

*"—First, face your past."*

The next instant, Subaru gasped when a voice seemed to whisper right into his ears.

"…"

Strength drained from him, leaving him no time to ponder what the voice might be.

His knees buckled, and Subaru's body went down like a doll, making no move to break his fall. Since he was in midrun, he tumbled onto the floor with limbs sprawled like a snow angel, ending up right next to Emilia by pure chance.

"…"

*I've fallen right beside her once before, haven't I?* he suddenly thought.

Before he could recall the memory, his first memory of death, Subaru's thoughts were swallowed up by the darkness—

6

As he always did, when Subaru awoke from slumber, he felt short of breath, as if his head were breaking the surface of the water.

The feeling was much like that of floating in a sea of unconsciousness, floating upward in search of the air called reality. Then, when his awakening lungs had breathed in enough of that reality, Subaru's mind awo—

"GOOD MOOOOOOOORNING, SOOOOON—!!"

"Hmrabhttnn?!"

That cool, refreshing morning, his poetic rise from slumber, was smashed to pieces by an incredibly destructive impact.

From above, something heavy squeezed the air out of his body, forcing Subaru to let out a cry much like a frog being squished. He batted the top of the futon away as he hacked and coughed.

"Hey, hey, heyyy, what's the matter? That's just my diving press to wake you up with *love*! Same as usual. Really gets those carelessness-is-your-greatest-enemy fires burning, huh?"

"*Koff! Koff!*... That's expecting way too...much from a guy who's asleep... Wait, just now..."

*What the heck happened?* he wondered, lifting his face with tearful eyes. As Subaru brought half his body out of bed, the other party pointed a finger to the ceiling right before Subaru's eyes.

And then—

"What is it with you? You've got the look of a guy looking at his father buck naked in the morning!"

It was his father—Kenichi Natsuki—as he posed *half*-naked there in the morning, blessing his son's awakening with a cackling laugh.

# CHAPTER 4
## PARENT AND CHILD

1

The annoying cackling, laughing voice made Subaru appreciate that yet another normal morning had arrived.

He was in his own, very familiar room. There was a bookshelf stuffed with manga and light novels on the wall, and the student desk he'd been using since a young age held a variety of small tools and the fruits of various hobbies scattered over it. In the back of the room was an old television used exclusively for gaming, and before that was the very familiar sight of his half-naked father.

Such was the morning scenery surrounding Subaru Natsuki atop the now-unmade bed.

"..."

But amid that very familiar scenery, he felt an odd stirring in his chest—

"Heyyy, are you ignoring me?! If you ignore me I'm gonna cry! I'm your real daddy related to you by blood and no spring chicken. Do you really think I can take that? There's no way. I'll die from embarrassment!"

"Same goes for me, then! Or rather, the press just now killed me. Now I will sleep forever."

Subaru responded appropriately to his half-naked father's statement and ducked under the futon. Faced with his son's cold demeanor, his father—Kenichi—groaned out in dissatisfaction.

"Well, whaaaat is this?! Is this your rebellious phase?! Shit, I thought it'd come someday, but I never expected it'd be this morning. I should've spent less time preparing breakfast and more time preparing to speak with my own son…!!"

"You say that, but what are you tryin' to do with a guy's legs… Hey, wait a— Ow! Owwww!"

"Okaaay, I've decided that today, I'll have a heart-to-heart talk with you! First, let's talk with our muscles! You just try breaking out of my figure-four leg lock infused with *looove*! Oh yeaaah—!"

With Subaru's legs bound in a lock atop the bed, Kenichi lay down facing the opposite direction as he applied pressure to the joints. Unable to resist, Subaru let out a painful cry, which Kenichi greeted with a laugh as he mocked his son.

"Gwahahah! What's wrong, what's wrong? You work out every day so you can grow big and strong, so aren't you ashamed of having such a hard time against one middle-aged ma— Ah, wait a second! Ow! Owwww!"

"You're a fool to pick a figure-four leg lock, it's weak against reversals. You're getting old, Dad! All I have to do is reverse my body and the damage flies the other way! Here's my revenge for you putting a figure-four leg lock on… Ah, wait! You can't reverse my reversal… Owow! Owowowow!"

As the victim shifted that morning, painful cries arose, boisterous voices filling the Natsuki residence to the brim. Thus did the horseplay resembling a father-son dispute continue until—

"Put a sock in it, you two. Your mom is getting pretty hungry over here and wants to eat breakfast."

When an uneven knock and a casual voice flew into the room, the pair engaged in a war of holds came to a complete halt. Both of them teary-eyed from pain, they looked at the entryway, where a single woman stood—a middle-aged woman with a foul look in her eyes.

At first sight, one might think the look grave, filled with considerable displeasure, but in truth, she wasn't the kind of person to think anything of the sort on the inside, something Subaru knew from seventeen years of being acquainted with her.

Subaru could derive all that from a single glance at her foul look, for the woman appearing was his mother, Nahoko Natsuki.

Nahoko's words made Kenichi go "Whoopsie!" He stuck his tongue out while leaping to his feet and said, "Sorry, sorry. I lost myself scuffling with Subaru there. You could've eaten without us, you know…"

"—? Why would I, when we can eat as a family? It's better to eat with everyone together."

When Kenichi turned his attention her way, Nahoko inclined her head with a mystified look. There was neither sarcasm nor resentment in her speech; it was simply how she really felt. His wife's reply sent Kenichi nodding strongly several times over.

"That's right, so very right. That's my bride! You really get it. Breakfast is much tastier when everyone's faces are gathered in one place! "

"The taste doesn't change. Everyone eating together means I can wash all the plates at once, though."

"Ah, you were talking about the cleanup? Sorry, I guess I got overly worked up by my lonesome."

Kenichi said a rather nice line, but Nahoko's statement bluntly shot it down. Nahoko looked curious as the blow sent her husband's shoulders sinking. Then she looked in Subaru's direction and said, "You're coming for breakfast, too, Subaru. Your mom worked hard for your sake today, after all."

To this, she added a thin smile, which only those close to her understood meant she was in a very good mood indeed.

2

"Whoa, this is amazin', Subaru. It's a super-special course. It's like a green forest."

Thus spoke Kenichi, gone from half-naked to clothed, as he went down to the first floor with Subaru. Standing by his father, who wore comically eye-catching glasses, Subaru gazed at the dining table and sighed.

"I'm straight-up grateful. Mm, I seriously feel that way...but what's up, Mom? Why is my plate the only one with a big pile of green peas plopped on top of it?"

Just as Kenichi had pointed out, before Subaru's spot on the dining table was a special course, a large heaping pile of green peas. Incidentally, Subaru really didn't like green peas. He was bad with green vegetables in general, but especially these.

"Hey now, you're always saying how you hate green peas, aren't you, Subaru? It's not good to be picky about your food, so I thought I'd take this opportunity to make you eat lots and put that whole business to rest."

"So you relied on a memory you'd eventually forget anyway and decided to correct my likes and dislikes. But what do you mean, this opportunity...? Is today some kind of special day or something?"

"Heh, you're so naive, Subaru. The day that is today...no, any day, any hour is precious time that will never return again in your life, so today may not be special, but it's special in its own way..."

"You can, um, stop now."

When Kenichi wedged himself into the conversation, throwing him for a bit of a loop, Subaru sat down with resignation on his face. Then the first thing he did was push the plate packed with green peas away from him.

"Anyway, I'll accept the feelings you felt for me on their own merit...but I'll pass on the green peas. I'm not eating these things even if it's Armageddon."

"Sheesh, that kind of like-and-dislike stuff will be a big hindrance to life down the road. Ah, Mom, there's some tomato in my salad. I hate tomato, so give me something else to eat."

"That's my father for you, damn it...the first part of what he says has nothing to do with the second."

The husband passed the tomato in his salad on to his wife, stealing the boiled egg from her salad in turn. Such trades between husband and wife were always occurring in the Natsuki residence. Glancing sidelong at that, Subaru pressed his hands together over everything on the menu except the green peas, which that morning consisted of tofu, miso soup, and honey toast heavy on the honey.

"I think you're always doing this, but why the eclectic Japanese-style food?"

"Mom used seaweed as an ingredient in the miso soup. I like strawberry jam on my toast, too."

The reply was not an answer, nor was it consistent with that day's menu. If he pointed that out, Nahoko would no doubt simply give him a mystified look. Accordingly, Subaru didn't trouble himself with pointing it out.

"Mm, this miso soup... That's Mom for you. You've gotten better at this behind my back, haven't you?"

"You can tell? Actually, I recorded a thirty-minute cooking channel video yesterday over lunchtime."

"No way she watched it."

Kenichi's statement felt strongly appropriate to the moment, and Nahoko's reply felt incongruous with equal strength.

Furthermore, if Nahoko's statement were dragged in line with the truth, it would likely go from her having recorded the show to her having *only* recorded it, most likely never to consider it again.

"Setting that aside, what are you gonna do about this plate of green peas? I tried to pass it to Daddy, Daddy passed it to Mom, and Mom passed it to me, and we've been going around in circles..."

"But Mom hates green peas. I hate even looking at them."

"And you were trying to overcome *me* being picky?!"

"Ah, don't misunderstand me, it's not just green peas that Mom hates, it's all food that's little and round like that. It feels icky to put them in my mouth."

"That's not a misunderstanding, then—if anything it just sounds even fishier than before!"

Deflated by his mother's impactful statement, Subaru grudgingly pushed the plate of green peas Kenichi's way.

"Well, it's the husband's place to take responsibility for the wife, so I'll leave it to Daddy to reap the fruits of defeat."

"Hey, don't make me feel all lonely here, Subaru. We're family getting along like few do these days, right? In other words, if Mom hates it, Daddy hates it, too."

"Man, I really feel for this forest of green, nobody's happy with it!"

In the end, Kenichi made a face like a mischievous brat as he said, "Guess we'll have to plop 'em into pilaf until they're all gone. Heh-heh-heh…" And thus, how to dispose of them was settled. No longer having to solo the green peas, Subaru readily promised to cooperate in their disposal. For her part, Nahoko declared, "I hate even looking at them," completely rejecting them in every way.

In the end, it became a competition between the two men to dispose of the green peas, and the family breakfast finally came to an end.

"It was a feast."

"Oh, it was nothing special. OK, let's wash all the dinnerware in the sink, then it's a race to school to help with digestion, Subaru!"

"I keep telling you, give it up with this cliché rushing-me-off-to-school routine. I'm gonna sleep till noon."

As the dinnerware was piled into the sink, Kenichi made the offer with a glint of his teeth, leaving Subaru to listlessly shake his head. Then, as he watched both parents head off, Subaru scratched his head as he went toward his bedroom—then his feet stopped.

"—Ugnh!"

A throbbing pain ran across his temples, making Subaru strongly rub his head and eyes. The light flashing on the backs of his eyelids made him blink, and he felt like he could hear something hot smoldering inside his chest.

—Something was off. Something about that morning was odd.

"Subaru?"

From the back of his head, the halted Subaru felt the gazes of his parents. Subaru knew just what emotions were infused into his father's gaze, his mother's gaze, the gazes of both his parents.

He didn't turn around. He silenced his head, practically fleeing—no, literally fleeing to his own room.

"What? Why, why am I getting these weird feelings like this...?"

Touching a hand to his own breast, Subaru sensed his rapid heartbeats, and even fear. Practically crumbling, he knelt on top of the futon, focusing his restless mind on the clock mounted on the wall.

The time was eight AM—school started at eight thirty, and it was a twenty-minute jog from home. If he changed clothes, he could just make it without being late.

"_____"

But Subaru made no sign of changing clothes as he stared at the movement of the clock from atop the futon.

Gradually, the second hand notched forward, and the minute hand moved to ten—crossing the deadline. From then on, he would not make it in time for school to begin. However he might struggle, that was absolute.

"...So it can't be helped. Yeah, it can't be helped."

Perhaps, if there'd been just a little more time until he could harden his resolve, he might have made it to school. But reality had imposed its time limit on Subaru to an exceptional extent.

He'd gone beyond it. Therefore, no more would the choice press upon him that day. And yet—

"...Usually, this would calm me down, wouldn't it? What gives...?"

His breath was ragged, his heart rate wouldn't settle, and Subaru desperately tried to suppress the shaking of his body.

This was the time for his daily ritual of fear to come to a close. Even though he knew that the same fear would come every day at the same hour, that day's had exceeded all bounds.

That morning, no one would censure Subaru any longer. No one would hurry him, or back him into a corner.

Whether to go to school—the time that tiny question would cause such powerful pain to Subaru had come to an end.

It had been several months since he had rejected school and become a delinquent. Though this had given root to a powerful sense of inferiority and self-revulsion, he became relieved every time he confirmed that the time to go to school had passed. This was something Subaru had repeated many times over.

Thus, the palpable sense of relief should have been well ingrained in Subaru's flesh. And yet...

"What is it, today of all days...?"

The sense of guilt and self-hatred, the clinging sense of unpleasantness...they just wouldn't vanish.

He didn't know where the sense of nervousness plucking at his chest was coming from. Without understanding how to set his breathing straight, Subaru agonized on top of the futon, smeared in disagreeable sweat.

Now that he thought back, something had been off from the moment he'd awoken that morning.

His father, Kenichi, hatching schemes like that to wake Subaru up was a daily fact of life. Once Subaru stopped going to school, becoming a good-for-nothing in name and fact, his father's approach toward him hadn't changed from before.

And yet, the physical contact, the conversing, the holds from his father, now hurt for a different reason.

Even if his mother, Nahoko, had all kinds of harebrained ideas that strayed from the mark, with those that misfired, like the one that morning, far more common than those that did not, she'd always put Subaru first—always, for seventeen years.

Even so, his mother's gaze that morning had instilled a sense of loneliness and thoughts of self-reproach well beyond the norm.

Everything was the same as usual, not a thing out of place. And yet, he'd sensed something off about his parents, and about himself.

"The heck. What the heck, what happened? Yesterday wasn't anything spec— Ugh!"

When he thought back to the day before in search of the cause of that morning's change in tone, fireworks scattered inside his head. The pain interrupted his thought process, feeling strangely as if it was preventing Subaru's attempt to touch on his own memory. To prove whether it was so, Subaru would have to challenge the sea of his memory once more—and this he did not do.

There was no special reason for the odd pain that morning. That day, his feelings of guilt had simply decided to assert themselves as pain. Probably he had been unable to look either of his parents straight in the eye because—

"Subaru, can I come in for juuust a bit?"

A voice came through the door, but the door opened before he could reply. When he let out a heavy breath and turned his head toward it, Kenichi was moonwalking his way into his own son's room. Subaru spontaneously smacked his forehead.

"...Coming in before I answer kind of defeats the point of asking me, doesn't it?"

"Hey, now. With the hard bonds tying me and you, father and son, together, that's not really nece— Er, it kind of is! Sorry, I wasn't considering that you're in puberty. I'll come again after you've taken care of things."

"Don't go back to form and lob weirdly realistic conclusions out like that! I wasn't even doing anything!"

When a crack was evident in the chain between father and son, he made a show of consideration. When Subaru spoke with a ragged voice, Kenichi went "Reaaally?" with a suspicious air and entered the room once more. Then he sat on the futon and crossed his arms in Subaru's direction.

"Well, it's fine. We'll leave what just happened as a secret shared by the two of us alone."

"There's nothing that needs to be a secret! Just be honest, sheesh! All you're doing is assaulting me before I get back to sleep again!"

"I get it, I get it— So, then. Let's get to the point. Actually, Subaru, I took time off from work today. Surprised?"

"...Yeah, I figured that. Daddy's not at the house on a Monday morning very often. And?"

"Don't be hasty jumping to conclusions. A father-son conversation is like boxing. The jab comes first."

Kenichi's laid-back smile and demeanor made Subaru feel like he was just drawing out the conversation. He was dancing around the main issue, using words and gestures to make light of things and giving himself and his opponent time to harden their resolve. This was a kind of habit in interpersonal relations Subaru knew well.

It was not simply because the apple did not fall far from the tree—there was a separate reason, one steeped in incorrigible idiocy.

"—Ow!!"

The instant he embraced that sentiment, a sharp pain ran through Subaru's head once more. He began to vaguely suspect just what was causing the pain. But Subaru averted his gaze from Kenichi as he said, "...And? Now that you've landed the jab, what's Daddy's right-handed punch, your conversation topic, gonna be?"

"Yes, let's see. Subaru, do you have a girl you like?"

"What is this, middle school?!!"

"Ohh, that overreaction is like making a confession, don't ya know?"

"What gives with you saying that with that smug look on your face? Exasperated sighs of lament don't mean anything, you know."

He'd meant to paper over the sentiment, but that blow had been an unexpected one. But, as a matter of fact, the assertion was off the mark, because Subaru didn't have any interest in such things at that time. He had neither the interest nor a belief that he ought to have one.

"Keh, well, aren't you boring. I laid it all out when you were little, didn't I? Girls have a weakness for promises that happened years ago and situations like that, so go make some and set up some flags, damn it!"

"If I sincerely took that as truth, I'd have every girl in town pointing me out as a dishonest bastard. I already have too many sins to deal with…you trying to drive me down into a living hell?"

"…If only you'd inherited my gentle mask. You've got Mom's I-don't-give-a-damn look, plus Daddy's short legs and bad jokes. Your status points are pretty low, huh?"

"I've been sayin' that since I had a umbilical cord…"

The tension dropped between father and son as they bantered about their hardwired genetic situations. As the diversion ran its course, Subaru returned to "So?" once more and asked, "What was the issue at hand, anyway? After this, I have an important duty to fulfill: sleeping two to three more hours. So if what you want draws a total *beeeep*, then talk to Mom downstairs, okay?"

"Don't brush me off all natural like that. Besides, this talk would just fly over Mom's head. My wife and your mom is the worst woman at guessing in the whole world. That's why I can't let her out of my sight, but…"

The natural way he tossed out fond phrases bored Subaru, his adolescent son, to tears. When Subaru hung his head, Kenichi went "Hmm," then twisted his neck a bit and smiled mischievously as he said, "Well, it happens to be nice weather out—how 'bout we dress up and have a little father-son talk outside?"

3

"Ohh, Ken. Not often I see you in the morning. They finally fired you, huh?"

"Don't be stupid. Nothing's getting done in that place without me. Felt bad to work so much that I'm stealing everyone else's job, so I've gotta lay off once in a while."

Kenichi lobbed his insult with a raise of his middle finger, smiling toward the owner of a nearby bakery as he passed on his bicycle. He proceeded to toss warm words the store owner's way as the latter vanished around a bend, adding afterward, "Sheesh, everyone talks like I got fired just 'cause they see me taking a day off. Is it so bad I'm nurturing a loving family here? And if I was fired, I'd get a new job before I got busted."

"…As a person you're nurturing, I'm praying you don't toss any heart-stopping surprises like that on me."

Hands thrust into his tracksuit pockets, Subaru watched the conversation with the baker from a distance, with sinking shoulders. "Hey, hey," went Kenichi at his son's demeanor, adjusting the position of his highly conspicuous glasses as he said, "It's bad enough in your own darned room, but there you are, making that suspicious face when I've dragged you out and the sun's shining this bright on a nice crisp morning like this. You might get stopped by a cop like that."

"If I got stopped by a cop, it'd be because Daddy dragged me out at a time like this!! I…said I didn't wanna, but you twisted my arm anyway."

"What are you sayin'? That foot dragging was just goin' through the motions. You really love everything about Daddy, don't ya, Subaru? Relax, I love you, too. Next after Mom, that is!"

Their stroll recommenced, and Kenichi's feelings didn't seem all that hurt as he gave Subaru a slap on his back. Subaru grimaced at the force of it, but that moment, his thoughts were stolen by an even greater ache in his breast.

After all, simply walking close to his father instilled so much pain, he felt like it would crush his chest.

"Don't be all guarded like that. It's not like I'm gonna talk about anything scary. It's an actual legit father-son talk."

"'Legit father-son talk,' eh?"

"Yep, legit father-son talk— Incidentally, Subaru, which would you rather have…a little brother or a little sister?"

"Being asked that at seventeen is nothing *but* scary!!"

He'd lost count of the unexpected blows, but this one left Subaru aghast, voice coarsened. Seeing his son like that, Kenichi went "I'm kidding, I'm kidding," showing off his teeth with a smile.

"Well, Mom and I are certainly still on lovey-dovey terms, but at our age we really don't wanna see more than one of you. So be happy. You're monopolizing my and Mom's love."

"Ahh, right, right. Happy, happy... You really are joking, right?"

"That sounds like the lead up to *Nooo, do you hate me that much?* and that kind of stuff, huh?"

When the possibility it wasn't merely a joke finally surfaced, Subaru wordlessly reflected on that possibility. Taking in the insecure, objecting gaze, Kenichi laughed *keh, keh* as he nodded.

Subaru and his father were walking on a footpath a short distance from home.

Subaru lived in a place with a mildly famous riverside doubling as a spring tourist spot, with cherry trees growing along the embankment. It was currently the wrong season for cherry blossoms, so the embankment was in full leaf instead. Subaru glanced at the trees as he walked with his father around town.

"Ken, what are you doing here in the morning? It's a late hour for starting pachinko, don't ya know."

"Oh my, Kenichi. By any chance, were you seduced by the aroma of curry in the daytime?"

"Oh wow, you're here, Ken? Now that's really funny. Isn't this bad for you? It's funny, though..."

The bright, sunny, average day made the time fly as father and son walked around town that morning, with numerous voices tossed their way.

—No, the voices were not being tossed *their* way. They were limited to the father, Kenichi, alone.

Regardless of whether male or female, young or old, there seemed no limit to the people who knew Kenichi's face. That went for the store owner in the shopping district, the housewife taking out the garbage, the senior high school girl with the *ganguro* look that was rarely seen nowadays, et cetera, et cetera—

"Kenny, it's been a while. You still hanging out with Ikeda, hmm?"

"That Ikeda guy? He won big at horse racing and used the money to retire and vanish ten years ago. He still sends New Year's cards, summer greeting cards, winter greeting cards, Christmas cards, and cards on his mom and pop's birthdays, though."

"I wouldn't call someone in touch that much 'vanished'..."

When Subaru inadvertently interrupted with a quip, he quickly covered his mouth. Overhearing his murmur, Kenichi and the solidly built old man he was speaking to looked over. The other man was wearing green overalls and a tag with the name of the riverside on it, so he seemed like a caretaker of some sort.

The old man spurring the conversation must have gone way back with Kenichi, his eyes going round as he looked at Subaru.

"Kenny, it's not often you bring someone along with you... Could that child be...?"

"Ahh, yeah. This is my son. Nah, I should correct that, my *beloved* son!"

"Ohh, I knew it! Somehow, he seemed like the spitting image of you when you were... Ahhh, maybe not so much. He takes after his mother, perhaps?"

"Errr, ha-ha... I get that a lot. Especially about the look of my eyes."

Amid the very average construction of his face, he'd inherited Nahoko's extremely characteristic three-whites-eyes look. In terms of outward appearance, about the only thing Subaru had inherited from Kenichi was the somewhat limited length of his legs.

When Subaru gave that noncommittal reply, the old man eagerly nodded.

"I am surprised, though. *That* Kenny got old enough to have a boy this big? Guess I'm getting old, too. If Ikeda was drowning, I don't have any strength in my body left to go swim and save him."

"Well, I don't think even that Ikeda guy is enough of a kid to go play in the river and drown..."

"I certainly hope not. Ikeda and your father just won't settle down like they should at their ages... Did you know they both used to be brats who walked around town kicking up all kinds of ruckus?"

"...Well, kinda."

Subaru's reply was on the awkward side. Receiving this, the old man knotted his eyes with a somewhat suspicious look. However, the next moment, the creases of his brow deepened further.

"Come to think of it…today's Monday, isn't it? What are you doing with your father at this hour?"

"—!!"

The question he did not want asked, the words he did not want to hear, made Subaru's heart strongly jump.

Next came the sharp, stabbing pain like that which had visited him in his own bedroom. Spontaneously, Subaru clutched his painful head and closed his eyes, wringing out "I'm sorry" as he turned his back upon the old man.

"Ah, hey, Subaru! Sorry, pops. I'll come again when we can take our time!"

"R-right… It seems I shouldn't have said that. Apologize to the lad for me, would you?"

The conversation exchanged behind him did not enter his ears.

At any rate, Subaru tried to run from the pain threatening to crack his skull, seeking a place where he could get the pounding heartbeats in his chest to calm down, fleeing from the embankment with rapid steps.

"It's nothing you need to apologize for—and the rest is his problem."

While he fled, he never heard Kenichi utter those words behind his back.

4

"Here, a cold, tasty cola packed with *loooove*. If you give it a nice, good shake, it's even tastier… Well, I'd like to say that, but this doesn't seem to be the time."

"…No one has time to pack anything with love on the way back from the vending machine."

Accepting it, Subaru felt the coolness of the can on his palm as he put his fingers on the pull tab. Then, after a moment's thought, he pointed the can's lid toward no one in particular before putting strength into his fingers—The instant he opened the lid, the contents spewed out with incredible force, reducing its contents by about a third. And, witnessing this—

"Tch."

"Don't click your tongue! I've seen this movie before! Aww, my hand's all sticky now!"

Shaking off his cola-bathed hand, Subaru clicked his own tongue at Kenichi's childish prank. Then he put the lightened can to his lips, swallowing down and healing his parched throat in one sitting.

He savored the carbonic acid bouncing down his throat, wishing it would wash away even the discomfort welling in his chest.

"So, you've calmed down?"

"...A little."

Replying with a sober look, Subaru sank his weight into the bench upon which his butt rested. As his son proceeded to heave a deep sigh, Kenichi, standing right in front of him, opened his can of cola and brought it to his own lips.

After fleeing from the footpath, father and son had ended up at a desolate public park for children. Naturally, it being morning on an ordinary weekday, there was no sign of anyone in the park, which liberated Subaru from the strange feeling of being backed into a corner.

Even then, the headache was asserting itself, but it had abated to the point that he could converse. He wanted to change the subject, and soon.

"...Incidentally, it took you a bit of time just to go to the vending machine and back. Did something happen?"

"Mm? Ah, nothing big. I just met a high school girl skipping class on my way to the machine. I lectured her about going to school, treated her to juice, traded e-mail addresses, and sent her on her way."

"There's no way I'm believing you got to trading e-mail addresses in that short a time!"

He had no words for the notion his father had gotten an e-mail address from a high school girl who was probably just going to the ladies' room for a few. "Is that so?" Kenichi asked Subaru, and he inclined his head as he said, "It doesn't take that much for a girl to give out her e-mail at least. My cell phone's address book has almost three whole pages full of high school girls' addresses I've picked up on the way."

"Even if I went to a government office or something I'd probably only get two. Daddy, you're not gonna get caught for some weird offense, are you?"

"Moron. I'm not interested in doing anything indecent with high school girls. They're children. The destination for my love was set long ago. My passions are for my family alone."

"Categorizing it like that makes it sound like I'm included, you know?!"

"...Well, I do love you. Like a puppy!"

"Like hell you do! Which one's the moron here?!"

Kenichi responded to Subaru's angry voice with a vulgar, cackling laugh.

That laughing voice left no refined echo upon the ear. And yet, for some reason, people didn't find it unpleasant at all. All Kenichi's actions were like that.

Everything he did was over the top, deprived of common sense, excessively theatrical, completely the sort of thing other people shunned you for, but for some reason, everyone took it in a really friendly way.

It was just that, merely by their going outside for a walk, the decisive difference between Subaru and his father was driven home to a distinctly painful extent.

"—!"

"Looks like you're in pretty bad shape across the board. That being the case, Subaru, how 'bout I carry you home on my back?"

"I don't need *that*, and I don't need to go back... Even if I go back, it'll be together and all."

If anything, his mother, Nahoko, was home, so Subaru's condition would probably get even worse.

He was coming to understand the cause of the pain arriving without cease. If his guess was right, the pain began to assert itself whenever he was in the same place as Kenichi and Nahoko, his father and mother. In other words—

"So what, even my body decided to finally chew me out?"

Did it mean his body had finally begun to cry out at the sense of guilt racking him from continuing to flee?

He spent day after day holding his knees inside his room as the hands of the clock reproached him for remaining inside his shell. He had an unpleasant feeling, almost as if someone were railing at him over his procrastination in a loud voice from inside his own head.

*I dunno who you are or from where, but what the hell do you know about me?*

"Hey now, Subaru. Let's change the topic—you have a girl you like, or something?"

With Subaru cowed into silence, Kenichi repeated the question Subaru had blown off once before.

The flippant way he asked it wasn't funny. The first time, Subaru had replied with a strained smile, but now that the question came a second time, it really got on his nerves for some reason.

With the aid of the unceasing headache, he felt like replying to the question with extremely crude language—

"*Subaru.*"

"Huh?"

Lifting his face, he tried to locate where the whisper in his ear had come from. But, however much his gaze wandered, he could not locate the speaker. The only person in the park besides Subaru was Kenichi.

Subaru's making that sudden, idiotic-sounding voice put a suspicious look over that very same Kenichi, who said, "What's wrong? You look like a guy just about to blurt out the name of the pretty girl he's not supposed to have."

"I really do look like that, so I can't say anything about it...but did someone call out my name just now? Daddy, don't tell me you've been practicing mimicking a pretty girl's tone of voice?"

"Daddy has a variety of little tricks, but that one is not among them. OK, gimme about a month."

"I wasn't giving you suggestions! Really, the heck was that?"

The voice had a beautiful echo to it that resonated in the bottom of his heart like a silver bell. It was exceedingly gentle, its reverberation making his chest grow warm, and had such power to it that it made Subaru forget the headache that continued intermittently.

Subaru didn't know whence it had come, but the voice had saved Subaru.

"So, back to the earlier question. Have a girl you like?"

"...What is it with all this? Even if I had one, why ask her name? Not like you'd know who she is, Daddy."

"You're the one who doesn't know that. For all you know, maybe I have the e-mail address of the girl you like on my cell phone?"

"Even a century-long love grows cold."

To that blunt retort, Kenichi went "Whaaat?" raining "Boos" upon him in dismay. Glancing at the behavior wholly inappropriate for a man his age, Subaru drank the rest of his cola in one gulp, leaving the can dry.

"You don't need to put it off anymore. You can come right out and say it: 'Why aren't you going to school?' and whatever."

"And here I was actually being considerate to someone for once. You're a son who can't read the mood— Well, it's not like you're wrong, that actually is what I wanted to talk to you about..."

"...I think I'm doing a bad thing to both of you."

"You don't really need to think about that. I had a vague idea you had something on your mind, and even if you weren't thinking, well, I can overlook a decent amount of that, so no need to dwell."

With Subaru airing his side of things a little, Kenichi drank his own pop can dry and sat on the bench. A gentle, refreshing breeze blew between father and son as they sat side by side.

The two proceeded to stare ahead, neither looking at the other's face as they wove their words.

"This might not exactly be the prevailing view, but I don't think school is everything. I mean, you won't hear that out of my mouth when I didn't take school seriously, either. I even skipped my graduation ceremony."

"And that's why, when you got your high school graduation certificate, you were with a woman two grades below you when she was graduating. My ears are octopuses from hearing that one over and over."

"Well I'll make you listen to it till they turn to squids. Since this is me talking, if you don't want to go to school, I don't really think you need to. Now that I'm my age, I do think *Sure would've been nice if I'd taken school seriously*, but that's not something you're gonna get for a while."

Kenichi seemed to be gazing somewhere far off as Subaru stared at the side of his face, internally cursing his father for being underhanded. Even though he normally played dumb and showed only his flippant side, he'd set the clownish behavior aside in a place like that.

It wasn't fair, not fair at all, enough to make him feel like crying.

"These days, human beings seem to live till they're eighty years old. Isn't that great? If you have eighty years, you can get one or two of 'em back while you're still young. Luckily, I earn some pretty decent money. Like this," went Kenichi, tracing a circle with his finger as he laughed with a vulgar look. Subaru didn't even make a sound to Kenichi to show he was keeping up, but his father nodded several times, showing no sign of caring.

"Going through life, you bump into questions without answers that leap out at ya. In my case, I move around and go looking for 'em, but for all I know, maybe you can find answers to some questions rolling around in your room. If you're mulling something over, I ain't gonna complain. If you give up, though…then I might give ya a piece of my mind."

"…Why?"

"Hm?"

"Why did you feel like talking about this all of a sudden today? It's not like it's some kind of special day, right? It's just a…green peas commemoration day."

"That plate sure was full of 'em, huh?"

Though he'd emptied the cola just moments before, it suddenly seemed very dry inside Subaru's mouth.

As Subaru seemed to gasp for air, his father patiently waited for a reply.

Watching from the side as Subaru became agitated, Kenichi went "Hmm," twisting his neck several times before saying, "Why, I wonder. I just happened to be off work, and I was wiping myself with a dry towel this morning, and I was like…the horoscope said Aquarius would have a great day, plus there was the look on your face this morning… Somehow, you looked just a little better, so I figured you might be up to talking about it."

"My face looked better?"

"I'm talking about the expression on your face. Your face itself is the same, and you still have that villainous look in your eyes just like your mother."

Setting the three-whites-eyes business aside, Subaru touched his own face with a hand as he mulled over Kenichi's words.

There was no proof for what his father had said. That his face was better meant that there had been a change. But whence in Subaru's way of life to date had such a change come about?

Nowhere. Therefore, Kenichi had to have misread him. Nothing had changed yesterday, nor would it tomorrow.

That was fine, and that was what he intended. If he kept it up, no doubt at some point Kenichi and Nahoko would realize it—just what, exactly, Subaru was really after.

"—Nhhha!"

The moment he thought it, an impact shot through his brain enough to make him think fireworks had gone off in front of his eyes.

His heart rate became like an alarm bell; he could hear the

exaggerated sound of blood flowing through his eardrums. The world going hazy before his eyes and his having a rising urge to vomit had a common cause: the unpleasant feeling inside his chest had begun to assert itself once more.

The sharp pain in his head, the uncomfortable feeling in his chest—both were trying to tell Subaru something.

"Hey now, you seriously look like you're having a hard time. Are you all right, Subaru?"

Naturally, Kenichi couldn't ignore the sight; he reached out a hand to Subaru's shoulder with a worried look on his face. When Subaru felt the touch of his palm, he lifted up his face, sweat on his brow as he tried to think of some kind of reply.

*"It's been hard for you, hasn't it?"*

"—?!"

Subaru's entire body ran hot when the silver bell voice made his ears quiver once more.

It was a voice full of affection and sympathy. The voice seemed to melt Subaru's strained heart, impeding his suffering as the swelling heat swallowed up the pain and the cracks therein.

The voice was scorching him. He chased after it. Without restraint, he clung to it to take back—

*"Thank you, Subaru."*

"You're..."

The sight of silver hair dancing in the wind was seared into his vision. She gazed straight at Subaru with eyes like radiant, violet gemstones. The words she wove with her lips were all filled with loveliness.

*"For coming to save me."*

*What, what, what, what, what the hell?*

*Who, who, who, who, who, who, who was this?*

*"—Subaru."*

His breath caught. His throat was hot. Something was welling behind his scorched eyes.

*"May the blessings of the spirits be with you."*

His fingertips trembled. He couldn't put strength into his legs. His lungs convulsed, and his soul began to scream.

*"I think you're the one who's reaaally incredible, Subaru."*

He covered his face with his shaking hands, holding back the sobs in his trembling throat. The welling heat was trickling from his eyes...

*"—Subaru, why do you come to save me?"*

The answers to his questions were already inside him.

The instant he found them, the ferocious emotions and the sense of discomfort inside Subaru both vanished.

The skull-splitting pain, the rising urge to vomit, the dizziness making the world grow hazy, the heartbeats growing more urgent as a decision seemed to draw near—where all of them converged, Subaru Natsuki found his answer.

He lifted his face, wiping away the tears that seemed due to trickle down any moment. As if to shake off the tears of regret on that sleeve, he strongly, strongly clenched his fist.

And then—

"Sorry to make you worry. I'm all right now."

"That so? If you're just down in the dumps, that's fine, but don't make me worry so much."

"Yeah, my bad. Besides, about the question from earlier..."

Shrugging off the hand of his father supporting his shoulder, Subaru turned toward him.

As they sat closely on the bench, his father's face was peering into his own with a look of concern. Now that he thought about it, he realized that even though they'd exchanged words many times that day, he had not looked straight at his father's face even once.

Wanting to flee even then, he smiled bitterly at his own weakness.

"I found a girl I like—so I'm all right now."

With the sight of the silver-haired girl still fresh in his mind, Subaru Natsuki confronted his own past.

5

"I found a girl I like."

When he put the words on his lips once more, Subaru had the palpable sense of his heart walking forward.

The inside of his head was clear. The pain, like a prolonged curse, had vanished. As he was then, Subaru had resolve sufficient to face his father and tell him everything.

Before his eyes, Kenichi blinked several times over, surprised by the confession disconnected from the conversation to that point.

"...Is that so?"

With a quiet voice, he lent the words of Subaru, the words of his own son, his ears.

His demeanor was a blessing to Subaru. Even though Subaru ought to have always known he was the kind of man to lend an ear like that, Subaru had continued to hold his tongue. But that had come to an end.

That was because there was someone gently pushing on his back, urging him forward.

"What might've shaken me up, what might've made me curl up in a ball, I remember it all now—no, I knew everything all along. I knew it, but I just pretended to not see the weakness in me that I thought only I noticed... But while I was pretending, someone..."

He couldn't hide it by saying *someone*. He knew who that *someone* was.

"I wanted...Dad and Mom to smack me."

"..."

"I was an unsalvageable little good-for-nothing idiot, a complacent piece of garbage, so I wanted you two to smack me...to make me give that up."

Without a word, Kenichi gazed at Subaru, his eyes never wavering. The face Subaru saw reflected in those eyes was altogether too weak, unworthy of pity, and thus, he continued.

"I've used any petty little tricks I could since a long time ago.

Whether it's studying or athletics, I easily pulled off stuff that not many people can do, leaving the people who can't do it all mystified."

Thinking back to his youth, he could have called what he'd had an adorable sense of omnipotence. At a young age, Subaru had been quicker on the uptake with both athletics and academics than the average person. As if by nature, he was more clever and fleeter of foot than those around him, inevitably becoming the center of attention among children his own age—

*"He really is that man's son."*

Thus was Subaru appraised; thus did the adults close to home praise him frequently.

Since that *him* was his father, the young Subaru had been proud to be valued as his son. For in the eyes of the son, the father—Kenichi Natsuki—was an attractive individual.

He laughed a lot, he smiled a lot, he cried a lot, he got angry a lot, he moved a lot, he worked a lot.

There were always a great deal of people around his father. He was adored by many, and his smiling face was the axis around which they revolved. And that very father announced in public that the two members of family—Subaru and his mother—were the most precious things to him of all.

Subaru took pride in that. He felt it gave him a special right to a boastful sense of superiority.

Someday, he wanted to be like his father—to Subaru, that was a natural wish.

"But at some point down the line… I don't remember it, but I lost a footrace to someone. I went from being number one to not being number one. Faster, smarter guys than me came out of the woodwork, and I dropped from number one bit by bit… I thought *There's gotta be something wrong with this.*"

The more the wrongness got to him, the more the star above his head seemed to move away, with each and every glimmering star between him and it forming the path he needed to take to get closer.

He harbored nervousness that the star might disappear. But even with that impatience within him—

*"He really is that man's son."*

Those words alone were Subaru's salvation, the hope to which he clung.

Even if he was not as fleet of foot, even if he was not as good at studying, those words bolstered the young Subaru's dignity.

More than training to run fast, more than doing his homework, he came to put stupid things first.

He sneaked into school at night with his friends, wandered aimlessly around the town, chased a famously dangerous stray dog from everyone's hangout spot—in this way, Subaru ran around protecting his pride to keep everyone from being fed up with him, thus protecting the meaning of his own existence.

"It's stupid to work hard. Having fast feet is nothing to be proud of. How I made everyone laugh was a lot stronger, a lot more impressive than that."

What others feared, he made his priority; what others detested, he made his own desire. Thus, he continued to challenge himself with precious care, with bold recklessness, so that he did not lose his place.

"But of course, the longer that continued, the next thing I was gonna do had to be even bigger. I couldn't do anything that was smaller than what came before it. I didn't want anyone to think I was boring."

Thus, Subaru's actions had to be more and more extreme.

Subaru Natsuki had to be braver than anyone, more extravagant than anyone, more liberated than anyone—he had to be someone everyone could continue to look up to.

That was the veneer he adopted. Using the veneer, he hid the fact that it was a veneer so even he couldn't notice it, and he had to do more, more, more, to deceive himself and the people around him.

After all, he was Kenichi Natsuki's son—Subaru Natsuki.

"I thought *I can do anything.* I made myself think *I can do anything.* That's how what I did got stupid, just me flailing around without any thought…"

And so he was like a moth drawn to the flame, seeking light, never realizing that it would burn him.

However, Subaru was not a moth, and the same went for Subaru's friends. His friends had gotten it a long, long time ago.

There hadn't been any particular trigger for it. The number of friends associating with Subaru's recklessness dwindled.

"I thought *Those guys are dimwits. You'll never have this kind of fun if you aren't together with me.* I'd make those guys regret it. They could just idly pass the time away with boring stuff. I was aiming for even higher places."

If he continued chasing the star like that, he'd lose sight of the other stars above his head.

Unable to see all the stars filling up the sky, Subaru desperately chased after the glimmer of the one star that remained, gazing at that star alone as he continued running after it—when he suddenly realized.

"There was no one left around me but me."

Naturally. With Subaru continuing to do things his own way, heedless of everything around him, even the people who'd thought it was funny at first would not follow as he escalated his exploits to new heights.

Not noticing this, he distanced himself from them, laughing derisively at them and calling them dimwits, but Subaru, now the only one left, found his thoughts harboring worry and doubt, and thus, he distanced himself even more. And thus did the cycle repeat itself until—

"Even though the sky has so many glittering stars, I lost sight of every last one."

Having lost sight of the starlight, and having lost all the friends around him, when Subaru was left all alone, enveloped by darkness, he finally came to realize it for himself.

—He wasn't a special person at all.

*"He really is that man's son."*

Those were the magical words that the young Subaru had embraced with pride. But somewhere along the line, the words transformed into a curse.

The curse rotted his heart. When he lost his place, he felt as if someone was chasing him, making him unable to breathe.

"By going outside, walking around town, I understood. Wherever I went, whatever I saw, there were traces of my dad everywhere... Of course there were."

In Subaru's confined world, he had come to admire his father. He'd wanted to see the same sights his father had.

To Subaru, who sought the same things his father had found everywhere he went, there was nowhere he could look within that confined world and not sense traces of his father.

In stages, the world became a scary place to Subaru.

What simultaneously rotted Subaru's heart was the realization he himself was mediocre, and the realization he didn't want either of his parents or any of the people who knew his father to know this; in other words, shame.

Subaru Natsuki, the son of Kenichi Natsuki, could not become known as a person who shrank in timidity from the public's gaze, a coward whose head harbored misconceptions and fear about a widening world.

From late elementary to middle school, through strenuous effort, Subaru managed to pass the time without standing out whatsoever.

Classmates who knew Subaru from his lower school years couldn't wrap their heads around the change in Subaru, but even they, children at an emotionally sensitive point in their lives, never noticed the darkness enveloping their fellow classmate's heart.

And what put him beyond salvation was that Subaru was crafty where the issue was concerned. Though he passed his school days without standing out, he continued to behave in the same old uninhibited manner at home.

"Even just remembering it, I shudder at how I passed the time back then. But that's how I managed to get through middle school... Even though we lived in the same town, most of my classmates stopped going to the same school as me. Guess because of test results?"

Even Subaru, who'd spent several years in such a backward-thinking fashion, harbored a faint hope from the radical change in environment. When he advanced into high school, the environment, one where no one knew his past, might generate new relationships—and if that was to happen, no one would see Subaru as Kenichi Natsuki's son.

Mustering all the meager courage inside himself, Subaru decisively stepped off the beaten path.

"Even for me, I totally blew my grand high school debut. A guy who couldn't have proper interpersonal relationships in little and middle school was never gonna cut it in a place with all new faces. I did bold and reckless stuff to shake off the tension, and the result was... Even an idiot could guess."

Even though it would be plain to an idiot, to Subaru it was not. The result hardly needed to be spelled out.

Subaru had never seen examples of how to approach other people beyond those of his father. He had nothing save his father as a reference for how to build relationships in a new environment.

Even if he knew stuff to make people laugh at a young age, to classmates undergoing psychological changes on the way to the second stage of their lives, it was nothing but poison.

From the first step into a new environment, he had gone badly astray. Thus, Subaru established his isolated position as a dork, someone who couldn't read the mood.

He wasn't ostracized. He simply spent his school life being treated like thin air. And then, as the days passed, one morning, he thought...

"*I just don't wanna go to school today.* It was a morning when errands meant Dad and Mom were both out, so even when it was past the usual wake-up time, I turned over and nodded back off—I was super surprised when I realized it was just before noon. After that, when I got up to change in a huge hurry..."

Subaru realized that his own mind and body were exceptionally at ease.

"After that, it was just a drag. I skipped one day a week, then it was once every three days, then once every two... It didn't take even three months before I stopped going to school altogether."

The days that followed hardly needed to be spoken of.

Once he stopped going to school, Subaru's heart was filled with a sense of relief. Yes, he was liberated from the painful times he underwent while at school, but that wasn't the main reason.

It wasn't a big reason, either. He'd become Subaru Natsuki, smug juvenile delinquent.

Looking at that Subaru, no one would think *He really is that man's son* anymore. But more than that, the exceedingly pathetic sight of Subaru like that would make both his father and mother stop loving him.

No matter how unsightly, how deplorable Subaru had become, both his parents had loved him.

That's what scared him the most. Nothing frightened Subaru as much as that fact.

And then, to Subaru Natsuki, Kenichi Natsuki and Nahoko Natsuki would say—

"'I don't love you. I hate you. You're...not my child.' I wanted you to do that, to say that, to throw me aside. I wanted to make you... give up on me."

With fleeting hope, he'd looked up at the sky, expecting to find the star that could never have been.

A human being as pathetic and mewling as Subaru was a fool unworthy of being Kenichi Natsuki's son. And thus, he wanted to be cast aside.

Not even Subaru himself realized that was what rested within Subaru's heart.

Unable to accept how weak and stupid he was, pushing onto others the task of cleaning up the mayhem that appeared in his wake, he averted his eyes, hating himself all the same.

In spite of all that, Subaru had not ended up shunned and abandoned by all, because someone had been there to support him.

*"It is easy to give up— However...it does not suit you, Subaru."*

The image of the silver girl imprinted on the backs of his eyelids now had a flickering blue radiance superimposed upon it.

With that, a warm breeze blew into Subaru's heart, making him pledge to move his listless limbs once more.

*"Subaru, I love you."*

With those words, she had given Subaru a push right when he should have been finished.

Because he realized that, because he remembered that, he set his heart on walking forward from zero—and to do that, he had to settle things with the past, the minus that came before zero.

*"—Yes. My hero…is the greatest in the whole world."*

"…"

Having listened to Subaru's long monologue to its completion, Kenichi closed his eyes, sinking into thought.

—In the end, the same as before, Subaru was forcing someone else to clean up after him.

Because he lacked the courage to identify his own flaws, because he didn't want to become the greatest villain in his own world, because he wanted to be the heroic main character, he kept making someone else play the villain.

He'd believed that if he did that—someday, Kenichi would break the door down, bringing it all to an end.

He'd spent day after day in foolish sloth, expecting that someone else would handle things.

It was with that deadlocked mental state that he had arrived in that other world. And, even in a place like that, Subaru had continued his conceited ways, until finally—

"Subaru."

Eyes closed, Kenichi stood before Subaru and addressed him by name.

When those words brought him back to reality, Subaru looked up at his father. To Subaru, ready to accept whatever Kenichi might say, whatever Kenichi might think, in its full, unvarnished form, he—

"Father head!!"

"Gahhh?!"

Taking an unexpected blow to his cranium, Subaru reeled as fireworks scattered in his eyes. Toward his son, eyes tearful from the sharp pain, Kenichi powerfully thrust a finger and said, "You see that, Subaru? That's my angry blow, the father head move I've filled with *love*."

"Wasn't that a heel drop?! What 'head'?! Was that just to throw me off?!"

"That's what stretching after a bath does for you. Got my leg pretty high up there, didn't I?"

Kenichi began stretching his supple hip joints on the spot. His father's demeanor defied his expectations, leaving Subaru half in tears, unsure what he should say.

Subaru had been expecting something else—

"Gotta say, though, Subaru. You're, well…a pretty big moron."

"Uhh…?"

Insulted by the rather disconnected words, Subaru couldn't get a single word out when Kenichi crossed his arms and continued.

"In the first place, there's a lot that rubs me the wrong way, but there's one thing that's the biggest. You're the one who thought you'd get me to hate you. The way you did it was by rejecting school. And you thought, somewhere along the line, your dad would blow a fuse and yell at you… That's stupid on a fundamental level, you know?"

"I can't really say I disagree, but…"

"I mean, if you want me to abandon you, you've gotta be more proactive about it. Who abandons his own kid just because he crawls into his own shell? If you want me to hate you, you should commit genocide on half of humanity for no particular reason. Then I'll hate you."

"That's a crazy thing to ask for!! You don't see many villains like that even in shonen manga!!"

"To me, what you wanted me to do is just as crazy."

The blunt retort silenced Subaru.

"Got it? Even if you were as slow-witted as a snail, a big idiot who can't even pick a banana hanging in front of his face, or even someone who bragged about harming yourself on some big high-profile blog..."

"I ain't that slow-witted or stupid..."

"But even if you were slow-witted, an idiot, or a moron, I wouldn't hate you or abandon you. That's how it should be, right? I'm your father, and you're my son."

Exhaling in exasperation as he spoke, Kenichi made a *nggh* sound as he stretched his back. When he sat, and Subaru, dumbfounded, gazed up at his father, Kenichi closed one eye.

"It's my son's twisted nature to be just short of dumb, just shy of an idiot, and on a straight line toward being a moron. If you really want, I can smack that out of you by force, but..."

"..."

"It seems like you got up again after breaking down to the point that I don't need to."

Perhaps Kenichi had seen something in Subaru's face. His words made Subaru slowly get up. When father and son faced each other head-on, the son's expression made the father moisten his lips.

"This morning, I thought *You've changed from before all of a sudden.* What happened to your face?"

"...I told you. I found a girl I like."

A silver radiance led Subaru Natsuki by the hand.

"Besides, there was a girl who said she would love even a guy like me."

A warm, blue light gently pushed on Subaru Natsuki's back.

"Those girls, they don't know me as the son of Kenichi Natsuki. When I'm with them, I'm just Subaru Natsuki... No..."

Shaking his head, he gazed firmly at the father before him and went on.

"I was Subaru Natsuki in front of everyone. All on my own, I worried about being some poster child and ended up crushed by a weight that wasn't even really there. I finally get that now."

"Took ya long enough. *I'm* the central pillar of the family. A guy who didn't inherit the job had better not carry any social burdens like that till you're a full member of society. I'll slap you silly otherwise."

"This coming from a guy who dropped his heel onto my head just now?!"

When Subaru complained again about the painful blow, Kenichi went "Sorry, sorry," smiling without a shred of guilt. Then Kenichi's eyes became tense. "More importantly, you said you found a girl you like, and you said there was a girl who said she likes you… What's up with that? Are you two-timing them? A guy like you…?"

"Whaddaya mean, a guy like me?! To be honest, even I think I'm not qualified! But I can't help it! So I have two number one stars, what's the big deal?!"

It was unforgivable no matter how he might frame it, but at the moment, those were Subaru's honest feelings.

He loved Emilia. He loved Rem. They had given Subaru the strength to stand, to walk, and to face his own past, even in front of Kenichi.

The light that the pair gave off rivaled the starry sky Subaru had once had above his head.

When Subaru was outside his room, unexpectedly invited to another world, he became desperate, suffered pain and anguish, cried out in tears, lamented and raged, laughed in delight, and finally obtained a new sky filled with stars.

"Well, it's fine if you can get by without making the two of 'em cry… By the way, don't make 'em cry. If you can manage that, I won't object. Looks like you've got your own way with people."

"If I had that, my high school debut wouldn't have been such a black stain on my past. I can't do it like you, Dad."

"Do you really think that? You're my son, y'know. Besides, seems like you've got a bunch of misunderstandings about me, but that one's the worst, I figure."

"That?"

As Subaru inclined his head, Kenichi wagged a finger atop his crossed arms.

"Yeah. I'm all bouncy like this in front of you and your mom, but Daddy completely behaves according to time, place, and occasion, okay? Maybe you wouldn't know it because I'm always in full-throttle family-love mode in front of you, but what, you think Daddy can pull an act like that and it'll just work on everyone...?"

"Wait, wait, hold on..."

"Ain't it obvious? No one wants to get close to a guy who's that high tension the first time you meet him. That's why you've gotta keep your collar straight until you get along better. You've gotta wait a while before you undo the buttons. If you start in April, gotta hold out until the end of June for that."

*The Shocking Truth: Father Revealed to be a Man of Common Sense and Appropriate Conduct.*

Ignorant of this until now, Subaru had been shallow enough to believe he could just mimic his father to become a popular guy.

"Why'd I agonize for all that time, then...!"

"Aww, don't worry about it. It's my fault for not noticing how much you looked up to me because I'm simply that awesome. Sorry that I'm just too big a presence in your life!"

"Even though it's true, I really don't feel like acknowledging it!!"

Patting the lamenting Subaru on the shoulder, Kenichi did what he always did: step on the naive parts of Subaru and grind them underfoot.

As he quipped at his father, Subaru felt something hard and heavy inside his heart fade away and vanish. The dark recesses were brightening with the approach of daybreak, and his vision opened to greet the dawn.

Subaru had confessed that he was conceited and self-serving, and yet the result was only relief.

Facing his past like that was making a statement: parting ways with his weakness and embracing what he wanted for himself in the future, his current self could walk forward with pride from now on.

That was why—

"Ha-ha-ha. Don't blush so much. You're still my son with my blood in ya. I'm sure you've got it in you to be half as cool as I am."

"Only half, eh? Normally, your genes get refined as you spend time in the world, right?"

"But half of you comes from your mom, y'see. Even if you've got my coolness in ya, the Nahoko part cancels it out, so I don't feel like I can expect much from the final judgme—"

"Sorry, Mom, he's got me there!"

Unable to stand up for his mother, who wasn't present, Subaru put his empty hands together and apologized. Laughing at the sight, Kenichi let his shoulders sink in exasperation as he moved on.

"This should lessen the burden on your shoulders a bit. The rest is talk about the future. It's all ahead from here."

"Ahh, yeah. Err, I really am sorry for causing you all that tr—"

"If you feel sorry for it, just spend a proper amount of time paying us back. You're the oldest son, so you'd better take real good care of me and your Mom later in life."

—When those words were spoken to him, Subaru was unable to move.

"..."

He'd had the resolve to apologize for how he had been to date. He'd had the determination to confess his current feelings.

These things, he had accomplished, finally dissolving that which had haunted Subaru for many long years, making him think he could face his father and mother again with sunny feelings.

He'd confessed everything about himself to date—

"Ugh!!"

But the instant the conversation broached "from there on," what permeated Subaru's entire being was—

"...I-I'm sorry..."

*　　*　　*

"Subaru?"

"I'm s…I'm so…I'm sorry…s-sorry, sorry…shorry…!!"

From in front of him came Kenichi's bewildered voice. But Subaru didn't see his face.

The flood of tears pouring forth clogged Subaru's vision, making the contours of the world vague. He covered his face with his palms, desperately trying to wipe the overflowing tears. However, as much as he tried, the tears were unending. They wouldn't stop. He couldn't stop them.

"I'm sorrrryyy… I-I…can't be together with… I'm so…s-sorry…"

He'd realized it.

Somewhere in his heart, he'd realized it long before.

He'd been invited into another world. The first instant the dazzling light of its sun shone down on him, making him squint, it had been like a revelation, and somewhere deep inside, Subaru had *known*.

He'd probably never return to his own world again.

His parents had raised him well enough for him to find the strength to repent before his father like that, confess the dark emotions roiling inside his chest, and yet gain forgiveness. All that was underpinning his resolve to walk forward once more.

"But in spite of that, I…haven't given anything back… I'll probably never see you again… I'm sorry, I'm sorry.

"…I'm sorry. I'm shworry. I'm sorry."

The tears would not stop. There, that moment, ferocious emotions seemed to churn inside him.

Yet even so, Subaru remained standing, not crumbling to the ground. Here, there was someone who held Subaru as he cried.

Supporting his son, now almost as tall as he was, he patted Subaru's back with his big, strong palms like he would for any crying child.

"…Goodness. No matter how much time passes, you're still a high-maintenance son."

6

"You've calmed down?"

"—Yeah, sorry. I really caused you a lot of trouble."

"Ya sure did. Look at my shirt. I've got tears and snot all over the middle of it. I can't walk around and have the neighbors see me like this, it's embarrassing."

Subaru was no longer crying when Kenichi flicked his forehead with a finger, the corners of his mouth curling into a smile. With that grin on his face, he gazed at Subaru who, after bawling his eyes out, wore an expression that was equal parts sad and apologetic. Kenichi sighed as he spoke again.

"I'm not sure what you were sobbing like that for, but it's embarrassing, so I'll keep it a secret. Be grateful to me for that at least."

"...Yeah. I'm grateful. Truly, from the bottom of my heart, more than anyone in the world."

"If you put it that way even I'm gonna blush..."

When his father scratched his own face with an embarrassed smile, Subaru lowered his listless gaze. Kenichi's shoulders sank when he saw his son's demeanor. Then he waved as if shooing a fly away as he pushed on.

"OK, crybaby, head home already. Daddy's still in the mood to stroll around a bit, so I'll head back after a little detour. I'll get weird looks if I'm walking around with a guy crying like you."

"...They'd wonder what in the world that father and son are doing at their age, huh?"

"Damn right they would. If I go back home with you together now, I'll get embarrassed by weird rumors between my friends, so..."

"You know, those are, like, famous last words, so watch out, okay?"

Poking fun at his father's statement reflexively, Subaru felt painful nostalgia running through his heart. Gritting his teeth and biting it back down by force, Subaru went, "Later," raising a hand Kenichi's way. "I'll head back first, then. Just make sure the cops don't stop you for anything, 'kay, Daddy?"

"Sorry, I ain't biting on that joke. Everyone round these parts knows me already."

"I wasn't joking."

Once again, he was saved by his father's unchanging demeanor. Subaru hated himself for that.

Just how much did he crave the chance to depend on and wish to be indulged by others? He really was incorrigible.

"…"

He didn't want to show Kenichi such weakness any longer.

Taking a single, deep breath, Subaru then turned his back on his father, setting his mind on becoming a stronger person. At that rate, he was set to walk out at a rapid pace, departing as quickly as poss—

"—Hey, Subaru."

From behind, Kenichi's voice brought his feet to a spontaneous halt.

"I'm sure you've got a lot of stuff goin' on, so I only have one thing to say to you."

"…"

"Hang in there—I've got high hopes for you, Son."

Subaru had always clenched a worry of betraying his father's expectations without ever letting it go. So to Subaru, his father's expectations were fear itself—

"—Yeah, you can count on me, Daddy."

His back still turned, Subaru extended an arm. He thrust a finger toward the heavens, speaking in a loud voice.

"My name is Subaru Natsuki. Son of Kenichi Natsuki—I can do anything, and that's how it's gonna be. Your son's hot stuff."

"Yeah, I know. I made half of ya, after all!"

"Hee-hee," went Kenichi, his faith-filled, laughing voice showering Subaru from behind.

When he heard this, Subaru's own lips broke into a smile.

Back still turned, he set off.

His knees weren't shaking. His heart wasn't wavering. He simply stared straight ahead as he walked forward.

Behind him was the man he had looked up to for so long. This time, Subaru would let that man watch his back as he walked on.

He did that while thinking to himself how much strength he had needed from others to achieve that one simple thing.

Then Subaru Natsuki continued walking forward, never to stop again.

7

With his arms through the sleeves his freshly ironed white shirt, Subaru put his legs through his good-as-new slacks. Waging a difficult battle, he tied his deep-green necktie in front of the mirror before finally putting on his navy-blue blazer.

"Student Subaru Natsuki, complete... Man, it's been around three months, huh?"

Checking his completed version reflected in the mirror, Subaru breathed out, his face proclaiming that one task was done.

There hadn't been a Subaru wearing his long-sleeved student uniform reflected in the mirror for quite a while. He recalled that tying the necktie of his blazer-type high school uniform every morning had been a real pain in the butt. Flicking a finger off the flat knot of the necktie, he turned his back to his reflection and picked up his schoolbag.

For all appearances, that much, at least, looked well within the realm of perfect preparation by a student preparing to attend high school.

"Unfortunately, it's about time the third homeroom period started. Ain't well within at all."

Scratching his head with a bitter smile, Subaru stretched his hand out a little on his way out of the room. Stopping just before he left, he looked back.

To Subaru, who'd never experienced a change in residence, that room was the only place he could call "my own room." Since entering middle school, he'd spent over five years in that room.

It would be the last time he saw that place, too.

"_____"

Subaru said nothing. He merely lowered his head in silence.

That single gesture contained five years' worth of feelings in it.

When his long, long period of bowing ended, Subaru lifted his head and departed the room with sunnier feelings. He proceeded to head down the stairs to the first floor, pushing open the living room door. And then—

"Oh my, when you asked me where your uniform was, I thought you might burn it, so I made all kinds of preparations…all for nothing, it would seem."

"Your son asks where his uniform is and the first thing you think of is burning it? Wait, when you guessed I'd burn it, your 'preparations' meant getting sweet potatoes and sausage skewers ready…?"

The reclothed Subaru was met by his mother, Nahoko, who seemed quite disappointed her off-the-cuff prediction had not borne fruit. Behind his mother, he saw that she was done preparing for a barbecue in the cramped kitchen.

After parting ways with Kenichi, Subaru had returned home and asked Nahoko where his uniform was.

Having shaken free of his past, her son had made the statement with a sunny look on his face—and *this* had been his mother's reaction.

"I give up on whether it's good guessing or bad, but this angle is definitely not what I expected…"

"Yes, yes, it looks very good on you. The outfit cancels out the foul look in your eyes. You look rather calm…"

"Mom, your current approach is taking all my serenity away from me!"

"—? What are you all riled up about? Hey, want to glug down some mayonnaise with Mom?"

With a mystified look, Nahoko presented the mayonnaise she'd placed on the table. The mayonnaise in the Natsuki residence was somewhat famous to all local mayo lovers.

Kenichi, Nahoko, and of course Subaru employed various mayonnaises, and glugging mayo was a daily sight during mealtime, getting out of the bath, and sometimes even in the middle of the night. Indeed, when Subaru fell into distress from lack of mayonnaise in that other world, he'd used modern knowledge to successfully recreate mayonnaise on that end.

Mayonnaise was inseparable from the Natsuki family. It was a must-have item.

"But right now, I don't feel like..."

"I suppose not."

The mayonnaise had Su written on the lid, marking it as belonging to Subaru. When he gently pushed the mayonnaise offered to him away, Nahoko gave a knowing nod.

"I mean, Subaru, you really don't like mayonnaise *that* much, do you?"

"..."

"You were just licking it with Dad and Mom because we like it so much, weren't you?"

Placing the mayonnaise marked for Subaru on the table, Nahoko murmured thusly in roundabout fashion. Hearing this, Subaru gasped in surprise. He breathed in, virtually wringing out his voice before gingerly posing a question.

"Wh-what basis do you have for...?"

"Well, Subaru. If it was the world or mayonnaise, which would you choose?"

"Er, probably the world..."

"You see?"

"That's a really bad example! Don't go 'You see?' with that smug look! Anyone picking mayonnaise there isn't picking out of love for mayo, but hatred for the world!!"

As he raised his voice at Nahoko's rather off-the-mark view, Subaru's shoulders heaved with heavy breaths as he glared at the mayonnaise on the table—on the inside, he wasn't calm in the slightest.

Whether he was a card-carrying member or not, Subaru had

pride as a mayo lover, enough that if someone asked him to pick between it and a deserted tropical island, he'd pick mayonnaise in a heartbeat.

But if asked the reason he was so hung up on mayonnaise in the first place, he'd have to say—

"I guess I hard-core have a complex for a happy family…"

"You'd slap *super* on it?"

"That'd make it a Super Family Complex aka Sufami, and that just sounds wrong."

Having engaged in such absurd conversation, Subaru let out a long breath with a pained smile.

Then he slowly picked up the mayonnaise atop the table.

"Ah…," Nahoko began.

"Mmm, delicious! Genuine mayonnaise really is way different! Can't enjoy this taste anywhere but my homeland! Over there isn't bad, either, but it's a pale shadow compared to the real deal!"

Wringing off the lid from the nearly full mayonnaise jar, he guzzled it down in one go. The tasty acidic flavor atop his tongue raced through him, with heat shooting down his throat that seemed to burn his chest.

This was the supreme, a-mayo-zing taste that mayo addicts could not help but love.

"Maybe I don't love mayonnaise as much as you two do, but I'm still a genuine mayo lover. I swear on the mayo lids of all the mayo I've licked to this day."

Incidentally, Subaru had kept the lids from his old mayonnaise jars, stuffing them into a corner of his room. They actually numbered 776—

"And this makes triple sevens. I'll have to stick it in my collection later."

"Ohh, congratulations on your third seven. Your father was really happy when he got his fourth a little while back."

"My love's literally incomparable to his!"

Nahoko accepted the empty mayonnaise bottle with an amused

look. His mother's comment made his sense of accomplishment feel somewhat tarnished, but Subaru immediately smoothed over his feelings.

"Well…guess I'd better head off, then."

"Ah, if you're going to the store, I want some cream puffs, so make sure to buy some."

"You see me like this, put your guessing gears in motion, and you say *that*?!"

As he spread both arms out to show off his school uniform, Nahoko went "I'm kidding, I'm kidding" and smiled at her son as she said, "Ah, you're going to school now? Mom's happy for you, but… won't you stand out in a bad way? If you can put it off till tomorrow, why not put it off?"

"Hey, stop putting a damper on your son's enthusiasm like that. Even if others are strict with me, I'm soft on myself and a slacker to the core, you know."

"If you were really like that, your mother wouldn't have such a hard time, Subaru."

When Subaru quipped at his own expense, Nahoko pretended not to get it as she shook her head. Her reply made Subaru narrow his eyes, but Nahoko went "All right then" and straightened her back as she said, "Well then, hold on a second. Mom's going to get her coat."

"What do you mean, wait… Hold on, you're coming with me?! Having a parent go with you to school when you quit being a hermit is, like, a level worse than a humiliation game!"

"I'm not going all the way to school. I'm just going out to the store to buy mayonnaise and cream puffs. What, I can't indulge you that much?"

"Huh?! That makes it sound like I was asking you to come with me?!"

The incomprehensible flow of events made Subaru's eyes bulge. "Yes, yes," said his mother in a perfunctory reply as she headed to her own room. It felt like a prelude to having a parent chaperone him to school for sure.

"No, no... Man, gimme a break here."

As he spoke those words, Subaru's cheeks faintly relaxed from relief.

At that point, even Subaru was aware the reason for his relief was that the time when he'd have to say goodbye to his mother had been pushed a little farther down the road.

8

"It's been a long time since I've walked side by side with you, Subaru."

"I suppose so. We were together when you went shopping at night quite a bit."

"*Sigh.* You know, given the flow of the current conversation, I'm speaking about daytime, not nighttime. You really must pick up on the context and the literary intent."

"Where that subject's concerned, you're the only one I can't accept hearing that from, Mom!"

Nahoko Natsuki was truly bedeviled by one of the world's dullest senses, possessing world-class bad guesswork. This was well understood by both men in the Natsuki family; indeed, it was virtually 100 percent certain that hypothetical or humorous conversations wouldn't work on Nahoko. That said, she herself was unaware of how complete her obtuseness was, which exponentially increased the stress arising from speaking with her.

Even understanding all that, though, Subaru happened to like speaking with his mother.

"I'm glad that it's warm today. What did you talk to your Dad about?"

"Ohhh, there it is, Mom's beginner-level 'first half disconnected from the second half' conversation topic! I know you don't mean anything special by it, but ummm..."

As they walked side by side on the way to school, Subaru tried to wrap his head around the question his mother had posed.

The details of his conversation with Kenichi involved Subaru's confessing his embarrassing internal complexes and bawling his eyes out, but that didn't amount to a proper explanation. Also, he didn't want to say it in those words.

It had been a necessary conversation, but he'd cut himself off from the emotions he imagined were unique to that place. No way in hell was he going to start crying again on a public street.

"Ahh, it wasn't really anything major. Actually, we talked a bit about old times with Mr. Ikeda."

"Ahh, Ikeda, yes. He moved after winning at the horse races, and his young wife there swindled the shirt off his back, so he had to do manual labor until the sun scorched his skin pitch dark, didn't he?"

"The tragic development in the second half of that is news to me!"

"Ill-gotten money really is no good for you. His heart may be in sorry shape at the moment, but his mind is still holding up, so he sends letters."

"So you experienced being stripped bare in an unfamiliar land, Mr. Ikeda... I can relate!!"

Though Subaru had been in a different world rather than a different country, he'd experienced things not so different from what Mr. Ikeda had been through. Though Mr. Ikeda was little more than an acquaintance whose face Subaru had known when he was little, for some reason, he harbored a strong feeling of fellowship with the man.

Subaru inwardly prayed for his good health. Beside him, Nahoko made a *mmm* sound, then said, "So, talking about old times made you want to go to school?"

"Ahh, well...that's the simple version, yeah. There were a whole bunch of triggers making me look back, and that led to it."

"So you stopped trying to do anything and everything just like your Dad, then."

"..."

When Subaru tried to keep things vague, Nahoko spoke with a gentle tone that did not permit him any escape.

A wry smile came over her, making it look as if she was about to break into a hum. The look in her eyes was the only sharp thing about her, but you could never tell what his mother was thinking by looking at her. However, Subaru had the distinct feeling she'd cut him off at the pass.

"You're a hardworking type, Subaru, and you do all kinds of things in haste. Thanks to your father blindly taking interest in so many things, you've had plenty of opportunities… It wore you out, didn't you?"

"M-Mom…how much did you realize I was…"

"Now, now, Subaru."

The true feelings Subaru had continued to conceal, even to himself, had been plain to Nahoko all along.

Subaru was still at a loss for words when Nahoko, pulling slightly in front, turned back to face him.

"It's often said the child looks at the parent far more than the parent thinks."

"…"

"But the reverse is also true. The parent is also always watching the child, much more than the child thinks. Subaru, even your mother has been watching over you the whole time, you see?"

Truly, he could do nothing but gape dumbfounded.

He'd been so convinced he'd kept his inner feelings hidden, but in truth, it had all been in vain. This in spite of the fact that he'd thought himself lonely and miserable with not a single person the wiser.

"I had to put suppositories in you when you were little, so I've seen everything, including the hole in your butt. Mom's even seen your body's intestines, something you've never seen, Subaru."

"Umm, I'm sorry, the conversation was flowing in a good direction, so I really didn't need that information."

Where one's intestines were concerned, that wasn't something one had many chances to see, let alone those of parents or siblings.

Though Subaru had been graced with the occasional opportunity to see his own intestines…

But in any case—

"About the mayonnaise, and the reason for not going to school…"

"If your mother could have done something about that, you can be sure she would have. Mom felt that no matter what she tried, it probably wouldn't work. But…"

Nahoko tossed in a little smile as she stared straight at her son's face.

"It seems like you managed somehow with the help of someone besides your mom or your dad. I think that's a very good thing. I really must thank that person."

"…Yeah, I suppose so. That person saved me from my incorrigible ways. She's the one who told the incorrigible me I *wasn't* incorrigible. That's why I can walk forward like this now."

When Subaru awakened to his own foolishness, she'd accepted him even so, so Subaru was able to stand there and face his past—and his father and mother with it.

"She's an amaaaazin' girl. Almost to the point she really is wasted on me."

"But you're not giving her to anyone, are you?"

"Damn straight. It ain't an issue of being the other's equal. If anyone's gonna do it, equal or not, it's gonna be me. I'll just raise my own worth from here on out."

"Yes, yes—you really are that man's son."

To Subaru, just how much meaning did those words carry?

This was the mother who knew the things inside Subaru of which he'd never spoken a word to anyone. Probably Nahoko had seen right through him. If she knew, and she was speaking those words with that knowledge, then…

"I wonder, if I can really do it right…if I can really have kids with her and do things right…"

"It'll be *fine*. I mean, your mother may be half of you, but if you act half as cool as your father, you'll do all right, yes?"

"You're acknowledging your own genetic inferiority in my body's makeup?!"

"I said you can act half as cool as your father…the other half, why don't you just be yourself, Subaru?"

Unmoved by what Subaru blurted out, Nahoko indicated that the path forward was very simple.

Upon hearing her words, Subaru was dumbfounded, thoroughly beside himself.

"So, Subaru, your mother thinks you will hang in there in your own Subaru-ish way."

"…"

"Incidentally, what happened to your father after the stroll together? Did you ditch him?"

"You ask that now?! Uh-oh, we're up to Mom's intermediate-level 'question that resurrects the past midconversation'!"

If Subaru cordially indulged her and ended up explaining the circumstances under which he'd parted with Kenichi, all his prior work would be undone. In the end, before being forced to speak about his bawling his eyes out, Subaru ignored the context surrounding the words and echoed his mother's words.

"In my own way, huh?"

"Yes. Over the course of thinking, *I wanna be just like Dad*, you'll end up just like Subaru."

Even though he'd ignored the question, Nahoko acted quite satisfied with the conclusion Subaru arrived at. Then his mother headed forward, but her feet suddenly came to a halt.

Having arrived at a fork in the road, Nahoko indicated the path to the right.

"Well, the convenience store is this way, so this is as far as Mom's going with you… Will you be all right?"

"I haven't been…maybe I have been wounded deeply enough for you to worry, yeah."

He couldn't laugh it off as Nahoko's overprotectiveness. Even if Subaru wasn't pathetic enough to completely lose heart, the concern with which his mother gazed at him did not cease. Therefore, to put his mother at ease, Subaru said, "I'm all right. There's some things I need to do and some things I want to do, but I'll chew on 'em all. I don't have even one reason to shut myself in anymore."

"That so? I'm glad to hear that. Good luck, then."

Apparently pleased with Subaru's reply, Nahoko nodded, then headed down the right path with a visible skip in her step. Subaru went down the left path, parting from his mother.

They were going their separate ways. Probably for far, far longer than his mother thought, at that—

"Mom!"

Unable to bear silently gazing at her back and watching her go, Subaru brought his mother to a stop with a loud voice.

His mother's feet, skipping as she sought more mayonnaise, came to a stop; she twisted her hips and looked back. Subaru seared the ever-normal, never-changing image of his mother into his eyelids.

"Ah..."

Goodbye. He needed to say goodbye. But Subaru hesitated to speak the words.

Even if he said goodbye and parted ways there, his mother still had no idea just how long she and Subaru would be apart. With his mother not knowing they would never meet again, Subaru would be spared seeing her cry. He didn't want his final memory of his mother to be her crying face, so was it not best that he leave his mouth shut?

Pulling the wool over her eyes out of consideration for her, and himself—

"There's something I have to do. So it'll be a long goodbye."

—was something the heart of Subaru Natsuki would not permit.

"..."

Nahoko greeted the spoken words with silence.

There, before she could react in some way, Subaru continued his words.

"It's kind of far away, so I won't be able to stay in touch. I think you'll probably worry about a bunch of things. I...can't firmly say

I won't do anything dangerous. If push came to shove, I'd say it's all pretty dangerous, because the girl I've gotta save gets herself in all kinds of dangerous messes."

His mouth moved rapidly. The information he wanted to enumerate, the words he wished to speak, poured out of him.

"I think Dad and Mom are both gonna worry about me a lot. You've worried enough about me where you can see me, and now I'll be somewhere you can't. But I'll be thinking of you no matter where I am, and I'll never forget about either of you..."

"Subaru."

"I'll never think *I don't wanna be Mom and Dad's child* ever again, and I'll never hate myself again. I know those words don't really let you send me off with peace of mind, but..."

"Subaru."

Even Subaru no longer understood what he was saying when Nahoko called out to him from very close.

When he looked up, his mother was standing right before his eyes. And then—

"Subaru—it's all right."

"...Wh-whaddaya mean, all right?"

"I know exactly what you're trying to say, Subaru. So you don't need to try so hard to find the words."

"You...know...? But how...!"

"Because...I'm your mother, Subaru."

There was not a single shred of logic behind the statement. So why did it feel irrefutable?

The backs of his eyes grew hot. He'd sensed the same thing only a few hours before.

Just how many times would Subaru need to bawl like a little child? How many tears had to flow before he could regain an unshakable heart of steel?

"I-I'm like...a little kid here... So lame..."

"If it's lame to cry when you need it, then that makes every single baby born in the world lame as well."

"That's not...what I mean..."

"Yes, yes, I told you, I get it. From Mom and Dad's point of view, you'll be our child no matter what your age, Subaru... When you want to cry, go ahead and cry."

The world began to blur. Tears came running out. Subaru hid his face behind the sleeve he used to rub it so his mother wouldn't see it. Out of respect for Subaru's stubbornness, Nahoko didn't peer any closer.

All she did was slowly stroke the short hair on Subaru's head.

As she stroked him, Subaru straightened his back.

"...Sorry, Mom. In the end, I can't do a damn thing for either of you."

"You know, I didn't give birth to you because I wanted something from you. I gave birth to you because I wanted to give. Subaru, your mother gave birth to you because she wanted to give you love."

How much of this, the very definition of love, Subaru had already received from her was simply incalculable.

"If you really want to do something for Mom, take those feelings and give them to someone else. And if you happen to give that love to a girl you like, Subaru...isn't that wonderful?"

"...Yeah, it's wonderful."

"Of course it is. What your mother says is never wrong."

With a satisfied smile, Nahoko toyed with Subaru's forelocks with her fingers. The feeling of those fingers tickled Subaru, making him smile back at her with his tear-marred face.

"Aw man, I'm super pathetic, just crying and crying..."

"It's fine to cry. Subaru, you cried so much when you were born. At first, everyone cries in an ugly way. A lot of things happen, and you cry in lots of places."

"_____"

"But if, after crying a lot, you end with a smile, everything's all right. What's important is not where you start, or what happens midway, but how it ends."

"So if the results are good, everything's OK, then?"

"You're taking that the wrong way. Consider this homework from your mother."

An opportunity to revise his answer would likely never come.

In the name of homework, she had offered him words of farewell. Accepting them as such, Subaru took them to heart. Surely, the day would come when the answer would emerge, and he would understand it, as if by natural design.

"_____"

It was neither a very manly nor a very valiant farewell scene.

Neither father nor mother—faced with a son who'd holed up for so long before saying goodbye while unable to even say where he was going—had spoken a word of resentment; instead, they were able to send him off with smiling faces.

For him, this place and his parents who were both too good for him—they were things he loved.

"—Well, I'm headin' off."

"Mm-hmm, go ahead."

Turning his head back at the end, he forced his cheeks to move and make a smile. Leaving that awkward, smiling face behind for his mother, Subaru turned his back to her and walked forward.

The commute to school would be anticlimactic. After the fork, all he had to do was go straight down the road, then up a hill, and then the school campus would come into vi—

"Ah, that's right. Subaru, Subaru, I forgot."

Then, just when he was all hyped up to get going, a scatterbrained voice called out to him from behind.

Subaru, worried about what the very, very end might bring, turned to see his mother raise a hand as she said, "Come back soon."

Then, with a little wave of her hand, his mother spoke those words with a pleasant smile.

The last night before he had been summoned to another world, before heading out to the convenience store, his mother had surely seen Subaru off the exact same way.

But at the time, Subaru, perhaps being in a sour mood, had said nothing, simply opening the door, and...

"_____"

This was the last chance for him to wipe away his regrets from that day.

His mom's advanced-level conversation piece was, "No matter how many detours you may take, you will always arrive at the right answer in the end." The instant he remembered that, a genuine smile, not a forced one, broke out as he called out to her.

"—Be back soon!!"

9

At the school campus, he didn't see a single student, or teacher, or anyone.

When he headed from the entrance to the foot locker, he opened the ill-fitting door that had remained closed for a while. He switched from outdoor shoes to indoor shoes, then walked into the linoleum-floored corridor.

Third year, sixth class, seat twenty-two. That was Subaru Natsuki's spot in school.

The classroom for third-year high school students, the senior class of the school, was on the first floor. His own footsteps echoed down the silent corridor as Subaru wasted no time heading to his own classroom. Then he stood in front of the door and took a deep breath.

"…"

Putting his hand on the door, he slid it sideways, opening it wide in one go. That instant, Subaru, blatantly arriving so very late, had reproachful stares converge on him from all over the classr—

"—I must say, you came far sooner than I expected."

No such thing happened.

When he surveyed his classroom after so long, the seats, including Subaru's own, in the back row and against the window, were empty everywhere he looked—save a single seat filled in the very center.

Then the individual sitting in that seat turned toward Subaru, seat and all.

"Welcome— Tell me, what did you gain from the time you spent facing your own past?"

Stroking her own white hair, such was the question that the Witch of Greed posed to him, her eyes filled with inquisitiveness.

# CHAPTER 5

## THE FIRST STEP FORWARD

1

The white-haired girl remained seated in her chair in the middle of the classroom as she gave a wry, charming smile.

Receiving her gaze upon him, Subaru leaned his upper body into the corridor, checking until he reconfirmed there was no one else around. Then he turned back toward the classroom once more, scratching his head.

"First, there's something I want to tell you…"

"Mm, you may speak it. I am very interested in whatever you might be thinking."

"That school uniform really looks good on you."

The Witch's eyes had an inquisitive glint as Subaru pointed and conveyed his impression.

For a moment, the Witch blinked at that impression, and then she gave a burst of irrepressible laughter.

"Ha-ha! Thank you. That makes it well worth rummaging through your memories to reproduce it. These clothes are seared into your memories particularly strongly. Perhaps you are rather fond of them?"

The girl—Echidna—rose from her seat, grasping the hem of her skirt as she twirled around on the spot. The sight of her white hair swaying down her back made her look like nothing more than an attractive teenage girl.

She wore a gray skirt and a navy-blue blazer. The red ribbon adorning her breasts marked her as a student of the same grade as Subaru, providing a vivid contrast to the white shirt underneath.

"It's just that I like longer skirts more than short, personally. Long skirts twirl around for longer, so it tugs at your thoughts even stronger that way."

"I see. Well then, I must ensure that my skirt twirls for longer the next time."

"Not that there's gonna *be* a next time! Also, it's not as if I really like everyone wearing that outfit. Here, it's just what you have to wear. It's as obligatory as a knight's dress uniform."

Echidna giggled at him, looking like she only took his explanation half seriously. Humphing through his nose at her, Subaru sat down in the empty chair in front of Echidna, turning to face her.

"I really thought you would be more surprised…"

"If you meant to hide it, you should've put more effort into the background. This goes for the commute to school, too, but there isn't a single adult or child inside the whole school, and that's impossible."

Even if he'd reasoned it was late afternoon of a normal day, the world simply felt too bereft of human presence. It was as if the world had been stripped of everything that was not useful information from Subaru's perspective.

"This world's way too convenient from my point of view… What's with this place? I was just entering the place called your tomb, and then…"

"You entered my tomb, possessing the qualifications to do so. Therefore, the trial began. That is all. Did you not hear the words? 'First, face your past.'"

Echidna, replying to confirm Subaru's impressions, crossed her hands behind her back as she tilted her head.

The beautiful girl's hair swayed with the wind, a gentle, cool breeze blowing into the classroom as the school uniform on her casually melted away. Sensing that each of her nonchalant gestures was a trap she had laid around his heart, Subaru consciously averted his gaze from her.

"It's gradually…coming back to me. What did you do to the memory of when we first met? I completely forgot about you until the moment this trial was underway."

"I told you, did I not? You are forbidden to speak of having met me at my little tea party to anyone else. It was faster and more reliable to affect your memory than trust in the tightness of your lips. Ahh, I would like you to relax… I did not play around with any other memories. I would never do such a banal thing."

"…What basis do I have to believe what you just said?"

"Perhaps your understanding of a Witch's true nature? I am the Witch of Greed, lust for knowledge incarnate."

Echidna crossed her arms as if embracing her own elbows, leaving Subaru unable to read what rested within her black eyes.

Whether to trust the Witch felt like a stupid question that did not require any elaborate thought. He'd already undergone terrible ordeals at the hands of the Witch of Jealousy and the Cult that worshipped her. The same went for Echidna.

"But first I want to set you straight about something. The fact is, you're the one who gave me the qualification for the trial."

"Set me straight, you say? Somehow, that sets my heart just slightly aflutter. How strange… I feel slightly elated that you would speak to me in such a manner.

"All I did was to upgrade you from an unpalatable thing to a maybe-unpalatable thing."

When Echidna's smile deepened, Subaru responded by tossing words her way that seemed intended to fend her off. "Tch," went Echidna, tapering her lips as her almond-shaped eyes gently narrowed.

"Everyone harbors regrets from their past. Living day to day makes it impossible to exist without regret—regret is a function built into all people."

"Don't put it pessimistically like that. That regret thingy turns into reflection, reflecting on yesterday lets you scrape by today, reflecting on today lets you bust through tomorrow. That's a function built into people, too, isn't it?"

"—Precisely!"

The air audibly leaped; this was caused by Echidna, speaking in a strong voice, bringing her hands together in a powerful clap. She drew close to the surprised Subaru, her face approaching so close that they could share breaths, opening her mouth as if to press him for more.

"Such a simple observation engenders what is, in the end, a minor difference. But which answer one chooses greatly affects whether one views the past optimistically or pessimistically. Most view the past pessimistically, repudiating the path that has led them to the present. And in that repudiation, they avert their eyes, never closing the lid upon what has happened."

"Um, your face is...close...!"

"Such a thing cannot be helped, for the you of yesterday was infinitely ignorant compared to the you of today. The you of now is at an absolute deficiency of knowledge compared to the you of tomorrow. In the sum amount of knowledge, and in the total number of memories, the past is inferior to the present, and the present is inferior to the future. That is a fact!"

Paying the overwhelmed Subaru no heed, Echidna spoke exceedingly passionately, punctuating her speech by strongly slamming both hands onto the desk.

"Accordingly, when people face the past, they sift through hesitation, bewilderment, anguish, and sorrow, all in search for an answer. I shall affirm whatever answer they arrive at as a result. I shall find no fault in any answer, for it is proof that you have faced your past, absorbing it and using it as your cornerstone as you overcome it."

"...So that's the objective of this trial? Huh, mission accomplished, I guess?"

"Facing your own past can mean accepting or rejecting it. What is important is arriving at an answer. One cannot overcome the trial with fear, anger, or cowering. However, I extol those who have either accepted their past or made a clean break with it. For that, I shall offer as many opportunities as one might desire... That is this trial!"

When Subaru took this as meaning he'd passed, Echidna made that powerful declaration, raising her clenched fist. Immediately afterward, Echidna audibly gasped as she came back to her senses, her cheeks reddening as she cleared her throat and said, "I became a t-trifle too excited. I am sorry for the unsightly display."

"I don't really mind. I did get to smell your breath a lot, but it smelled like citrus fruit. More importantly...from what you're saying, I passed the conditions for clearing the trial, right?"

"I believe you have displayed sufficient results for me to declare that this portion is finished."

Echidna touched a hand to her chest, her face full of satisfaction, like one savoring the aroma of luxuriant black tea.

"In regards to your trauma and your lingering feelings of guilt toward your past, you have found an answer to both. This, I wish to praise with thunderous applause."

"One portion... Wait, you saw me bawling my eyes out, didn't you?!"

"So sowwy, before I knew it, even my eyes were moist."

"Shaddap!! Don't tell a soul, it's embarrassing!!"

Subaru couldn't keep his cool at her being a Peeping Tom in regards to his farewell with his parents, both longing and regret bared. Her inquisitiveness that instant was a slight against Subaru's family.

"But what a pity...it seems you already had your answer for facing your painful past."

"Ahh?"

"I welcome any answer. But it is my belief that an answer means more when one must take an excessive time to arrive at it. I was hoping that you would arrive at your answer as a result of racking your brain...but it would seem the trial unfortunately came too late for you to amuse me to the fullest, more's the pity."

Echidna made a morose sigh. Knotting his brows at her words, Subaru slowly realized it for himself.

If Echidna's desired outcome for the trial was for Subaru to face his past trauma in the form of both his parents, overcoming that past after much agony, he could only give his condolences.

"A girl told me, a totally helpless no-good guy, that I'm her hero. That's why I've already accepted how much I come up short. I don't need to face my past now to teach me *that*."

"So you resigned yourself to it in a different manner. It is not at all amusing that this has gone contrary to my will. Should you meet that girl on the outside, I would like you to convey that a Witch bears a grudge against her."

Subaru's breath caught at the way she so casually stated that extremely frightening complaint. He knew he was at the limit of his ability to avert his eyes from comprehension he did not wish to accept.

Echidna's presence, the world without people, and her saying she was reproducing a school uniform from his memories—even an idiot would realize that...

"Not that I even need to ask. This world, it really is..."

"Yes, that's right. This is a fictitious world reproduced using completely faithful reliance upon your memories. Therefore, naturally—your real parents remain with no knowledge of where you are and what you are doing, and are no doubt worried about their son, vanished without a trace."

"Really faithful in every way, though? They talked about a whole bunch of things I didn't know about..."

"Did you truly not know these things? Perhaps you saw a letter sent by an acquaintance of your parents once? Did you not meet an old man who knew your father when he was young? Did you truly not suspect even once that this image of your father was at odds with what you believed?"

When Subaru seemed to cling to her, Echidna indulged him, pounding home point after point.

"You thought they didn't know, but in your heart, did you really want to conceal it? Can you truly say you didn't want a fictional father and an idealized mother to know all along, out of the self-serving desire to be loved in spite of them knowing?"

With Subaru cowed into silence, Echidna drew her face close to his, the tenor of her speech gradually diminishing to a whisper as it gained an ever-more-suspicious-sounding ring. Then, when she was close enough to breathe on him, she said, "That is a little too idealistic, a little too convenient—do you not think so?"

"_____"

Echidna gracefully smiled as those soft, seemingly adoring words dug deep into Subaru's heart.

At odds with the age-appropriate appearance she had displayed to that moment, this was the malevolent smile of a Witch. In the face of that captivating smile, infected with a Witch's seductiveness, Subaru closed his eyes and—

"Don't mock my parents out of some half-baked resentment, Echidna."

"…What?"

"I gave my entire answer to *them*. Both my mom and my dad accepted it. I told them everything I hadn't said, and they said everything I wanted them to say: *Hang in there, come back soon.*"

Subaru stood up, put his hands on the desk, and put his forehead to Echidna's. Subaru watched the Witch's black eyes blink in surprise as he pounded his own chest.

"Those voices, those smiling faces…every last bit was what *my* imagination poured into them—they're not vases for you to pour your half-baked ideas into. Don't look down on them. Those are *my* parents."

"_____"

"I told them everything I had to say. I'm not gonna be led astray by words from someone like *you*."

Turning her bladelike words back upon her, Subaru snorted and set his hips down on the chair once more. His brusque crossing of his legs, rough nasal breathing, and hard glare made the Witch look taken aback as she exhaled.

"Goodness, to not leave any room for doubts in the answer you have given… You truly know how to make a little Witch cry."

"Sucks to be you. I reeeally love Mom and Daddy."

He puffed out his chest as he asserted it, though he couldn't quantify just how long it had taken before he could do so.

Echidna greeted Subaru's stance with a resigned shake of her head.

"In a true sense, this trial is over. I hope for great things for the next question."

"Yeah… Er, next question?! The hell, the trial isn't just one thing?!"

"My, did I not tell you when you first entered the tomb? 'First, face your past.' You should have paid more attention to the *first* part…"

"Stop talking like a Japanese language teacher!! And that deceptive face really annoys me!!"

Subaru was shocked at the notification that it would be a longer fight as Echidna leaned an elbow against the desk, forming a mischievous smile.

"The condition for liberating the Sanctuary is to pass the tomb's trial, three parts in total. I am pleased I was finally able to speak to you about this. My chest is aflutter that I have surprised you to quite this extent."

"Yeah, I've got a real lively look on my face 'cause you didn't tell me about this back at the tea party, damn it…"

She'd no doubt been full of frustration concerning the uncooperative visitor arriving for tea with far too little information. Unlike that previous time, he had more he wanted to ask her about, but—

"Either way, you're not gonna hand out cheat sheets on the contents of the trials or how to answer, are you?"

"Of course not. Stealing my fun from me after my death would simply be far too cruel."

"Don't talk about this like some geezer's fun, sheesh…"

Wincing from the witchy reply, Subaru slowly rose from his seat.

There was no longer anything he wished to speak to Echidna about. Nor was there any reason to stay in that place, that fictional world, for long, save for lingering attachment. He'd said his farewells to the regrets in his heart; that was enough.

"Hey, Echidna."

"What is it? Ahh, a grudge to vent, or perhaps you wish to punch me once? Certainly, you have the right to do that much. I know my amusement comes at your expense. But I *am* a woman. At least avoid the fa—"

"Thank you."

"_____"

Echidna's face froze when she heard those words.

The sight of Echidna in shock, eyes wide open and taken aback, felt a little creepy to Subaru as he spoke.

"Even if it wasn't real, even if I didn't really say those things to the two of them, thanks to you, I was able to say out loud what I wanted to tell them. To put it bluntly, even if it's the result of your shitty curiosity, I was able to say goodbye to them— If nothing else, I'm grateful for that. So thank you."

"...You are an incredibly interesting person, one I am no longer able to understand to a degree that is...frightening."

Echidna's reply contained neither jest nor falsehood; rather, it felt as if she was speaking from the heart for the very first time.

After hearing her reply, Subaru shrugged, smiling like a mischievous boy.

"I'm honored to have frightened a Witch. So how do I get out of this world?"

"This world has served its purpose. It has already begun to disappear. Nothing save this building still holds its proper shape—exit the building, and you should find yourself in the tomb where you started."

"Well, that's pretty convenient."

When Echidna's answer prodded him to look out the window, the distant sky was indeed warped like some kind of mirage. Having fulfilled its duty, the false world was vanishing back into a distant dream.

With it went the father who had given Subaru a push forward, and the mother who had sent him off.

"They already taught me the important stuff, though."

The emotions filling his chest and the hot sensations in the backs of his eyes made Subaru rub his eyes once with his sleeve. Then he lifted his face, and there was room for tears no more.

Subaru turned his back to the Witch and faced the classroom's exit to bring that world to an end and—

"That's right, one more thing. It seems like you want me to challenge this trial again going forward...but I can't do it."

"...Meaning what?"

Echidna knitted her refined eyebrows as Subaru paused on the verge of leaving the room, turning only his head back toward her. Subaru lifted a finger toward her, wagging it left and right as he spoke.

"It's not my job to clear the trial and liberate the Sanctuary. This is a commemorative exam, just 'cause I happened to have an exam ticket on me. It'll be a different kid who'll fulfill your expectations."

He remembered Emilia, who had challenged the tomb and had surely undergone the same trial. It was her duty to liberate the Sanctuary. Subaru's challenge had been completely unplanned; he couldn't raise Echidna's hopes.

So he said that last thing, waving his hand toward the Witch he was probably seeing for the last time...

"Will that truly be the case, I wonder?"

Subaru Natsuki never noticed Echidna's deeply suggestive whisper as he was enveloped in white light.

Then he left the world of the trial—

2

The instant he awoke, the first thing Subaru felt was the bitter taste of sand and dust inside his mouth.

"Blargh!! *Ptoo, ptoo!* Some weird rock's in my mouth... *Bleh!!*"

Feeling drool and something else shaped like a rock on the tip of his tongue, Subaru retched as he instantly sprang up. When he surveyed the area around his dirty body, he saw an empty room shrouded in thin darkness.

The cold, chilly air and musty, acrid scent—they reminded him that he was in the tomb.

"That's right, I completed it..."

Now that Subaru was awake, his mind finally caught up as he recalled all that had happened since he collapsed.

He'd been pulled into the trial, had been reunited with his parents, spoke with them, then returned to reality. There didn't seem to be any gaps in his memory from start to finish. He remembered it all.

"Not like I can forget bawling my eyes out like that... Ahh, I'm glad."

Leaving his father and mother was a sad, nostalgic memory, but also the ritual that had hardened his resolve.

Relieved he had not forgotten it, he clenched his teeth as he belatedly recalled why he had rushed into the tomb in the first place—the answer was sprawled on the floor right next to him.

"Emilia!"

Kneeling, Subaru saw Emilia lying on the cold floor beside him. Peering at her face, he confirmed she was breathing. He was initially relieved by that fact, but the pained look on her sleeping face stabbed into his chest.

"—ah, ngh..."

Emilia was moaning, with sweat on her brow, as her face twisted in anguish and fear. Every so often, she shook her head in denial, as if she were desperately trying to run away from something—

"A past you don't want to look at…something you have to face and deal with, huh…?"

Subaru didn't know how much time had passed, but Emilia had entered the tomb long before him. That Subaru had come back first in spite of that meant she was having an exceptionally difficult time with the trial.

Emilia moaned faintly, like she was begging for help, as if ready to break into tears at any moment. The sight of her like that made Subaru's breath catch. Wanting to somehow ease her suffering, he touched her cheek with his finger. That instant—

"—!"

"Emilia?!"

Emilia's slender body sat up fast, almost like she'd been zapped with a jolt of electricity. The dramatic reaction made Subaru reach out with his arms, hugging Emilia against his own chest.

Then, when she shuddered like she was having spasms, he called out to her over and over.

"Emilia! Get it together, Emilia! Emilia!"

"—Wuu... Su...baru?"

"—! Y-yeah, that's right. You can tell it's me? I'm so glad."

Subaru's arms had been wrapped around Emilia while he desperately cried out. After some time, the anguished expression on her face finally eased as she slowly opened her eyes.

She seemed to be coming to her senses, letting Subaru breathe in relief after calling out her name since the episode started.

"This is... Er, I was..."

"Take it slow, don't panic. We're inside the tomb in the Sanctuary. You came in here to fulfill a very important duty...and, er, sorry for taking so long!"

Remembering that he was embracing her, Subaru abandoned his explanation midway and pulled back from Emilia's body. When Emilia hazily turned her head toward him, Subaru scratched his cheek and tried to pick up where he'd left off.

"Emilia?"

"That's right... I began the trial, and then..."

Emilia's thoughts returned to the moment right before she'd lost consciousness, to the test. But her reaction had clearly been abnormal, and the sight of her set Subaru's heart deeply astir.

Emilia embraced her own shoulders, as if remembering the shuddering from mere moments before. Her face was pale, drained of blood, and he could hear her teeth chattering.

"I-it...wasn't me...! I...said it wasn't...me...but..."

"Wait, Emilia? Calm down, please. Emilia, look at me, Emilia!"

"No...don't look at me like that... No, no, no, you're wrong... Don't...blame me...!"

Subaru's voice never registered as Emilia cowered on the spot, covering her face with her palms in denial. Her tearful words turned

into sobs, and her crystal clear voice was so full of grief that it pained his heart.

When Emilia crumpled onto the floor, Subaru still had no idea what had happened.

"It's all right, it's all right. I'm here. You're not alone. It's okay."

As Emilia shuddered in tears, Subaru tried his best to console her, to protect her, to care for her. He gathered her in his arms and gently stroked her back.

During that time, Emilia continued to sob, seemingly unable to hear Subaru's voice.

"...ve me, Dad. Save me... Puck, Puck...*Pucckkk...*"

It was not the man at her side consoling her, but the absent spirit whose name she continued to call.

3

"She finally calmed down a short while ago and is now sound asleep."

Ram whispered the news when she came out of the room after Subaru had questioned her with a glance. Given her considerate demeanor, what had happened inside the room behind her must have been something else.

While relieved at her reply, he wasn't relieved enough not to turn his worried eyes toward the closed door.

"That expression isn't like you, Barusu. Normally you have such a sloppy face. Now that I have seen that somber grimace of yours, I truly have no wish to see it ever again."

"Nobody asked you... Sorry, making you worry about me like that."

Ram reacted to those words with a "Ha!" and walked away. Before following in her footsteps, Subaru bit his lip as he turned his eyes toward the door one last time.

Perhaps repeated regrets over his insufficient strength, his weakness causing failure to pile upon failure, had steeled his heart.

"Ohh? I wonder, is Lady Emilia already weeeell?"

Cutting short his lingering sentiments at the closed door, he chased Ram deeper into the building. When he stepped into the room farthest back, he was greeted by Roswaal, lying upon the bed.

The place was at the back of the building in the Sanctuary devoted to Roswaal's convalescence. From what Subaru had heard, it was actually Ryuzu's house, but it was currently on loan, the needs of the lord of the land being the highest priority.

—Thanks to being able to use that room, he had ended up carrying Emilia, fallen into disarray at the tomb, into the very same building.

"Yeah. Right now she's sleeping in her room. Thanks to Ram, she shouldn't have to see any nightmares."

"I used aromatic tea that acts as a sedative. Normally it would not work, but the Great Spirit is not currently at her side, so..."

After Subaru replied to Roswaal, Ram put a hand on her pouch as she added her words to his. The tea ingredient seemed to be a different one from what Ram had previously used to lead Subaru astray with an illusion; that there were multiple types rather surprised him.

It went without saying that he ought not to be concerned about bad effects inside his body, but—

"I still have this nagging suspicion you've been serving me poison all that time..."

"Too large a dose of any base ingredient for tea will become poison, nothing more. You are a petty man to hold a grudge all this time."

Speaking those words with a composed expression, Ram stood right at Roswaal's bedside. For all intents and purposes, the room was host to a one-on-one meeting between Subaru and Roswaal—no other connected persons were welcome.

"Garfiel dragged his feet, but Ryuzu being so sensible was a huge help."

"Due to her age and senioooority, she has learned the value of discreeeetion. Even Garfiel understands that they cannot achieve their objectives without our cooperation, you see."

Roswaal's words made Subaru recall how they'd looked when

Subaru had parted ways with them at the tomb. The liberation of the Sanctuary was Garfiel & Co.'s cherished desire. If their side didn't cooperate, the other side might resort to force, but—

"If we intend to liberate them, they'll lend us a hand, huh? Damn complicated situation to be in…"

"Because Lady Emilia is with us, our interests are aligned. The obstinacy their side has displaaayed to date should ease… Incidentally, I heard that a follower of yours was preeesent?"

"Follower… Ah, you mean Otto? He's, well, we stuffed him in the Cathedral for tonight. He actually came to the Sanctuary because he wanted to meet you in the first place, Roswaal, but…"

"Buuuut what?"

Roswaal had one eye closed as Subaru scratched his head. The reason for Otto's absence was exceptionally clear.

"We're talking internal camp business from here on. I don't intend to drag a half-outsider like him into our problems past the point of no return."

"I see, a wise decision. It would seeeem that you do not enjoy involving friends of yours in your troubles."

"I wouldn't exactly call us friends, but…well, pretty much, yeah."

Having mulled over and accepted the circumstances, Subaru shrugged his shoulders, making no great effort to deny the point. From there, despite the absence of Emilia, the subject of their discussion—

"How about tonight we hammer out important stuff for this camp that we've been kicking down the road?"

4

"You were the instigator behind the hunt for the White Whale, you dispatched the Archbishop of the Seven Deadly Sins of the Witch Cult taking aim at the mansion and the village, you formed an alliance with Lady Crusch, candidate for the throne. That seems to be your meritorious seeervice record."

Roswaal's white-painted brow wrinkled as the detached tone of his voice deepened.

When Subaru attempted to speak about their internal affairs, it was Roswaal's mouth that summarized the ferocious combat occurring in his absence that Subaru should have spoken about first.

When they were enumerated like that, even Subaru thought his exploits sounded unreal, but he made no effort to deny them; all of it was pure fact.

"I had not asked in detail before the evacuation...but I cannot think the contents anything but fiction."

"I thought you might say that, but there's no point hiding it, and I hadn't boasted about it before! Now come on and praise me!!"

"Yes, yes, good boy, good boy."

"Put some heart in it!!"

In contrast to the serious Subaru, Ram treated him as flippantly as ever. However, the dull edge to the sarcasm behind her words was likely due to her surprise that Subaru had truly done all of those things.

And the same seemed to go for Roswaal, silent as he strove to comprehend those facts.

"These are unexpected, unanticipated results."

Lowering his eyes with extremely deep feeling, Roswaal spoke thus as his breath trickled out.

Subaru, utterly convinced Roswaal would praise him in some halfway frivolous manner, was dumbstruck by his reaction. Then Roswaal fixed Subaru in his differently colored eyes as he said, "Subaru. Do you recall the declaration you made at the beginning of the royal selection?"

"Like I could forget it. Like I should ever forget it. I remember each and every word."

Suddenly, he recalled the abominable memory, and the shame and self-loathing of it scorched his breast.

Even if the numerous people of power and influence in that place had laughed it all off, Subaru alone was not permitted to forget, so that he might never repeat the recklessness, naivete, and stupidity of forgetting what was really important ever again.

But Roswaal responded to Subaru's reply with a solemn nod.

"In that light, I think your meritorious service should be rewarded. You have proven the words you spoke in that place—upon our safe departure from this place, I shall appoint you knight."

"_____"

"Subduing the White Whale with the duchess and taking down an Archbishop of the Seven Deadly Sins are exploits that should be commended. You shall be known as Subaru Natsuki, knight. No one will laugh at you anymore."

In the name of helping Emilia, he'd opened his big, fat mouth as a youth ignorant of his position.

His naive dreams were broken on harsh reality time and time again. He had fallen first into despair, then madness; then he'd cast everything aside as he raced forward with vengeance in his heart, only to be saved by deep feelings of love— These were the events that had brought him to where he was now.

The prestige Roswaal promised would demonstrate all that time had actually meant something.

It would mean everything Rem had done would also be rewarded; though memories of her actions existed in the minds of none, save Subaru himself.

"…If doing so gives meaning to that battle, I…gratefully accept."

"You should be proud of these exploits. With your own power, you have won the right to stand at Emilia's side."

"…It wasn't…my power alone."

Subaru murmured it quietly enough that only he must have heard it. When Roswaal knitted his brows as a result, Subaru tightly closed his eyes for a moment, audibly cracked his neck, then continued.

"You acting serious really throws me off. I'm grateful we can move this talk along, mind you."

"You wouuuund me. Am I not always serious? Besides, I promised, did I not? That I would face you directly the next time."

"...*You* as in me and Emilia. Emilia really should be here, but she's not..."

"Oh myyyy. You are quite mistaken."

When Roswaal averted his face, apparently uncomfortable at being misunderstood, Subaru's breath caught a little.

Roswaal closed one eye as he corrected Subaru's correction, leaving the gaze of his yellow eye alone—that was his tell when he was hiding something deep within himself.

Subaru got a bad feeling when he looked at Roswaal's eye and considered the earlier statement.

"What do you...mean by that? Why did you go out of your way to leave Emilia out of this?"

"Is it not rather oooobvious? Dirty matters should be discussed only between trusted coconspiiirators. I am not so gracious as to include someone I do not fully trust in such a meeting."

"You mean you don't trust Emilia? What the hell are you talking about out of the blue like that?!"

When Roswaal, resting his back against the bed, calmly revealed his opinion, it drove Subaru into a rage. Of course it did. He was practically saying Emilia was not worthy of his trust. He—Roswaal L. Mathers, none other than Emilia's backer in the royal selection.

"You're the one who nominated Emilia for the throne! Where do you get off saying that you don't trust Emilia...!"

Giving in to his anger, Subaru closed the distance between them to say what was on his mind. He violently rubbed his brow with his fingers over and over as if it were a spell meant to convince his head, flush with blood, to calm down.

It was his bad habit to suddenly lose it in the middle of a conversation. Just how much had he run in circles at the royal capital because of that short temper? He focused on deep breathing. *Breathe in, breathe out.* He did this a second time, and then a third.

"...Let's...talk about everything in order, starting with this coconspirator business."

"Very well. Once you understand that point, it should serve as a reply to your earlier misgivings."

Subaru chained down his anger, which made Roswaal appear quite satisfied. Subaru crossed his arms and glared at the man, silently prodding him to continue.

"Now then, first, the true meaning behind my use of *coconspirator* in regards to you…it is quite simple. I wish you to continue providing Lady Emilia aid as you have done to date. Do as much as your feelings dictate until the day she sits upon the throne."

"That goes without saying…but what the hell will you be doing?"

"Naturally, I shall do the same. Lady Emilia shall have my full support for victory in the royal selection so that she may become the ruler of this kingdom. You see, you and I share the same goal. Thus, we are coconspirators."

"If that's all you were planning, I'd just call you an ally. *Coconspirator* means something different."

Gritting his teeth as Roswaal presented his terms, Subaru controlled the tone of his voice. He didn't think Roswaal would invoke the word *coconspirators* if his motives were limited to the proper ones he had just presented. In the first place, there would be no reason to exclude Emilia from the conversation if that were true. Besides—

"What you're saying is full of contradictions. If you seriously wanted to put Emilia on the throne, what's your excuse for slacking off before coming here to the Sanctuary?"

"What do you meaaan by *slacking off*?"

"That's obvious! It was common knowledge Emilia publicly entering the royal selection would set the Witch Cult off on a rampage! Everyone said, 'Oh, Roswaal has to have prepared countermeasures,' so where the hell were they?! If that's not slacking off, what is?!"

Subaru replied to Roswaal's feigned innocence with anger as he pounded home the suspicion he'd wanted to express for some time. Once he'd reached a boiling point, his dissatisfaction had only grown and grown without pause—

"For starters, you hid info on the Witch Cult from Emilia, didn't you? Emilia didn't know a damn thing about the Witch Cult. She didn't understand at all what would happen when she joined the royal selection. If she'd known, everything could've gone differently! None of that would have had to...!"

As Subaru spoke, those hellish scenes came rushing back to mind, hells he had peered into several times over.

The villagers slaughtered, the children cruelly put to death, how Petra's corpse had stripped his mind bare, how Ram's dead body had carved a hole out of his soul, how Rem's death had robbed him of even the ability to mourn, and how Emilia's death—

"...You should have been there. If you'd been there, none of that would have happened. So why...weren't you there...?"

"Barusu..."

The unconcealable pain and anguish in his voice made even Ram's cheeks stiffen.

No tears flowed from him. However, with a disheveled face, Subaru accused Roswaal. Only Subaru, who had seen those hellish scenes, had the right to accuse him.

"If you'd stayed behind and protected everyone...I..."

"But while I was absent, you fulfilled my duty in my place, exploits that would make even a knight's heart swell in pride..."

"—! That's not the point!"

His gratitude for being honored with the prestigious title of *knight* rapidly diminished.

Certainly, being awarded the knightly title gave firm meaning to that battle. However, to the Subaru of the present, that battle, in and of itself, was a symbol of his mistakes. If that battle had never happened—

"Barusu, please, calm yourself."

"Ram...!"

When Subaru unwittingly took a step forward, Ram glared at him from right up close. She shielded Roswaal behind her back, quiet anger resting in her pink eyes.

"Master Roswaal is injured. Even so, he can surely put a stop to any violence from one such as you with a single finger... I shall permit no rudeness when I am present, Barusu."

"You're okay with this? It's the same for you, he left you behind like a sacrificial pawn! Roswaal curled his tail and ran from the Witch Cult! Are you telling me I'm wrong?!"

"I accept that without reservation. Ram forgives all Master Roswaal's deeds, including however she might be treated, or even eventually cast aside."

"Then you forgive Rem being sacrificed for stupid stuff like this, too?!"

The incomprehensible loyalty in Ram's reply set off Subaru like nothing else.

He had avoided the issue several times, telling himself it wasn't the right time, putting off the truth he needed to speak to her about Rem—and how her memory had faded from the world, now existing only within Subaru's heart.

With the master she had served for many years, even with her older twin sister who was her other half, Rem—

"—? I know not of whom you speak, but no other name means anything to me. To Ram, Master Roswaal is everything, and all others come second."

The words Subaru had spat out, giving in to his emotions, were cut down by Ram without the slightest hesitation.

Though Subaru had not planned it that way, her words were solid proof there was no memory of Rem within Ram, presenting him with the painful reality he had repeatedly ignored and avoided.

"_____"

Drained of strength, Subaru retreated a distance greater than the step forward he had made. The sight of Subaru's shoulders sinking made Ram knit her brows, whereupon Roswaal weightily shook his head.

"Ram, stand aside. This conversation is between him and me only. I permit you to attend, but I do not permit you to speak. You understaaand, yes?"

"...Yes. I have no excuse for intruding."

Ram bowed, then attended Roswaal's bedside once more. As

Subaru watched the exchange, he felt something like a breeze blowing through his exceptionally empty chest.

Both of Roswaal's eyes narrowed at the sight of Subaru hanging his head at that desolate reality.

"Tonight, I respond to you in earnest. This is what I have decided. Thaaaat is why I shall respond to the doubts you toss at me with the truth."

"…"

"Why did I conceal information from Lady Emilia that I should have disclosed? Why was I absent from the mansion when the Witch Cult was coming to attack? These questions have a single answer."

Subaru put strength into his neck and lifted up his head. When accepting someone's reply to your suspicions, you at least had to look him in the eye.

As Subaru did so, Roswaal closed one eye and said…

"—I guided events so they would be resolved without me needing to confront the Witch Cult."

"…Huh?"

Subaru was dumbstruck, unable to digest the meaning of the words Roswaal had spoken openly while looking him in the eyes.

When he crunched, chewed, and swallowed the words down, tasting their meaning with his brain, the contents permeated his very soul.

"I don't…get it. Then you mean…what? You ran? You actually did get cold feet when the Witch Cult was coming, and then…? How… could you!"

"Is it truly incomprehensible? That I, among the kingdom's sages, a prominent man of influence…I, capable of a violent rampage even greater than the menace of the Witch Cult, would avoid battle with the Cult?"

"Damn right it is! You of all people could've easily taken care of all of—"

"That is precisely why I did not. Had I resolved the matter, no credit would have gone to Lady Emilia, nor would there be any fame to be won by you, would there? That would have rendered it meaningless."

"Wh-wha...?"

Subaru genuinely couldn't comprehend what was being said to him.

The statement would have been a hundred times better if it had been a joke or Roswaal toying with him. But Roswaal's face showed nothing that could fulfill Subaru's wish; Roswaal kept one eye closed as he continued.

"The effect was tremeeendous, was it not? Indeed, ever since the Witch Cult was driven off, the attitude of the residents of Earlham Village toward Lady Emilia has been the complete opposite of what it once was. She has gone from a Witch beyond their comprehension to the savior whose efforts protected their very lives...and their assessment of you has similarly risen, yes?"

"Y-you... Do you even understand what you said just now...?"

The jolt inside Subaru's throat made his voice quiver indistinctly. However, the sounds that were not garbled made Roswaal cock his head, his lack of comprehension clear.

It was that demeanor that gripped the bottom of Subaru's heart in incomprehensible fear.

Roswaal had essentially said this: His understanding of the menace of the Witch Cult had been in no way deficient. He had anticipated that the Cult would launch an attack. And, so forewarned, he had used the expected disaster for public relations purposes.

But—

"That's just judging by hindsight. It ended up that way, that's all. If you'd resolved it all, Emilia definitely...maybe Emilia and the villagers would still be in the same place. But—!"

He recalled the scene from the previous evening—Emilia exchanging words with the residents who had evacuated to the Sanctuary, where they had entrusted their hopes to her.

Certainly, that scene might never have become reality if things hadn't gone as Roswaal had planned them.

"But that's all hindsight!! Did you even think about how many people would die because you weren't there to save them?! Certainly, the casualties were minimized. I worked my ass off for that! But they weren't zero. People died!"

"Allow me to express my regret for the harm that befell our allies. It is, of course, only natural that our enemies are dead. The Witch Cult force was laid to waste, not a single member surviving. I could not have done it better myself. For this, you seek to apooologize to me?"

"—!! No! No, no, no, that's not it! That's not it at all!"

In revulsion, Subaru weakly shook his head, rejecting Roswaal's words.

Why wasn't he getting through? Why didn't he get it? Roswaal's intent had been just too cruel, too heartless. It was fine to charge straight toward your goal, but couldn't he just *listen*?

But this wasn't simply charging forward. It was as if he was ignoring every obstacle that had fallen upon the roadway before him.

"...If I'd stayed a piece of garbage that couldn't accomplish anything, where would you be then? The result would be that nobody was saved, not Emilia, not the villagers."

As a matter of fact, Subaru had laid eyes upon that result multiple times over. If anything, that result was inevitable.

In most worlds, entrusting the matter to Subaru Natsuki had led to the worst-case scenario.

"—I left it in your hands...because I trusted you."

Subaru wanted to know if that reply was sincere. When he heard it, all he could do was laugh out loud in despair.

"...That means you don't intend to give me a serious answer."

"Perhaps it is not the answer you hoped for, but I have stated the truth. I decided that tonight, I would not deceive you in any way. If I cannot speak of something, I shall say so, and if something is inconvenient, I shall hold my tongue, but I swear to you that no words I have spoken are lies."

Roswaal's words were solemn. However, they invited too much distrust for belief. From the conversations they'd had to date, Subaru had no faith left over to take his words at face value.

Despite Subaru's silent distrust, Roswaal's expression did not falter as he continued.

"I say again: Where this matter is concerned, I made the decision to trust you. I trusted that you would strive for Lady Emilia's sake, that you would exhaust all efforts to achieve an alliance with Lady Crusch, that you would put your life on the line to successfully fend off the attack by the Witch Cult, and thus increase your renown."

"What do you know about me?! You've known me for only two months. Do I look like a man who can accomplish things like that?!"

Subaru was indignant. He was fed up with eloquent, pretty-sounding phrases that only made his ears hurt.

His teeth were bared, his beady eyes grew tense, and Subaru pointed straight at Roswaal as he howled.

"There's no way in hell. When you parted ways with me, I was a piece of garbage through and through. It was only after that I changed from garbage to something halfway decent. What came after was only because it was the only thing left to find inside of me— What did you see that lets you trust me like that?"

It wasn't a discussion. If the other party had no intention of being serious, conversation was futile.

Roswaal's demeanor toward the raggedly breathing Subaru had not changed one iota. Therefore, that gaze itself was his reply. He intended neither to correct Subaru's view nor to state the objective truth.

"...It would seem our conversation for this evening is at an impaaasse."

Roswaal declared the conversation over, almost as if he could see straight into Subaru's inner being. Subaru had no objection, either. At the very least, not until he was ready to engage in a *real* conversation.

"Though your esteem of me has plummeted, I cannot call that a pure disappointment... Incidentally, I think I hardly need to confirm, but concerning tonight, Lady Emilia..."

"I'm not saying a word. Like I could tell her anyway. Besides, whatever you're planning, whether you're laughin' behind whatever face you make or not...what matters now is the result of Emilia's own choices."

Her determination to challenge the tomb's trial, her promise to liberate the villagers urging her onward from the barrier, her resolve toward the royal selection from that point on—Emilia had chosen all these things for herself.

It was absolutely not because she was dancing to Roswaal's tune, manipulated by his shady schemes.

"Though you are governed by anger, within your mind, you correctly grasp the situation. For the sake of Lady Emilia's royal selection, there must be no discord created between her, myself, and the villagers."

"_____"

"Meaning you have become an adult—you are a worthy coconspirator indeed."

"...There's no good death waitin' for you."

"I am aware of this. I shall without doubt fall into hell. Therefore, I must exhaust all efforts to bring my ambition to fruition in this era before that day comes."

Subaru breathed hard at the stifling situation as Roswaal gave him the adoring gaze a predator had for his prey. Subaru returned that gaze in enmity before turning his back.

The conversation was over. He didn't want to spend another instant in the man's presence. But—

"I have one last thing to ask you. I'm not sure you'll want to give me a straight answer, though."

"What is it? My earlier promise, to answer truthfully, remains in effect. Ask whatever you wiiiish."

"It's about Beatrice."

The instant Subaru invoked that name, all composure vanished from Roswaal's face. "Beatrice," he murmured to himself, regaining the aloof, clownish demeanor that had reigned until the moment before. "You pay a great deeeal of attention to that girl. What is it you wish to ask?"

"I had a chance to speak with her before coming here to the Sanctuary, and though she wouldn't tell me much...she said all the answers to my doubts can be found here. If you're in a mood to speak seriously, what do you think she meant by that?"

When their conversation in the archive of forbidden books drew to an end, Beatrice had spoken those words to Subaru with a tearful face. Frederica had also said Beatrice was one of the very few people related to Roswaal with whom he shared his thoughts.

If that was so, then Roswaal might understand just why Beatrice had had that sad look on her face.

"Before I reply to that question, there is something I wish to ask for myself."

"...What, then?"

"To aid Lady Emilia, you entered the tomb. By whatever twist of fate, it seems the tomb's punishment did not go into effect... Did you meet someone within the tomb?"

The question Roswaal posed made Subaru sink into thought for one brief moment.

Despite hearing that it was dangerous, Subaru had rushed into the tomb to rescue Emilia. Though Subaru had, in fact, undergone the trial, he hadn't spoken a word of that to Roswaal.

One reason was that the flow of conversation hadn't given him much of a chance, but the biggest reason was Subaru's lack of trust toward him.

Roswaal had decided to use even the Witch Cult's onslaught to increase Emilia's popularity. If he knew that Subaru had challenged the tomb, Subaru couldn't even fathom what schemes he might come up with this time.

In the first place, it was unclear to whom he was referring. Subaru hadn't met——in the tomb, or anyone else.

"What are you talking about? It was inside a tomb. Like there was room to meet anyone. A zombie, maybe?"

"I do not know what you mean by 'zombi,' but...no, that answer is suffiiicient. Thus, my reply to your question is simple: it is not yet time to speak about the matter."

"Ha! So that's your story in the end. When will you be able to talk about it, then?"

"That depends on you. Though, if possible, I would like tonight's pact to be invoked as soooon as possible."

"—?"

His manner of speech was deeply suggestive, but Roswaal did not seem ready to explain any further.

Thinking back, Subaru felt deeply despondent at how evasive Roswaal had been from start to finish. Everything, even the prestige that came with the title of knight, had been for the purpose of setting up a favorable conversation with Subaru.

"Well then, Subaru. Let us share pleaaasant conversation again."

"..."

Subaru, showered by Roswaal's sarcastic-sounding words even on the eve of his departure, vengefully slammed the door shut.

5

"Subaru?"

Subaru scratched his head at the fact that he'd been addressed by name despite entering the room with great care. When he quietly closed the door and turned around, the girl on the bed—Emilia—seemed to have just awakened from a deep sleep as their eyes met.

"Sorry, did I wake you?"

"No…I woke up a little earlier. I was surprised you were sooo quiet, Subaru."

"Keeping the noise down when I walk has become a habit. But my scheme has been foiled. I was actually thinking I'd play a prank on Emilia-tan while she slept…"

"A prank…? You mean like writing on my face?"

"You got me! I definitely don't have the courage to try a worse prank, either…!"

The way Emilia tilted her head, the thought of other things between boy and girl not even crossing her mind, took the wind out of Subaru's sails. Regardless, now that she'd awoken, he sat by her side and checked the state of everything else.

The color of her face and her breathing were both normal. Her face was cute, too. She'd returned to her normal self without any noticeable issues.

"I'm sorry, Subaru. I reeeally lost it when I woke up in the tomb."

"Eh, ah, that's fine, that's fine. More importantly, I was worried you might have bumped something when you first fell down. It really is a lot easier on both of us if I can watch you without being separated."

"…Yeah, it might well be."

"Mm?"

Subaru, replying in what he thought was his usual flippant tone, narrowed his brows at Emilia's reaction. She lowered her eyes, looking as if she was thinking about something as she clutched Subaru's sleeve.

It was as if she were unconsciously grasping his hand to allay her worries. Subaru stared at the gesture when—

"—? Ah!"

Following Subaru's gaze, Emilia was startled when she realized her fingers were grasping the sleeve of his tracksuit. She proceeded to release her fingers, her face reddening as she waved her hand to and fro.

"I-I didn't mean to. Huh, that's strange. Why did I do something like…"

"My, my, Emilia-tan finally wants me enough to subconsciously reach out her hand. Hey, if you want to rely on me for everything, you can just come out and say it."

"That's…totally not it. My hand probably just…slipped."

"You sure denied that fast, and what do you mean by slipped?!"

Emilia shook her head at the half-joking assertion, wearing a strained, embarrassed smile. Subaru did not press the issue. After all, she didn't seem to want to talk about the worries subconsciously connected to her actions just then.

And naturally, those were related to the trial that night…

"Can I ask you something about the trial? What kind of past did you see inside?"

"—!! Subaru, how do you know about...?"

"If it's tough to talk about, I won't ask about the details. I have a past I don't wanna talk about, too."

"Th-that's not what I... How...do you know that the trial showed me my past?"

As Emilia's violet eyes opened wide, her words made Subaru let an *ah!* out of his throat.

Certainly, no one was supposed to know the details of the test within the tomb before entering, and even then, they would only find out if they were challengers themselves. Of course, Subaru could have just told Emilia that he'd undergone the trial just like she had, but—

"_____"

Looking back at Emilia's trembling eyes, Subaru swallowed the words with which to convey that fact. Given that she was already shaken and discouraged, he feared that telling Emilia he'd taken the same trial, but had overcome it, might push her farther into a corner. Nor was this the only reason not to tell her.

Accordingly, Subaru closed his eyes, pushing the role of the villain onto someone absent from that place.

"That jerk Roswaal was keeping quiet that he knew about the trial. He said something about facing your past, but, ah, I don't really know the details past that..."

"Is that so... Did Roswaal...say anything else?"

"Err, maybe that it's three parts in all, and seeing the past is the first one?"

A barefaced lie, Subaru's reply made Emilia look dispirited. "Three parts...," she echoed.

At least she didn't question Subaru's assertion that Roswaal was the source of the information. In reality, he'd heard it from ——, but he avoided such a problematic explanation.

"Setting the number of problems aside, today's challenge...didn't go all that well, did it?"

"...Mm. So it would seem. I tried hard, but it suddenly ended midway..."

"Sorry, I think that's because I woke you up. Seems being touched from the outside wakes you up. Come to think of it, I feel like I got told that from the start."

"Who...told you that?"

"...Who was it, I wonder."

The creases of Subaru's brow deepened as he tried to wrap his head around it. The thought easily rolled off his tongue, but where had the idea come from? When he thought about it, nothing came to mind, so he put off forming a conclusion.

"Let's switch topics. Tonight was no good. But that just means you can take it again. You can take it as many times as you need to... So the rest is up to how you feel, Emilia-tan."

"How I...feel?"

"I could tell from the look on your face as you slept that it wasn't a warm, fuzzy past. But if it's not you who liberates this Sanctuary, there's no meaning to it... That's what I think, anyway— For that, are you going to challenge it again?"

"_____"

When pressed to choose, Emilia took in a deep breath and fell silent. Her trembling fingers went to her own neck, touching the green crystal that dangled from it...but her only family made no response.

Emilia was hard-pressed for an answer as Subaru watched her, silently awaiting her decision.

If, for example, by any chance, Emilia recoiled from challenging the trial again, too afraid to face her past, Subaru did have an idea.

It just took someone else qualified to do it instead. And that would be Subaru Natsuki. But—

"—Subaru, you idiot."

"Hey, I'll accept any answer you... Wait, what's with the sudden insult?!"

"If you say that with gentle eyes and a gentle voice, there's no way I'll say I can't, is there? I'm not a very smart girl...but even I know that this is my duty."

"Emilia..."

"Don't pamper me. Trust me… Maybe I don't sound very convincing saying that after today, but…"

Right after speaking with such strong resolve, Emilia flushed as she lowered her eyes. However, her words made Subaru exhale at length. "That's not true at all," he said, shaking his head.

Emilia had said she'd do it. Then she certainly would. From all the time he'd seen her, not just that night, Subaru genuinely trusted her.

"Hey, I'm with you for makeup tests or anything else. I trust you. I'll wait."

"Mm, thank you."

When Subaru smiled at her, Emilia finally regained the strength to send a charming smile back at him. It was a small, fleeting smile, but the resolve it contained made Subaru lose himself in the sight of it for a moment.

"But the one thing that pains my heart is…the trouble it must be for the people of Earlham Village…"

She'd promised them she would definitely liberate them from the barrier and return them to their village. She hoped that they were not people to shun someone upon learning of her failure, but she couldn't help its weighing on her mind.

But Subaru had an idea where that was concerned.

"Can you let me handle that part?"

"You have something in mind?"

"I do. I don't plan on causing Emilia-tan or the villagers any trouble."

"…Understood. I trust you, Subaru."

When Subaru thumped his hand on his chest, Emilia narrowed her eyes and immediately nodded. Subaru was a little surprised at the instant decision, whereupon Emilia gave a tiny, pleasant smile.

"As if I'd doubt you now, Subaru—I trust you."

"…"

Those words left Subaru quietly closing his eyes, thinking hard in his own mind.

Emilia's trust was a product of Subaru's actions to date—and even if those had proceeded according to the sketch drawn by Roswaal's own hand, it would not be that way from here on.

"—No way I'm gonna let everyone dance on top of your palm."

He would not permit Roswaal's will to intervene as it had so far.

And, there in the Sanctuary, it was Subaru Natsuki's job to prove it.

6

Three days later, Subaru executed the plan that he had mentioned to Emilia.

"I must say, I am impressed you managed to persuade Garfiel."

Otto shared his thoughts while Subaru checked the condition of the dragon carriage with Patlash, his favorite land dragon, hitched to it.

Subaru's back was turned as he responded with a "Yeah" before continuing. "It took a little time, but it's a big help that I somehow got through to him."

"Though from my perspective, it was difficult to believe he would listen to what we had to say…"

"…You might be a merchant, but you're not a good judge of people, are you?"

"I suppose not! Having associated with all kinds of company to date, and never earning even the slightest bit of profit without a great deal of toil, it's enough that even I doubt my own eyes!"

Otto responded to Subaru's barb with a shrill, resentful comment of his own. But Subaru understood why he felt that way. To begin with, the point of taking Otto to the Sanctuary was that Subaru could fulfill his promise of granting him an audience with Roswaal.

"And yet, to think I would go three, no, four whole days without meeting him once, only to return to the village where we started…"

"I'm sorry about that. But you won't be able to talk to Roswaal until the heat dies down. If you want me to introduce you with a ton of sparks flyin' in the air, I can force the issue, but…"

"No, no, no! Please, there's no need! I do *not* want to become involved in a strange situation like that!"

Otto's recoiling like that had been partly responsible for the delay in introducing him and Roswaal.

Scratching his cheek, Subaru focused on what lay ahead of their dragon carriage—the other carriages for evacuating the villagers assembled at the entrance to the Sanctuary. There were a total of fifty villagers and cooperating traveling merchants in seven dragon carriages, all moving in one rather large convoy.

Subaru and Otto had arranged to bring them along on their return to Earlham Village.

The condition that was required for it to happen—that the barrier enveloping the Sanctuary be lifted—remained unmet, but...

"Lady Emilia ain't got a choice. From the moment she stepped inside the barrier, she either lifts it, or she ain't leavin'. They ain't got no value as hostages no more, so go ahead and return 'em to their village..."

"—Garfiel."

As Subaru watched the villagers prepare to embark, a figure with blond hair and a bad attitude approached. The man who always had a dangerous look in his eyes glanced over, glaring at Subaru and Otto as they stood side by side.

"Waaah!"

That gaze made Otto let out a small cry as he meekly retreated to the other side of the dragon carriage. Even considering the impact from their first meeting, it was quite an attitude.

"Don't boss him around too much. He's a super-important... Wait, why is he important again?"

"If you're wonderin' out loud, how the hell am I supposed to know? Besides, him actin' like a chicken is his problem."

Garfiel crinkled his nose as he sourly folded his arms. But though his actions were frequently crude, Garfiel was a man unexpectedly attentive to details. Subaru had learned that thanks to having come into contact with him repeatedly over the last few days.

"Who'd have thought you were taking care of the villagers who'd evacuated..."

"What's that? Can't be helped, damn it. Not like I can have the old hags pushin' themselves too hard, and a lot of 'em don't wanna get friendly with strangers either... The less trouble the better."

"Meaning my suggestion put us in the same boat?"

"Pretty much. 'It's the Maringo Island way' and stuff."

Subaru was tempted to ponder how he was managing to hold such a normal conversation with Garfiel. But Subaru ignored that and lightly bowed his head to Garfiel once more.

After all, without Garfiel's cooperation, the freeing of hostages wouldn't have been possible.

"Cut that out, it's embarrasin'. I told you not to bow your head an' stuff."

"Even if you say that, I have to do this much. I know you guys have your own circumstances, and you accepted this because it suits your own interests, too, but..."

Welcoming strangers into the Sanctuary meant exhausting some resources.

The settlement did have its own fields, and Roswaal had arranged for the regular delivery of supplies, but a prolonged emergency situation wasn't good for either population.

That was why Subaru had brought the matter up with Garfiel, who had in turn spoken with Ryuzu and the other residents, resulting in that morning's freeing of the hostages.

"That's why I'm grateful. The villagers, their feelings are a little mixed, but they're happy, too—besides, we really stuck it to Roswaal."

"Yeah, that makes me feel good, too. I'll accept yer thanks, then."

When Subaru gave a mischievous grin, Garfiel revealed his fangs and let out a hearty laugh.

Not only had the proposal been Subaru's idea, but Roswaal had approved when he had been informed after the fact. From what Subaru had picked up through Ram, that had to have given Roswaal plenty of heartburn.

Ever since the nighttime discussion a few nights earlier, Subaru had stubbornly resisted meeting Roswaal again. At the very least, he didn't intend to forgive Roswaal until the latter made a proper apology.

That was unfortunate for Otto, but—

"Subaru!"

Just when there was a tiny break in the conversation, a voice clear as a bell called out Subaru's name. When Subaru looked back, Emilia was waving as she walked toward them.

"...We'll talk again later. When we're on the road."

Noticing her approach, Garfiel whispered only that into Subaru's ear before moving off from his side. He walked off with an exaggerated swagger as Emilia arrived, cocking her head to the side as she posed a question.

"Err, did I butt into your conversation with Garfiel?"

"Oh, that's all right. It's not like it was anything important, and Emilia-tan's my top priority."

"I'm reeeally happy to hear that, but right now the villagers should be your top priority."

When the corners of Emilia's eyebrows lowered as she gave a conflicted smile, Subaru nodded in reply to her request. Then she turned her mind's attention toward the villagers' dragon carriages, where preparations to return were underway.

Subaru had a strong grasp on the complex feelings Emilia harbored inside.

"I really do think lifting the barrier and heading out like a big parade would be great, but..."

"...I'm sorry. It's because I haven't overcome the trial even after several days. But I don't think it's right they shouldn't be reunited with their families because of me."

Her voice full of feelings of self-reproach, Emilia bit her thin lips in apparent regret over her own powerlessness.

—In the three days since they'd first challenged the trial, the tomb's methodology had become clearer bit by bit.

Just as Subaru had remembered, it was possible to undertake it any number of times. However, it could only be undertaken once per night. Emilia had made an attempt every night without rest—only to be met with failure each time.

When night fell, Subaru watched Emilia confront her past at the tomb, and he saw the pain break her heart, causing her to return tearful and haggard.

Repeated painful experiences had resulted in a rising pile of failures. Moreover, he couldn't even begin to imagine how much her spirit had been worn down in the process.

"Anyway, you can't get impatient and force yourself. Since ancient times, no one has managed to accomplish anything good with those two things. I'll get the villagers back home and come back here right away...but it still won't be till tomorrow that I can make it. You can put off tonight's challenge if you want, you know."

Subaru couldn't remain in the Sanctuary to be at Emilia's side that night. Because of that, Subaru had proposed several times already that she take a break from challenging the tomb. But Emilia firmly shook her head this time as well.

"It's all right. It's true I'm...a little impatient...but I'm the one who said I'd do this. I don't want to disappoint the villagers or the people of the Sanctuary."

"...Gotcha. All right, then. I won't say any more."

"Thank you. Also...though you should also be mindful of the villagers, be mindful of Frederica."

Now that they'd checked off what each had to do, Emilia worriedly added that at the end.

Her worry was rooted in their lack of knowledge about where Frederica stood. If Ram's warning was anything to go by, Frederica was involved with those opposed to the liberation of the Sanctuary. Subaru hadn't the faintest idea how she'd treat him and Otto upon their return to the mansion.

"—If Frederica bears Lady Emilia ill will, the mansion should be an empty shell right about now."

"...Huh? Ram? What'd you come here for?"

Ram, slipping through the line of dragon carriages, came over and promptly joined their conversation.

Much like with Roswaal, Subaru wasn't feeling particularly positive about her. Considering the issue of Rem and her behavior—namely her taking Roswaal's side—Subaru was standoffish with her.

Ram feigned ignorance of the discord with Subaru, narrowing her almond-shaped eyes as she spoke.

"Greetings, Barusu. I have merely come out of my way to see you off in Master Roswaal's stead. As a lord, it pains him greatly to not be present as his people begin to depart."

"You've got some nerve to be…"

"In addition, he sends a message to Barusu for his return to the mansion. If Frederica concerns you, I believe it is all the more important you should hear it."

When Subaru clicked his tongue at the preamble, Ram dangled the existence of information he could not afford to dismiss in front of his nose. Truth be told, it was very difficult for Subaru to endure going along with it, but…

"What should I do, then, if Frederica is a concern?"

"Lady Emilia is so forthright. You should learn from her, Barusu."

Ram employed Emilia to sarcastically pester Subaru, clapping her hands with excessive glee. Then, as they caught their breath, Ram continued in a quiet tone of voice.

"He said that if you are concerned about confronting Frederica, rely upon Lady Beatrice."

"Rely on Beatrice? Hey, listen closer when people explain stuff. That's a majorly high-difficulty thing in itself. In this situation, just meeting her isn't simple at…"

"It is you who should listen, Barusu. Please be quiet until I am finished— Certainly, it is not easy to speak to Lady Beatrice. That is where Master Roswaal's message should come into play."

The grave accents of her voice made Subaru swallow his words and indicate for her to continue. His gaze made Ram lick her lips before she spoke.

"He instructed, upon returning to the mansion, to say this: 'Roswaal said ask your questions.'"

"Questions…?"

"Ram does not know the details. However, Master Roswaal stated that once this reaches Lady Beatrice's ears…the situation shall change. I came only to deliver this message to you."

Ram made that declaration with a composed look, showing that she was not of a mind to entertain any questions about the matter. Subaru mulled over her demeanor and the words she had spoken. In the end, he grimaced because he didn't understand their meaning.

"So if I tell Beatrice that, she'll listen to what I have to say…is that it?"

"Who knows? That surely depends on you, Barusu… See the villagers home safely, please."

Placing a very strong emphasis on that last part, Ram turned her back to him and left, her business concluded.

Taken aback by her attitude, Subaru scratched his head.

"Ram…no, Roswaal's probably hiding something, damn it."

"…"

"Emilia?"

"Eh? Ah, yes, nothing. No worries."

In the blink of an eye, Emilia's gloomy expression vanished as she straightened her back and turned to face Subaru. Then she smiled pleasantly at Subaru once more before she continued.

"I don't know how far we should trust the advice from Roswaal that Ram gave us, but…don't be reckless— May the blessings of the spirits be with you."

To a spirit mage, this was an important phrase, special words to send others off. Subaru answered with a solemn nod.

"Though that might not sound very convincing coming from me right at this moment."

"That's not true— I'll be back. You hang in there, too, Emilia."

Instead of telling her not to be impatient or reckless, he tried to say something else. Rather than reinforce her worries, he tried to convey his trust to bolster her spirit, even if it only helped a tiny bit.

"…Mm-hmm. You, too, Subaru."

Emilia nodded, and it was right around then that the preparations to depart were complete.

7

With Emilia, and subsequently Ram, seeing them off, Subaru and the others set off from the Sanctuary in their dragon carriages.

At a steady pace, it wouldn't even take a half day to reach Earlham Village. The main concern on the road ahead was the barrier that blocked the passage of those who were mixed and led people astray, but—

"If ya know the right path and yer a pureblood who doesn't trigger th' barrier, ain't no problem. Ain't like either o' us wanna keep more people with grudges than we need."

"Beyond that, I'm grateful that you offered yourself as a guide to make sure we don't get lost, but…"

Garfiel was inside the dragon carriage, sitting in his seat at an angle and having a great time. Sitting opposite him, Subaru leaned on an elbow and sighed.

"You're not guiding us. Hell, you're practically falling asleep. Did you ditch the job?"

"Naw. It's just, that black land dragon of yers is too damn good. She's got a perfect grasp of the road from just runnin' down it once, so there ain't nothin' for me to do."

"Aside from her taste in men, my Patlash really is perfect, isn't she…?"

Subaru was very fond of his favorite dragon whose specs were so high they had earned Garfiel's seal of approval. But that she'd picked Subaru as her owner might have been indicative of a certain flaw in her character.

Either way, her amazing performance was why Subaru had ended up one-on-one with Garfiel. Over at the driver's seat, Otto made a point of having nothing to do with the conversation.

And so their chatter naturally drifted to the topic that they had set aside until now.

"So. Before ya head out, there's somethin' I wanted to talk to ya about. Unless yer real bad at guessing, I think ya can imagine what it is."

"...Sorry, setting aside opinions on whether I'm good or bad at guesswork, there's a whole bunch of problems I can think of. Unless you tell me the specifics, no way I'm gonna understand what you mean."

"Well, ain't that rough. In that case, I'll lend ya a hand in solvin' yer problems."

Garfiel spread his thighs where he sat, turning a sharp gaze toward Subaru. Subaru's breath caught as he recoiled from those eyes that were not so much *piercing* as they were *cutting*.

"The way you say that doesn't sound like a good omen to me... In other words...?"

"Hey, third rate—you took the trial, didn't you?"

"_____"

The question Garfiel posed in a low voice, like the guttural growl of a beast, ran right through Subaru.

When Subaru narrowed his eyes at the question, Garfiel shook his head.

"Don't hide it. I ain't picking on ya. I'm wonderin', like, people not qualified take the punishment once, and then they're free to enter the second time an' after... That's just a guess, not like anyone's tried it."

"If you wanna tell Roswaal to try it, I'm not gonna stop you."

"Me, I'd love him to try, too, but Ram'd smack me to death, so I'll pass."

With a pained look and a flippant tongue, Garfiel bared his fangs and laughed a little.

As he'd pointed out, he'd come to the conclusion that Subaru had been able to enter the tomb because it was his second time. There was no way for Garfiel to be sure, but it seemed he intended to make something out of it.

"Let's say for the sake of argument that's true... What do you plan to do about it?"

"Now, hold on. I figured ya wouldn't cop to it. That's just a what-if, so I'll talk about somethin' easier for ya to agree to. This is 'Gam and Gum Bridge Building'–level stuff."

Garfiel unleashed another one of his trademark mystery phrases, and while Subaru felt his mouth go dry from the incredibly not-casual level of pressure it suggested, he drew in his chin, indicating he would at least hear out the proposal. Accepting this, Garfiel continued.

"It's real simple. If yer qualified...then you take the trial in Lady Emilia's place. Lift the barrier for me and my people."

"—!! Wait, I can't do that! That assumes Emilia's gonna fail!"

Garfiel was proposing that Subaru challenge it in Emilia's place.

Certainly, the thought had grazed Subaru's head several times over. As a matter of fact, Subaru had already passed one of the three parts of the trial, leaving two obstacles to go. If pressed, he would admit he held a strong desire to challenge it.

But that was something he wanted to avoid. If he did that, all Emilia's struggles to date would be for—

"Don't get me wrong. Me and the old hag wanna be freed from the Sanctuary. An' we don't much care who does it."

"That's..."

"You wantin' Lady Emilia to do it so she can have the old hags and the hostages thankin' her—that's your problem. Includin' wantin' her to overcome a hateful past and take the sting off it, that's all your problem—it ain't got nothin' to do with us."

Subaru couldn't summon a rebuttal to Garfiel's words.

Looking at it from Garfiel's point of view, of course that's how he saw the Sanctuary situation. Just as he'd said, having Emilia undertake the trial, and hoping that she would overcome it, was essentially the solution to a personal problem.

When Subaru hung his head at this sound argument, Garfiel sighed as he added more.

"—Is the past really something ya gotta overcome in the first place...?"

"Eh?"

"For three days I've been watchin' Lady Emilia challenge the trial, same as you. It's breakin' her. Seein' her come out all messed up like that—I can't stand to watch."

Crinkling the skin of his nose, Garfiel brought up the heartbreaking sight of Emilia right after emerging from the tomb.

The number of times Emilia had failed to overcome the trial were adding up. But it wasn't just that—it was the sight of her turning back: broken, panicked, calling for Puck, then finally sleeping as if her strength was exhausted.

The ordeal was excruciating. But what lay beyond her after she overcame that was—

"I believe Emilia will overcome it. That's why I'll..."

"And yer free to hope she does. But can Lady Emilia really overcome her past? Could it be that crying and going all *I'm scared I'm scared* is what she really wants to do? Me, I can't really tell."

"What Emilia...really wants..."

The words Garfiel threw out struck Subaru like a shower of cold water.

Subaru had meant to respect Emilia's wishes and devotedly support her until the matter was resolved. However painful it was to climb that wall, as long as Emilia challenged it without fail, he would continue lending her a hand.

—Emilia, challenging the tomb in spite of her trembling legs, heedless of the cry of her heart.

"..."

Right then, when Garfiel said it out loud, Subaru arrived at the possibility for the first time.

—The possibility that she wanted to be rescued, that she was searching for salvation.

—If, in her own heart, she truly wanted someone else to fight in her place...

—Then who should be that someone, if not Subaru himself?

"...That's one more thing I've gotta really talk to her about when I get back."

"Huuuh?"

"Nothing... Setting aside whether to accept your proposal or not, it sure does sound like it'd help solve my current problems. Gotta say, you really are a surprising guy."

"Ha! Don't say stupid stuff. Me, I just wanna improve my odds even a lil' bit."

Clenching his fangs in annoyance, Garfiel turned his face away from Subaru. Rather than this being a cute reaction in the vein of concealing a blush, he seemed genuinely irritated, which brought a pained smile to Subaru's face.

But when it came to his assertion about improving the odds, there was a lot there Subaru could agree with.

"What do you wanna do when you get out of the Sanctuary?"

"...Well, ain't that outta the blue. What I wanna do once I'm out, huh?"

"You've been twisting arms left and right to get the barrier lifted and escape, right? I was thinking you had to have something you wanted to do on the outside..."

"..."

He'd innocently raised the topic, but Garfiel looked completely taken aback. It was as if he found the question unexpected, or even as if it was something he'd never thought of before.

"...That's somethin' only a person who can freely come 'n' go would say. If ya can go wherever the hell ya want, ya can understand how me an' the old hags feel, right?"

Finally, Garfiel slowly spat those words out. Subaru felt like he'd been insulting, but Garfiel stood up, giving him no opportunity to apologize.

"We're close to the barrier. This is as far as I go with ya. Take care of the rest, ya hear?"

"You bet... Er, I'll be coming back real soon. Not like I have zero worries about stuff, though..."

He was worried about returning to the mansion. On top of that, he felt a duty to make sure of certain things.

Petra's safety was obviously one concern, but even more than that, making sure whether a certain sleeping girl was safe—

"...Well, crap. Can't be helped."

"Garfiel?"

Garfiel scruffed up his blond hair as he harshly clicked his tongue.

Surprised by the gesture, Subaru turned toward him as he put a hand into his own waistcloth. Then—

"—Take this with ya."

"This crystal…it's the same as the one Frederica had."

The piece of jewelry Garfiel took out of his pocket and offered Subaru was a necklace of a blue crystal on a string. The gem looked identical to the one Frederica had possessed.

The twin blue crystals were undeniable proof that Garfiel and Frederica shared some kind of bond.

"I don't intend to talk about our circumstances. Just…it's trouble for us if ya don't come back. So I'm givin' this to ya. In a pinch, show it to Frederica."

"…Taking this before I head off makes me worry I'll get teleported by the barrier all over again…"

"If ya don't need it, just give it back. But havin' it might help ya in a pinch."

When Subaru turned the crystal over in his palm, Garfiel reached out like he wanted to take it back. With a grand gesture, Subaru escaped from his hand and stuffed the crystal he had received into his pocket.

He didn't know what lay between Garfiel and Frederica. They were likely blood relatives—the barrier that supposedly rejected the passage of anything considered mixed seemed like a literal impassable wall between the pair.

If, perhaps, the barrier was the reason Frederica had been scheming—

"I have to find out what Frederica meant to do. So, well, wait for good news, 'kay?"

"Ha! What's this good-news business? If it ain't like 'Balulumoro-roi makes the sun go down,' then no way I'd ever tell the difference."

Subaru, in his attempt to bid Garfiel farewell on a positive note, drew the first smile from Garfiel he had seen that wasn't related to his ferocity. However—

"I still have no idea what makes the sun go down."

Subaru remained ignorant of just what the mystery phrase pressing against his back meant.

8

Eight hours after setting off from the Sanctuary—and six since parting ways with Garfiel—Subaru arrived back at Roswaal Manor, just before sunset.

"Will you really be all right without me there with you?"

Otto spoke with a concerned, subdued voice from the dragon carriage halted in Earlham Village.

Now that the refugees had been safely transported back to the village, Otto and Subaru watched as moving reunions broke out between family members who had been temporarily separated.

Otto was no doubt keeping his voice down because he didn't want to interrupt the reunions.

"Yeah. I'll head back to the mansion by myself for now. If nothing happens, I'll send my thoughts over to you straightaway, so hook up with me after getting that, 'kay?"

"Mr. Natsuki, you have so many distractions, I am concerned that my accepting your precious thoughts might leave you in dire straits… I'm joking, but let me speak seriously. If you are trying to be considerate toward me, then…"

"I won't say that's completely inaccurate, but…you're my insurance."

When Subaru scratched his cheek and spoke those words, Otto tilted his head and asked, "Insurance?" Nodding back toward him, Subaru explained.

"At the very least, you're the only other person here who knows our circumstances. If you figure something really did happen to me, I want you to avoid doing anything crazy and report back to the Sanctuary."

"…I would rather not speak of such things, even if it's only just in case, but…"

"Well, since you're our crew's Mr. Dependable Merchant, I'm countin' on ya!"

"Yes, leave it to… Wait, since when have you arbitrarily lumped me in with your faction?!"

When Otto went shrill at being entrusted with a job he didn't remember accepting, Subaru forced a smile and set out from the village. Straddling Patlash, he raced like the wind up the road from the village to the mansion.

"_____"

"What, are you worried about me? It's all right. I'm not gonna cause you any trouble."

When they arrived at the front gate, Subaru dropped off Patlash's back and rubbed the tip of her nose. His favorite land dragon responded with a lively gesture, rubbing him with her head, and accompanied Subaru on his way to the mansion's entrance hall.

The day had stretched into dusk. The orange sun shone on Roswaal Manor, nestled between the mountains; gradually, he sensed night approaching from the sky to the east.

"…First, door number one."

Subaru spoke those words as he stood before the doors and put his hand on the knocker. Taking a deep breath, he strongly knocked with it, announcing the arrival of a guest to all within the building.

For a time, he waited for a response from inside, but—

"—Door number one, no good. Proceeding to door number two."

When the supposedly present servants didn't reply, Subaru suppressed a sigh as he gently pressed his hand to the doors. When he applied a little pressure, he found that they had been carelessly left unlocked. Without much difficulty, he slipped through the gap between the doors and trespassed on the mansion.

"_____"

The worried breath given off by the land dragon at the very end, a moment before the doors separated them, weighed heavily on Subaru's heart.

Steeling himself, Subaru turned his eyes toward the interior of the mansion he hadn't seen for three days. At the very least, the broad entry hall was quiet, with no sign that anyone was near him.

The words Ram had shared prior to his departure abruptly rose from the back of his mind—if Frederica did bear any ill will, she was no doubt already gone from the mansion.

If the worst case was that Frederica had gone off somewhere, he didn't care. The problem was—

"Whether she left by herself…or took Petra and Rem with her."

He wasn't thrilled with either possibility, but he especially didn't want to think about the latter. He had the handkerchief on his wrist and the crystal Garfiel had entrusted to him. Relying on the presence of those two things, he advanced, stepping farther into the mansion.

"—?"

His brows scrunched up at his sense of foreboding. Subaru was on the verge of calling out to the occupants in a loud voice.

Without the sight of the people who ought to have been there, the familiar mansion corridors felt like unknown territory. When Subaru walked into the hallway of the main wing and peered within, he was greeted by a strange sight.

As far as he could see, every single door in the corridor had been opened.

"…Doesn't seem like someone did this to air the place out."

From what Subaru could tell, only the doors had been thrown wide open; there was no sign anyone had touched the windows. All the rooms were impeccably tidy.

Though that served as proof of Frederica and Petra's capabilities as servants, the empty tidiness clawed painfully at Subaru's chest.

Something was wrong. Something felt off. Something was very… unnatural…

"_____"

A detestable feeling, a foul timidity crept around inside Subaru's body. With a deep breath and a hand to his chest, he held it in check by force.

He'd already noticed that this was a bizarre emergency situation. After the many dangerous situations he'd found himself in, Subaru's survival instincts were currently ringing loud and clear: there was some kind of issue there in the mansion.

If he'd followed his initial judgment call, Subaru would have immediately left the mansion and rendezvoused with Otto. The best plan was to tell his allies of the strange occurrence in the mansion so that they could devise a way to address it.

If the mansion hadn't contained so many people he wanted to save within its walls, that's exactly what he would've done.

"_____"

He understood it was reckless and irrational. Even so, he had to be sure.

Subaru didn't know how long it would take to return here with allies. The more time passed, the greater the chance the girls inside the mansion would be spirited away. He couldn't weigh them all on a scale. He just couldn't.

"Who...to put first...?"

Gripping the handkerchief on his wrist, as if to make sure it was still there, Subaru's brain tossed and turned enough to bring it to a boil.

The people in the mansion related to Subaru in some way numbered four, all girls. Among them, Frederica was the lowest priority. At the moment, it was unclear to Subaru where she stood. Besides, she probably possessed combat capabilities. If any of them could deal with problems as they arose, it was her.

As Subaru stepped forward with trembling, wavering knees, he realized if he had to go over them one by one and decide whom he had to check on first—then he could only think of Rem.

"_____"

He had any number of excuses he could cite.

Asleep and immobile, Rem was completely defenseless. With her existence forgotten, there was no way to be sure what value it held to a potential enemy, so he couldn't simply leave her alone.

"In her own room...!"

She had to be asleep. There was no reason she would have moved. Rem ought to be sleeping in the same room that very moment.

With so many conditions piled together, wasn't it natural he would check on her first?

Subaru repeated unnecessary excuses over and over inside his head as he headed to the east wing of the mansion—to where Rem's bedroom was located.

His breathing in disarray as his lungs convulsed, he clutched his chest as his loudly beating heart protested in concern. He abused his knees with rapid, tottering steps as he carefully hurried to catch up with the anomaly.

"_____"

Along the way, every door in the main wing had been flung open. This continued into the east wing, remaining the same as he reached the floor that contained Rem's bedroom.

Rem's room was at the end of the corridor. The doors of every room before it remained open.

"Shit...Rem!!"

Clicking his own tongue as he climbed up the stairs, Subaru ran toward the back of the corridor.

The color of the evening sun thickly filled the corridor through the windows. Some kind of sweet aroma was mixed in with the serene air.

Breathing hard, Subaru's own body was dyed orange as he quickened his ragged steps.

His heart beat louder and faster, sending painful throbs and a feeling he could not describe racing through his eyes. Horror poured in, intruding upon his brain and leaving him able to think of only one thing.

He had...to find out...if Rem...was safe—

"—Wh-whoa?!"

As Subaru's thoughts raced, his feet suddenly tripped two rooms short of his destination. Subaru's chest slammed into the corridor's floor, leaving him gritting his teeth at his own folly.

Clenching the fist that had landed on the carpet, he tilted his head and came back to his senses. His feet had snagged on something—that's what had tripped him. He'd been focused solely on the doors of the rooms he'd been passing when something slender at his feet had made him fall.

With everything dyed in the glossy light of the setting sun, it was difficult to tell what its original color had been. But the thing was slender and long, stretching out without interruption, and when Subaru's eyes followed it to its end point he realized where it came from. It was no great mystery.

—It had simply tumbled out of the rent side of Subaru's abdomen.

"—Huh?"

The right flank of his track suit had been cut clean. That was where the yellowy intestines had tumbled out.

A large amount of blood was pooling beneath him. He wasn't sure if his right foot had stumbled over his small or large intestines, but at any rate, his innards had been expelled, seemingly clinging to their owner.

"...*Oghu.*"

The instant he confirmed this fact, his throat was blocked by a rising clump of blood, and the world was dyed crimson.

His trembling fingers tried to stuff back in the innards pouring out due to the pressure exerted by his belly, but he didn't have the strength. Then his knees failed as well, and before he realized it, he had tumbled forward onto the carpet.

He didn't know what had happened. Only that his belly had been fatally slashed—

"—I told you, didn't I? I promised you, yes?"

Suddenly, there was a voice.

Straight ahead, from the direction that Subaru's fallen head pointed, someone was talking to him.

He couldn't lift up his face. His consciousness was draining away with his organs, mixing with the coursing blood and spreading thinly across the floor. Subaru desperately gurgled, as if trying to cling to a world that was growing more distant.

*It's over*, his instincts proclaimed.

He understood that, but somewhere in his heart, Subaru rejected dying for nothing.

It wasn't over, it couldn't be over, not until he gained something, obtained something. If he didn't return with something, anything, somethinganythingsomethinganythingsomethinganything—

"_____"

There was the high-pitched echo of shoes striking the floor. A shadowy figure stood in the corridor, dyed crimson from the spring of fresh blood.

She wore a black outfit on her slender physique. Her long, black hair was tied back in a triple braid. Adoringly, with a coquettish look, she gazed down at his dying moments.

When he sensed those things, along with the sensation of having his *belly cut*, Subaru understood.

—*Why…are you here…in front of Rem's room?*

"—I told you to take care of your bowels until the next time we meet."

It was a declaration of love that had gone astray, the pure affection of a murderer that no one else could understand.

As Subaru Natsuki's consciousness grew hazy, that was the only thing that grazed the fingertips of his soul.

Hazy, hazy, hazy. Dark, dark, dark. And finally…

Everything vanished. It was the end. And then…they began anew.

The curtain of Subaru Natsuki's fourth loop…had risen.

# AFTERWORD

Yes, yes, yes, hiya, I am Tappei Nagatsuki! I am also the Mouse-Colored Cat! This time, I wanted to thank you very much for buying and reading *Re:ZERO -Starting Life in Another World-*, Vol. 10!

Huh?! I'm getting déjà vu, like I've somehow written a greeting like this very recently?!

So, while I was stricken by a sense of familiarity, it is *not* déjà vu. It's that Volume 9 and Volume 10 are being published back to back in November!

With the anime broadcast ending in September, it's a treat to be able to read about the immediate aftermath in Volumes 9 and 10, but not so great for the author. Truly, the days were spent going from the frying pan into the fire.

From start to finish, this was the fault of the author for blithely saying "Hey, once the anime's finished I'll be able to pick up the publication pace!" No, that is not the case! If anyone would be at fault, it would be you readers for saying "That sounds really fun, please do it!" And I would never lay blame like that!

The delight of all the readers at back-to-back publication in November is the fruit of Nagatsuki's soul as an author! Also, the fruit of the senior editor saying in a great burst of hot energy, "We can do it, we can do it! Mr. Nagatsuki can do it!" And you see? We did it!

Back-to-back publication in November was pretty hard to pull off, enough that I forgot about that silly conversation until just before going to print. Back-to-back publication added various burdens, which of course included Nagatsuki's own workload.

Furthermore, this time, with Volume 10, *Re:ZERO* enters a brand-new arc! By a new arc, I obviously mean changes in the scenery and the characters appearing onstage. So that means Otsuka has designed plenty of new characters. Of course, I would call all the characters he's designed gems, so it was quite an ordeal, even for a superhuman like Otsuka!

Yeah, who was that guy who mouthed off on his own to the tune of "Once the anime's over I'll raise the production pace"? Who, me?! It was me.

Mr. Otsuka, I'm so sorry. Maid Petra and School Uniform Echidna are *sooooooo* cute. As this is the general consensus of everyone who has read Volume 10, best regards for Volume 11 and beyond!

Also, the story has changed from the web version, where it got fairly *gnnnnh*, so if readers also have fun with things *besides* the illustrations, that is a very good thing, yes.

Even if what precedes them is more of a jumble than usual, things tighten up once the words of praise and thanks begin, so let us begin.

Senior Editor I, thank you sooooo much for your work on Volumes 9 and 10 following the anime! You were a huge help in so many areas! For Volume 9, it related to how to portray the climax of Arc 3, and for Volume 10, how to set up Arc 4 going forward. I intend to race forward at high temperature that is in no way inferior to Arc 3, so let's look forward to Arc 4!

To Mr. Otsuka the illustrator, I mentioned you in the middle of the afterword already, but thank you very much for the many character designs this time around. The Witch, the punk, the girl, the maid—you gave them all such adorable touches that I can't help but gush. I'm counting on your fine service during their hardships and exploits hereafter!

To designer Kusano, this marks the fourteenth *Re:ZERO*-related book you've done, but where rankings are concerned, number 10 is right there at the top. Kusano, I've come this far because of your sense of how to attract people's eyes. Thank you very much. Let's strive to aim even higher in the future!

To Daichi Matsuse and Makoto Fuugetsu, who are in charge of the comic versions, thank you very much for sticking with me all the way to *Re:ZERO*'s anime finale event. I think it was a really good thing to get us all together right on the verge of it ending. Best of luck on the way to completing Arc 2 and Arc 3!

To others in the editorial department of MF Bunko J, the various bookstore and enterprise-side persons, and the anime staff and cast for whom my feelings of gratitude have yet to diminish in the slightest, and everyone else involved in *Re:ZERO*, thank you.

And last but not least, my greatest of thanks to all you readers who have followed this tale thus far.

The long third arc is over, and with this volume, the fourth arc begins. If the theme of Arc 3 is "self-awareness," the theme of Arc 4 is "self-reliance." New hardships block the characters' paths, so by all means, watch as they aim to do whatever it takes to overcome these obstacles.

Thank you very much for your time, and I hope to see you again for Volume 11.

*September 2016*
*Tappei Nagatsuki*
*(Written while challenging the sudden cool spell with a*
*Hawaiian shirt for as long as possible)*

Kenichi

Nahoko

BOOO
(DAZE)

- Drooping eyes
- Angled eyebrows
- Short legs

- Almond eyes
- Drooping eyebrows
- Ditzy

Gaucho pants

I designed them so that you could tell at a glance that they're Subaru's parents. Reading about them from the text, I really liked both of them a lot!

Shinichiro Otsuka

Kenichi

"Ha-ha-ha! So there you have it, this is Kenichi Natsuki, magnificent previewer!"

"I am Nahoko. Ah, I'm Ken's wife… Also, did something happen to you?"

"Suddenly hearing what you called me before marriage threw me off, but you said what you needed to say so it's all OK, my bride. So let's get *down* with this preview stuff!"

"Errr, concerning the next volume of this story…*Re:ZERO*, was it? This is where you talk about new information, I think. Also, this is Subaru's story? I wonder what kind of story it'll be…"

"Ohhh, you really got it, which is a totally super-rare thing! You can do it when you really try, Nahoko!"

"Tee-hee, I can certainly do it when I try. Today was nonflammable garbage day, wasn't it?"

"There it is, Mom's beginner-level 'the first part's disconnected from the second part' conversation piece! Let's set aside talking about the garbage for now and try to keep the conversation focused."

"Okaaaay. The next book after this one is Volume Eleven, expected to come out in December…the month before New Year's? Others came out in September and October, too, so it seems to be a rather busy schedule."

"Well, that just means they're in that much demand.

"And at about the same time as Volume 10 comes out, disc Volume 5 of the *Re:ZERO* anime will be out

Nahoko

with a novella, and on top of that, there's talk of a book on the setting called the *Re:ZEROpedia*, too! Even with the anime finished, there's lots and lots to do. Feels like Subaru's won't be gettin' a chance to rest anytime soon."

"Come to mention it, Subaru's written it's his dream to become an author, and that 'I'll become like Dad, and then marry Mom.' So adorable."

"There's Mom's intermediate-level conversation piece, 'sudden resurrection of the past'! All of a sudden, that Subaru guy gets his dark past revealed when he isn't even here!"

"I just thought, the more everyone knows about Subaru, the more they'll like him, and the harder that child will try."

"...Yeah, I suppose so! I think that, too! Why, you truly are perfect, bride of mine! 'No matter what detours you may take, the final answer is always the right one!' Right?"

"Of course I am perfect. I am Subaru's mom and Ken's wife, after all."

"That's my wife for you, and that's my son. Better keep at it, Subaru... I have high hopes for ya."

"Yes, hang in there, Subaru."